# The Edge of Grace

Christa Allan's sophomore book, *The Edge of Grace*, is a powerful work of art, delving into waters not often stirred in fiction. It made me squirm and it challenged me to consider how I offered grace. The only thing it did not do was leave me unchanged.
—ANE MULLIGAN, editor *Novel Journey*

*Edge of Grace* needs to be required reading for every church book club out there. Once again Christa Allan tackles a difficult subject, this time homosexuality, with grace, laughter, love, and intelligence. With sometimes chuckle-out-loud humor annd heart-breaking pathos, Allan walks the reader through a horrific hate crime against her lead character, Caryn's gay brother. With winsome words and honesty, Allan brings the reader into a world of prejudice and pain as Caryn must confront her own misconceptions. In the end, Caryn is able to "woman up" and dig deep down where she finds love and God waiting. Allan reminds us that love does indeed conquer all and we all live lives on the edge of grace.
—JOYCE MAGNIN, Award-winning author of the Bright's Pond novels

# THE EDGE OF GRACE

Christa Allan

Abingdon Press fiction
a novel approach to faith
Nashville, Tennessee

*The Edge of Grace*

Copyright © 2011 by Christa Allan

ISBN-13: 978-1-4267-1311-8

Published by Abingdon Press, P.O. Box 801, Nashville, TN 37202

www.abingdonpress.com

All rights reserved.

The persons and events portrayed in this work of fiction
are the creations of the author, and any resemblance
to persons living or dead is purely coincidental.

Published in association with WordServe Literary Group, Ltd.,
10152 S. Knoll Circle, Highlands Ranch, CO 80130

Cover design by Anderson Design Group, Nashville, TN

Library of Congress Cataloging-in-Publication Data

Allan, Christa.
The edge of grace / Christa Allan.
    p. cm.
ISBN 978-1-4267-1311-8 (trade pbk. : alk. paper)
I. Title.
PS3601.L4125E34 2011
813'.6—dc22

                    2011016133

Printed in the United States of America

1 2 3 4 5 6 7 8 9 10 / 16 15 14 13 12 11

*for Johnny Bassil and Ricky Johnson*
*who taught me that grace is truly amazing*

### ACKNOWLEDGMENTS

The first chapter of this novel made its debut at an Abingdon authors' retreat in 2009. It grew from there to what you're holding today because of the encouragement of those writers and the unwavering support of Barbara Scott, then the fiction editor at Abingdon Press, and Rachelle Gardner, agent at WordServe Literary. They championed this story, never doubting that one day Caryn and David would be as real to readers as they were to me.

Along the way, when my arms wearied from paddling to keep myself afloat in the sea of doubt, I was rescued by the faith of friends. Jenny B. Jones challenged me to writing sprints that kept my hands out of the chocolate, and Joyce Magnin provided free laughter therapy. The Truby-adorers Bonnie Grove and Allison Ariel Lawhon prodded and poked and persisted, always believing a truer story awaited. Shelley Easterling Gay continued to answer my frantic messages and won my heart as the weekend on-call reader of all things messy.

I'm grateful for my straight friends who came out of the closet to share their stories of gay siblings and spouses and parents, the courage of the student who asked me to sponsor the Gay-Straight Alliance at school, and the monthly Girls' Night Out posse that kept me sane and fed.

My children braced themselves for round two of novel writing, refusing to listen to me whine (I think they may have enjoyed the payback). And bless my husband, Ken, who often came home to uncooked dinners, unwashed clothes, and undone me, and managed to take care of all of us. He also kept the cats corralled and off my laptop keyboard.

Without the support of the team at Abingdon Press, this novel would still be in my computer: Tammy Gaines (who first heard the idea over a New Orleans lunch), Fiction Editor Ramona Richards, Sales Director Mark Yeh, Brian Williams, Nancy Hall, Meagan Roper, and Marketing Manager Julie Dowd.

My agent Sandra Bishop of MacGregor Literary has been a lifesaver, mostly saving me from myself. She seems to have an endless supply of floaties.

Like my debut novel, *Walking on Broken Glass*, which dealt with alcoholism and recovery, this one too is rooted in my own life experiences. My brother and his partner of over fifteen years loved me through the fog of confusion and, when it cleared, opened their arms to welcome me home.

God truly brought me to the edge of grace and waited patiently for me to walk across the border.

# 1

The last two words I said to my brother David that Saturday were "oh" and "no," and not in the same sentence—though they should have been.

On an otherwise ordinary, cartoon-filled morning, my son Ben sat at the kitchen table spiraling a limp bacon slice around his finger. His last ditch effort to forestall doing his chores. I was having a domestic bonding experience with the vacuum cleaner. My last ditch effort to forestall the house being over-taken by microscopic bugs, dead skin, and petrified crumbs. I'd just summoned the courage to attempt a pre-emptive strike on the intruders under the sofa cushions when the phone rang.

I walked into the kitchen, gave Ben the "don't you dare touch that phone with your greasy bacon hands" stare, and grabbed the handset.

It was David. "I wanted you to hear this from me," he said.

An all-too familiar sensation—that breath-sucking, plum-meting roller-coaster feeling—I'm thinking he's been fired, in a car wreck, diagnosed with cancer, six months to live, but, no, it wasn't as simple as that.

He told me he was leaving in a few days for a vacation. With a man. Leaving with a man. Crossing state lines from Louisiana to Mexico to share sun, sand, and sheets with a person of the same sex.

My universe shifted.

He came out of the closet, and I went into it. For perhaps only the second time in my life, I was mute. Not even sputtering, not even spewing senseless syllables. Speechless.

"Caryn, are you still there?"

No. I'm not still here. I'm miles away and I'm stomping my feet and holding my breath in front of the God Who Makes All Monsters Disappear.

I think I hear God. He's telling me I'm the monster.

Wisps of sounds. They belonged to David. "Did you hear what I said? That I'm going away?"

I hung up. I didn't ask "Why?" because he'd tell me the truth my heart already knew.

"What did Uncle David want?" Ben asked.

I spun around and made eye contact with my unsuspecting innocent. "Get that bacon off your finger right now, mister. Wash your hands, and go do whatever it is you're supposed to be doing."

He shoved the bacon in his mouth, his face the solemn reflection of my emotional slap. From the den television, the Nickelodeon Gummy Bears filled the stillness with their ". . . bouncing here, there, and everrrrrywherre . . ." song.

"And turn that television off on the way back to your room."

"Okay, Mom," said Ben, his words a white flag of surrender as he left the room.

Now what? I decided to abandon the vacuuming. Really, was I supposed to fret about Multi-Grain Wheat Thin crumbs and popcorn seeds when my only sibling was leaving for Mexico with a man?

The phone rang. Again.

"You hung up on me," David said.

"I don't know what to say." I opened the refrigerator. The burp of stale air cooled my face as I stalked the shelves of meals past and future. I'd find solace in one of those containers. Maybe more than one. I'd solace myself until the voice on the phone went away.

David reminded me there were alternatives to hanging up.

Alternatives? You want to talk alternatives? How about I'm hung up on your alternative lifestyle?

Between the sour cream and a stalk of tired celery, I found an abandoned crusty cinnamon roll in a ball of crinkled foil. I unwrapped it and plowed my finger through the glop of shiny, pasty icing smeared inside and said, "But you and Lori just finished wallpapering your bathroom. You remember her, right? Your fiancée?"

"Lori knows," he said.

I grabbed the two fudge brownies with cavities where Ben already had picked out the walnuts.

"Uh huh." I fought the urge to hang up again.

"Is that all you're going to say?"

No, that wasn't all I could say. I was going to say I was ever so sorry for answering the phone. I wanted to say that I hate you. I wanted to say that of all that things you could have been, gay was not what I would've chosen. I wanted to say that I didn't want to imagine you in bed with a man. I didn't want to know that what we had in common was that we both slept with men. I wanted to say that if our mother hadn't already died of cancer, she would've keeled over with this news.

"Lori and I are working this out," he said.

9

I fumbled for words like keys in the black hole of my purse. My brain rummaged for syllables and sounds, buried under a clever adage, a witty phrase. But all I could choke out was an "Oh."

"Don't you even want to know who I'm going with?" He sounded small, like he was the one being left behind.

"No."

Then, with a level of intimacy I reserved for nighttime marketers of exterior siding, I told him good-bye.

I walked to where I'd left the vacuum handle propped against the den wall, flipped the switch, and pushed the vacuum back and forth, back and forth, back and forth. I pictured the unwary bugs caught in the vortex. I knew just how they felt. I'd been in this wind tunnel before, when Harrison died and without my permission.

Sometimes husbands could be so maddening.

And, once again, Harrison, where are you when I need you? Who am I supposed to talk to about this? Not Ben. Not my father. Don't give me that condescending "life isn't fair" mantra. You're right. It's not.

I yanked the cord out of the wall, pressed the button that zipped it into the belly of the beast and steered the machine toward Ben's room.

My almost seven-year-old sat on the floor of his bedroom tying his navy Sketchers when he saw me at the door. "Hey, Mom. I washed my hands." He held them up, wiggled them in front of his face as proof. "See?"

"Where are your socks, Ben?"

Harrison again. Caryn, the world's not going to stop spinning because the kid's not wearing socks.

Ben doubled the knot, pulled the laces, and looked up at me. His sprinkle of freckles and his cleft chin, totally stolen from his dad, weakened me. How could there be anything wrong in the universe when his precious face slips into that soft spot in my heart?

"I couldn't find two socks that matched. Besides," he stood and stomped his sneakers on the floor, "these are almost too small. My feet get all squinchy when I'm wearing socks." He pulled the elastic band on his basketball shorts up past his waist. We both knew the shorts would slide right back down in minutes. A battle he always lost. "So, can I go play Wii with Nick now?"

My only child wore shoes that crushed his toes. How did I miss that? "Why didn't you tell me your shoes were too small?"

"No big deal, Mom. Anyway, remember you said we'd go shopping with Uncle David before school started." Ben grabbed his frayed purple L.S.U. cap off his desk lamp. "Can I go now?"

"Sure. Just be home for lunch." I hugged him, and when I felt his arms lock around my waist, I wondered how I still deserved him.

I must have latched on a bit too long because he started to squirm away. "Mom. You okay?" Ben stepped out of my arms, turned his baseball cap backward over his sand-colored hair, raised his arms, plopped his hands on the top of his cap, and waited.

"Of course," I said, tweaking his nose, hoping he heard the lie in my voice and didn't see the truth in my eyes. "Plug that cord in for me on your way out, okay?"

"Got it. See ya." The front door slammed. It opened again. "Oops, sorry about that," he called out, and then the door closed solidly.

Well, Harrison. Door closing. That's one lesson learned.

I moved Ben's lamp to the back of his desk and straightened the framed picture that the lamp had slid into when he'd grabbed his hat. Bacchus, his first Mardi Gras parade captured in the photograph. I'd always called it the "man" picture. Ben's crescent moon smile as Harrison hoisted him on his shoulders, my father and David flanking Harrison, both grinning at Ben and not the camera.

One man already gone. Now David. At least the David I thought I knew. Wasn't that the David that just last week sat next to me in church? The church he'd invited me to for the first time a month ago? How could he have done that? He's certifiably crazy if he thinks I'm going to church tomorrow. That's not going to happen.

I mashed the vacuum cleaner switch on and returned to the sucking up of dirt. It seemed all too appropriate for my life.

# 2

Ben told Nick you looked sad. And you didn't ask if he'd brushed his teeth after breakfast, and he warned me not to ask about his Uncle David." Julie stepped in the foyer and closed the front door. "Figured code orange. I zipped right over."

Neighbors for years, Julie and I color-coded our traumas; Julie called it our Homeland Sanity Advisory. Below yellow, phone calls would be sufficient. Yellow or above, always a face-to-face.

Standing in the den, the bug-sucking beast still at my side, I must have looked like Martha Stewart, the prison months. But Julie looked me over and didn't say anything about my stupor or my morning bed-hair, which probably poked out from my scalp like clusters of brown twigs.

"Drop the handle," she said and marched right past me, looking all the more stern with her copper hair pulled into a neat ponytail at the nape of her long neck. A woman on a mission. I plodded behind her and hoped her trail of lemony-rose fragrance would settle itself on me and maybe compensate for the shower I needed.

Julie grabbed two glasses from the dish rack by the sink, filled them with iced tea, handed me one and walked over to the sofa with hers.

"Come. Sit." Julie patted the suede sofa cushion next to her. Its original pewter shade had been softened by the patina of lazy weekend movie watching, shuffling visits of family and friends, and the bouncing of a round-faced toddler.

I sunk into the sofa as she wedged an over-sized throw pillow behind her back. Julie kicked off her beaded flip-flops and plopped her toenail-polished feet on the glass coffee table between a chipped stoneware vase and a wicker basket holding an assortment of pine cones.

"Okay. Give it up. And don't give me the microwave version," Julie demanded. "You're still wandering around in your jammies, so I know it's gotta be big."

Julie and I gave up boundaries years ago. She was the sister my parents never gave me, and the only person allowed in the dressing room when I shopped for bathing suits. Once someone charted every dimple in your thighs, it wasn't a long way to knowing every dimple in your life.

"It's . . ." Deep breath . . . "Well, it's David." I set my glass on the July issue of *Good Housekeeping*, right over the picture of the Year's Best Banana Pudding. The room felt as steamy as asphalt after a hard August rain. I leaned against the back cushions, closed my eyes, and flipped through the memories of my life that'd unfolded on this sofa, in this room, with Julie by my side. Gain seemed outscored by loss. But, no matter what, we'd always depended on faith and friendship to buoy us as we navigated life's rivers. Like today, when an undertow threatened to yank me away.

She leaned toward me. "What happened? Is he okay?"

I opened my eyes. Gazed out the den window. Fingerprint smudges and splattered lovebugs almost blocked the view of the weeds that had overtaken what was supposed to have been a vegetable garden. I waited for the tidal wave of sorrow that would deplete itself in my sobs. Nothing. Maybe empty's the new full. Like orange is the new pink or something.

The words tumbled out of my mouth like marbles dropped from a jar. "David called this morning. He's gay. He called to tell me he's gay. Well, not that he said he's gay. No, I guess he didn't have to say that because he said he was going to Mexico with a man, by himself, and why would he being doing that if he wasn't, right?" I rubbed my temples with my fingertips. Was I massaging reality in or out? "My brother's gay."

I waited for Julie to react. I stared. I waited.

Whatever anxious concern she'd carried, she must have flushed it out with the tea she'd just finished.

"Uh-huh. Go on." Julie shifted, recrossed her legs on the table, and looked at me.

Her expression was, well, expressionless.

A sour bubble of anxiety popped in my stomach. "Uh-huh? Go on? Go on to what? To where? What do you mean? You did hear me, didn't you?" My voice stretched so thin it grated leaving my throat.

"I heard you. I'm just not all that shocked," she said with a tender weariness—like when I tell Ben for the umpteenth time to stop digging snot out of his nose when we're in the grocery store—and patted my hand. "Caryn, click your heels together. It's time to leave Oz. Your brother's gay. He's still your brother. The same brother you loved seconds before the phone call."

"Seriously? You're telling me this is okay?" She couldn't be. Of all people, Julie would share my outrage, not intensify it.

"He's your brother. Want to ignore him? Sure. Who's left? Your father married the step-monster after your mom died. That's all you've got. You're going to adopt her?"

She was on the verge of endangering her best-friend status. "Don't be ridiculous."

"There are some advantages here. Maybe we could think about those."

"No, let's not," I said. "And why are you smiling? This isn't funny. At. All." I didn't need a mirror to know I wore my injured-morose expression.

"I'm not laughing at you or your brother. I'm still surprised you didn't suspect this. In fact, I'm a bit shocked—"

The dryer signal blared from the laundry room and startled me. It reminded me today was still an ordinary Saturday. "Julie, I'm stunned. Horrified. The thing is, this is my brother. My only brother. My only sibling. It's different somehow when it happens in your own family. I mean, how would you feel if we were talking about your brother?"

She shrugged her shoulders, raked her bangs off her forehead with her fingers, and looked at me as if seeing me for the first time. "How would I feel? I wish my brother was gay. Instead, he's unemployed, he drinks too much, and he's an idiot."

"You don't understand. You can't understand." I rolled up the short sleeves of my cotton T-shirt. If only I could sweat out the pain and frustration. "It's not that simple. If he was your brother—alcoholic idiot or not—you'd be afraid to close your eyes because when you do, there's a snapshot of him and his other holding hands on the beach." I gulped my tea hoping it would lower my body's thermostat.

"Okay. So in that snapshot, my brother's throwing up on the beach."

The annoying, insistent dryer blared again. "I'm going to turn off that obnoxious buzzer of yours and get us a refill. Don't go anywhere." Julie smiled, kicked her shoes out of her way, and headed for the laundry room.

Because I am a mother and doomed to guilt, I wondered if his gayness is my fault. If I hadn't been such a nerd in high school, I could have saved him. If I hadn't devoted my college years to Harrison, I could've spent more time with David.

Julie returned, and my train of thought ran off the tracks. "Here you go." She placed my glass on the coffee table and sat on the sofa facing me. "Look, I suppose I haven't sounded sympathetic, but I'm sorry this is so painful for you. Thing is, Caryn, I don't feel sorry for you because you have a gay brother. Maybe it's all semantics, but I do feel sorry for your having to struggle through this. Without Harrison. Without your mom. But you don't have to do this alone." She reached over and hugged me. "Would it help you to talk to Vince? I could go with you."

"As in Pastor Vince? No. Definitely no. It's hard enough to talk to you about this." As if I'm going to tell the pastor I barely know that my brother, who's been going to services there for years, is gay.

"Okay," she said, but with a voice that made it sound not okay. "But that's what he's there for you know. And for all you know, Vince might already know that."

"I know, but he and I just met last week to talk about cater-ing his daughter's wedding. One issue at a time. Besides," I twisted my watch around my wrist to check the time, "that catering contract could be big."

She swallowed the ice she'd been crunching. "Like the boys say, 'Get cereal.' Get serious Caryn. Like David being gay has anything to do with your catering business." She grabbed her flip-flops and slipped them on her feet. "And don't worry about Ben. Trey wanted to take the boys to the real bowling alley. He's probably tired of them beating him on Wii."

Julie stood and tugged the hem of her blue plaid Bermuda shorts. "Ten pounds ago, these shorts wouldn't have crawled

up my legs every time I sat. It's all your fault. The white chocolate bread pudding and seafood lasagna you've been forcing me
to taste test. It's all settling right here." She poked her thighs.
"See?"

"Well, when Caryn's Canapes is self-sustaining, I'll ask our
accountant if I can write off a liposuction for you. In the meantime, I've got my own lumpy thigh issues to contend with." I
hadn't squeezed into pant sizes under two digits since Harrison
died. And lately the sizes were moving in the direction closer
to my age. Not so good. But it was collateral damage in the
catering business. I had to sample what I intended to serve.

"Speaking of your accountant, he asked me to let him know
if you were okay with the bowling plan." Julie tapped out a text
to Trey on her cell phone. "It's not a problem, right?"

"Not at all. Maybe he can hand out some of my cards while
he's there. Could get us both closer to plastic surgery."

⚬⚬⚬

Julie left not too long after giving Trey the bowling go-
ahead. She invited Ben to spend the night at their house, so I'd
have time, as she said, "to wallow in a bubble bath of self-pity
and move on."

She knew, of course, I'd back up more than move on, at
least for a while. We'd been through too much together for
her to think I'd wake up in "I'm all over it now" land. But even
Julie didn't know how much of a foreigner I was there. Even
after all these years.

Ten years ago, the Pierces moved across the street about a
month after we'd thrown away our last moving box. Trey and
Julie, we discovered when we'd strolled over with a welcome-
to-suburbia bottle of generic red wine, had sacrificed the ambi-
ance of a rented shotgun home near MidCity for a residential

starter home for the couple ready to "go forth and multiply."
Harrison and I were still newlyweds, trying to figure out what
to do with three toasters, a crystal punch bowl, and five place
settings of our china pattern.

Eventually, Harrison and Trey did their male-bonding-
getting-acquainted thing, then started spending Saturdays on
the golf course. Julie and I brought books to the clubhouse
pool, stretched out on lounge chairs, and pretended to read.
Mostly we critiqued body shapes and gave thanks we weren't
the ones hustling a three-year-old out of the water screeching,
"I gotta pee-pee in the baff-woom."

On Sundays, Trey and Julie headed to Mary Queen of Peace
Church and lunch with one of their parents. Meanwhile, at
the Beckers' house, Harrison kept the sheets warm while I
attended Grace Memorial, praying for enough rain to ruin the
chances of his playing golf and sufficient forgiveness for being
so petty.

The past few years were almost equally unkind to Julie and
me. My mother Lily died of cancer the year after Julie's father
had a massive heart attack driving home from a New Orleans
Saints football game. Julie's still trying to explain to her mother
why she can't sue the team.

I learned to gauge the depth of Julie's grief by the spike
of her humor. After her dad's funeral Mass, she passed me a
note she'd scribbled on an old church bulletin. "Your dad. My
mom. It could happen." I blew my nose and coughed my way
through a laugh.

My reaction to grief, however, headed in the opposite direction. Plummeted to pathos. So, even as she left that morning
after hearing about David, Julie knew she couldn't cushion me
from the fall. No. I had to hunker down in it, like an animal
rolling around in a decomposing carcass, until I gagged from

the stench of self-pity. Then I'd bolt out of the putrid mess I'd made and gasp for small breaths of acceptance.

After Harrison died, I felt as if I'd been shoved from a plane without a parachute. Five years later, I still wonder if maybe I've just landed on a ledge and the real bottom, the one that's a well of crud, was still waiting for me.

---

Lori. Should I call Lori? I should call her. Maybe. Why didn't I think to ask Julie? She's the self-declared queen of Google for what to do when you don't know what to do. But can you really do a web search on "what to say to your almost sister-in-law when your brother announces he is going to play for the other team"?

I carried the glasses to the sink and finished picking up what was left of Ben's breakfast. Two crispy blistered shells of the biscuits that he'd excavated the soft doughy insides out of. I tossed them out the backdoor to feed the sparrows.

I wouldn't endure one more phone call until I showered and changed out of my mismatched pajamas. Better yet. The bubble bath Julie suggested. A bubble bath so hot I'd have to ease into it one body part at a time. With Ben away, I could soak at leisure, let my fingertips wrinkle like raisins. Maybe some inspiration would soak in as well, and I'd know what to say to Lori when I called her later.

My cell phone vibrated, skittering across the enamel topped kitchen table like rocks in a tumbler. David's number flashed in the display. I let it go to voice mail and headed to the bathroom.

Vanilla Birthday Cake, Pink Grapefruit, and Apple Pomegranate. I couldn't escape food even in bathing. Julie had given me a basket of what she termed "guilty pleasures" for my birthday that seemed more fit for my pantry than my body. "The closest you'll get to buying bubble bath is that new strawberry-scented dish cleaning liquid," she'd told me after I'd unwrapped the gift. After months of caring for Harrison, the idea of a bath that didn't require sheet changing, a sponge, and a basin of lukewarm water seemed not only foreign, but extravagant.

I eased into the spacious garden tub, the heat of the water singeing my skin as I inched down and submerged myself up to my neck. When I reached up to hold on to the sides, bubbles splished over the top. My body felt in the tub like my foot in my father's shoe when I was a little girl. I remembered Harrison asking the agent when we looked at the house if the garden tub could accommodate two people and could we see if it was comfortable. My elbow in his side and her stare happened simultaneously. He'd looked from me to her and back to me. "I meant with my clothes on, of course," he said. The day after we'd moved in, we discovered two people fit quite well if one of them didn't mind leaning against the faucet.

Tonight, the blanket of bubbles on the water's surface crackled like leaves in a fire. I closed my eyes, breathed in the fragrance, and soaked in the promise. I willed the swirl of anxious questions—what will I tell my son about his uncle? what will happen to David's reputation in the community? what am I supposed to tell people now?—out of my muscles. I waited for them to seep through my pores, pushed out like toxins to dissolve in the heat that surrounded me.

Maybe Dad could be the role model for Ben now. I opened my eyes and blew tunnels through the bubbles. But that didn't work out too well for David.

# 3

I called Lori's land line and not her cell phone because I hoped she wouldn't be home. Then I could leave a message, feeling quite proud of myself for having made the effort to contact her. And I could finish blow drying my hair.

Wow. Bet the God I used to believe in heard that and "Tsk, Tsked" me in disappointment.

Could I be any more of a wimp? Probably. But, since her machine didn't pick up the call, I wasn't going to find out now.

"Hi, Caryn." Lori's voice sounded as if it'd been rolled over by a tractor.

A jolt of surprise when I heard my name. Of course . . . caller ID.

"Hi. Did I catch you at a bad time?" Great, Caryn. Nice lead-in to a disaster.

Quiet.

"Lori?" Did she hang up on me already?

"I'm here."

"David called me this morning. He told me about Mexico." I leaned against the antique enamel table we used as an island in the kitchen and traced the wispy cherry red curlicue design on its stark white top with my finger. "I'm overwhelmed. I didn't know. I don't understand."

"Wait just a minute," she said, and I heard what sounded like a door shut. "My parents are here. I walked outside so I could talk. They're trying to help, but . . . they're furious, and I just don't have that kind of energy right now."

Six months pre-wedding, Lori's parents deserved to be a little combustible, especially since they turned down the wedding cancellation insurance. Months ago, David had told me the company, Change of Heart, covered everything except if the bride or groom had a change of heart. At the time, we all laughed at the irony.

I stopped my invisible tracing and eyed the empty coffeepot. "Did he tell you this morning?" I found a bag of Community Dark Roast in the pantry, propped the phone between my ear and shoulder, and measured six full scoops into the filter.

"No. Last night. We were supposed to meet my sister Nita and her husband for dinner. But David called me at work yesterday afternoon and asked if we could meet them another night. He just said he needed to talk. I should've known it was a disaster waiting to happen. Nobody says 'we need to talk' when it involves something good." Her words were laced with tears.

"Lori, I know what a struggle this is for you. I can talk to you later or tomorrow . . ."

"It's okay," she said. I heard her sniffle against a backdrop of muffled voices, then silence before she asked, "Can you hold on?" It was a question tinged with impatience.

"Sure. Of course." I poured water into the coffeemaker's reservoir, flipped the on switch, and sat on one of the cane bar stools to wait for Lori and the coffee. I heard a barrage of one word replies, "Fine. Sure. Whatever. Okay. Yes. Thanks." Like drumbeats between smatterings of untuned instruments.

"I'm back. My parents couldn't decide if they should order Chinese for lunch or go to the grocery. I think they're doing both. Thank God." Relief echoed in her voice.

Two cups of coffee later, I learned how Lori lost her fiancé. Her friend. Her future.

Lori said she and David talked until after midnight. He told her he loved her, he cared for her, but he couldn't marry her. Make that, *wouldn't* marry her.

"Another woman. Of course that's what I thought first. You know, somebody blonder or taller or thinner or smarter or richer. One of those '-ers,' " she told me. Lori said she was prepared to fight, to do whatever it took to win him back. Until he dropped the "G-bomb," as she referred to it.

David told her he'd fought himself because he wanted the dream package: a wife, kids, the white picket fence and the happily ever after. But something never seemed right. He said he hoped making a commitment, the engagement, planning a wedding would make a difference. And it did. But not in the way he thought. It just proved none of those things actually made a difference in what he'd known to be the truth about himself.

I listened, ping-ponging between anger and sadness, wishing I could press a "pause" button to ready myself to ride the next wave of revelations.

"And then he said he was gay. I can't fight gay. I don't have the right equipment." Her words landed with the force of sandbags.

She told the story in that "he said, then I said" narrative, draped with all those totally unrelated details we tend to summon when immersed in our own epic tragedies. Each word a brushstroke painting the scene in our brains, so we can't convince ourselves later that none of it happened. I knew the color of David's polo shirt ("that lime one I bought him at Neiman's for his birthday"), and what they were drinking ("I didn't have any wine in the house; I sipped Earl Grey tea. How pathetic."), and even the temperature of her den ("my teeth were chattering, the room was so cold; I don't know why I didn't make it warmer . . .").

After David left, Lori told me she'd called Nita. She said her sister and Jeff must have rolled out of bed and into their car because they made the twenty-mile trip in half the time. "They slept here, then called my parents in the morning. They thought since they had to leave, Mom and Dad should be here with me." She sighed. "You'd think I was on suicide watch."

Lori must have caught my strangled "Oh" because she snapped back quickly. "No, I've not gone there. I won't. But if my mother and father don't leave soon, I might be on murder watch." Her voice dropped to a whisper, so I figured they must have returned from their food buying frenzy.

"It sounds like you have company again. Call me after they leave . . . or whenever." I walked over and turned off the coffeemaker and carried the empty carafe to the sink. "I'm as blown away by this as you are. It's like suddenly I have a new brother. I don't even understand who this David is or why."

"Guess I didn't either. And that scares me. All these years thinking I knew how I'd spend my life, then it disappears. Who would have thought . . ."

"I understand. I really do," I said, reminded of the familiar knot of loss laced so tightly I doubted it would ever unwind.

"Yes, I suppose you do understand more than anyone in my family. But I'm sorry. I didn't mean to bring back memories of Harrison."

I couldn't tell her it wasn't just remembering Harrison. The life I thought I knew as David's sister was disappearing too.

After talking to Lori, I regretted sending Ben away for twenty-four hours. This was a time I could use a distraction or at least a legitimate reason to stand in line to buy tickets for a Disney animated film.

I cleaned the glass carafe, then dumped the wet coffee grounds in the garbage. Not very eco-friendly of me, as David once reminded me. One weekend when he stayed to help take care of Harrison, David told me I could use the grounds as an organic flea dip rub or mix them with egg whites to make facial mud packs. "If this is the helpful info you're including in those real estate e-newsletters you're sending out, don't be surprised to find your client list dwindling," I told him. Not long after that, he bought one of those snazzy single-cup brewing systems. Guess convenience trumped being green.

The coffeemaker reassembled, the dishwasher started, and the emptiness of the house reverberated. I looked around, seeing not furniture or flooring or keepsakes, but an emotional assault. I didn't need to be held hostage by memories on a combat mission, lying around my house, waiting in picture frames and used bottles of Aramis cologne, and notes on birthday cards, all of them ready to ambush me.

"Well," I said to the pantry, "this soldier isn't going into battle on an empty stomach." I found a box of granola cereal, poured some in a coffee cup and spooned vanilla yogurt over it. I leaned against the island and considered my options as I ate.

I could wander around Whole Foods Market. Usually on Saturdays there was something to sample on every aisle. I could taste-test myself through the store and consider it research for my catering business. Or I could go to the bookstore and hunt for a cookbook I didn't already own. Or I could call Julie and meet them all at the bowling alley. Or I could defer to my standard coping mechanism when faced with an overdose of reality. I could take a nap.

Naps became my drug of choice after Harrison died. How else could I forget those days potty training my son and diapering my husband? Days I wanted to call Ms. Easterling, my ninth grade teacher, and tell her I'd grasped the definition of situational irony and could pass the test now. Remembering the medical supply company replacing the bed that made me a wife with the one that sentenced me to being a caretaker. Some days I'd stumble to Julie's with Ben in my arms. She'd take him from me, and I'd succumb to exhaustion in their guest room.

There were days I'd hear Ben's sweet lilting almost two-year-old voice as he toddled from room to room, accompanied by the waddling wooden duck he pulled behind. "Where Daddy? Where Daddy go?" Only when I slept could I escape the echoes of his forlorn confusion.

But like most addictions, the solution for making the pain disappear became the problem. Unless I entered eternal sleep—and there were certainly those days I'd considered it—I'd still be doomed to face life without Harrison.

I scraped the last bite of cereal out of the cup. Now I'm doomed to life without a straight brother. No nap was going to change that either.

I called Julie and told her the pity party had ended early.

"The guys just started their second game. If you're desperate for entertainment—I know I am—head on over," she said.

I tossed my cell phone in my purse without checking for missed calls, turned on the house alarm, and left. Driving to the bowling alley, I reminded myself to apologize to Ben for snapping at him this morning after David called. My poor child's toes curled in on themselves inside his shoes, and I fussed at him for his innocent question. He physically lost his father; he didn't need to emotionally lose his mother.

And Harrison witnessed it all now. And more.

———∞∞∞———

Blindfolded, I'd know if I landed in a bowling alley. Stale cigarette smoke and sweat swirled between layers of spilled beer and soft drinks, marinated in French fried grease, and topped with a sharp chemical spritz. Clearly, recipes were overtaking my life.

The smell settling on my shoulders, I searched for a tall woman with hair the color of a new penny. Even Julie's voice wouldn't break the rumbling thuds of bowling balls exploding into thundering crescendos of pins.

A few lanes from where I stood, Ben darted in my direction. "Mom! Mom! You came. Cool!" He high-fived me and showed off his clunky black and silver bowling shoes. "Mr. Trey rented these, so I gotta give 'em back when we leave."

I followed him, stepped into the pit and tossed my car keys into one of the empty chairs. I sat next to Julie who manned the scores. "Surprise. I made it."

She smiled. "I knew you loved me more than you loved Rachel Ray."

"Actually, you barely edged out John Besh and his recipe for Strawberry Ravioli." I patted the top of her head. "Where are your boys?"

"After Nick's ball landed two lanes over, Trey thought the kid might need a break. They're at the snack bar," she said. "So, you get to watch Ben solo."

Ben finished tying his right shoe and gave me a thumbs up.

"Okay, Ben, show your mom how the pros do it," Julie said.

Ben grabbed a green speckled ball from the rack and shuffled to the foul line.

He swung his spindly arm back, forward, then flung the ball toward the pins. It landed like a meteor hitting concrete, slid into the head pin and then spun into the gutter. I watched his thin shoulders sag, and I wanted to knock the other pins down with the sheer force of my will. How dare they disappoint my child.

Ben turned around, shrugged his shoulders, and grinned. "I got one!"

Julie patted my hand. "See. It's all a matter of perspective. Maybe it's time to follow your son's lead."

A kernel of annoyance dug itself under my thin skin. "Not now, okay? I get it. You're not talking about bowling." I smiled at Ben as he waited for the return to burp up his ball. When he stepped up to the lane, I returned Julie's hand pat. "And I'm not going to talk about David."

"And that's exactly the problem—"

"Problem? What problem?" I heard Trey before he appeared from behind me juggling three fountain drinks, his shirt pocket lumpy with bags of candy. "Hey, Caryn, glad you made it," he said, not seeming at all surprised that I did.

Julie reached for a drink. "Just girl talk," she answered. I knew that tone. She used it when Trey asked the price of her new shoes. "Not much," always meant "Don't ask, you really don't want to know." Trey rolled his eyes in my direction. He probably figured he was shut out of a girl conspiracy. But I felt shut out of a Julie conspiracy. It was quite un-Julie-like to not divulge code-orange information to her husband. Though neither of us had moved, the space between us widened.

Somewhere between my confusion and curiosity, Nick materialized from behind Trey. He handed me one of the two drinks he held. "I saw you come in when Dad was ordering our stuff. We got an extra for you."

# 4

Baking the Cranberry Walnut Biscotti to bring to Julie and Trey's house the next morning, I redefined hell: every appliance that bings, buzzes, and burps will be there. Without off buttons. Maybe my baking therapy had burned itself out. The year after Harrison died, I gave away cakes, pies, muffins, cookies, bread. No one ever worried I'd end it all like Sylvia Plath kneeling in front of the oven. I had too many other things to put in there.

When friends of friends started asking for my pumpkin bread during the holidays, my catering business began. Actually, David suggested it. He and Lori had taken Ben to the park after David asked, "When's the last time your son breathed air that wasn't controlled by a thermostat?" My blank stare answered for me.

They returned about two dozen loaves of bread later, lined up on the counters like bloated bricks. The scent of cinnamon soaked the kitchen. That's when David, using his official big brother voice, nestled the words "allocation of resources" among a slew of others, and, next thing I knew, I owned a catering business.

David always had big picture brain. I'd look at a pile of manure and think, "shovel." My brother would see the same pile and look for a horse.

"Where'd that brother go?" I shot back at my reflection in the glass oven door. The timer screamed, took a breath, and screamed again. "Okay, okay. Gimme some time to put on the mitts." I opened the door and pulled out the baking stone, the citrusy scent making itself at home in the kitchen. Once I slid the stone on a cooling rack, I took off the mitts, and reset the timer for ten minutes. "The tyranny of the timer," I said to the speechless biscotti and laughed at myself. But the laughter soured with the memory of years when time was my enemy. Never enough or too much of it.

My phone rang while I searched the cabinets for a cookie tin. I reached over the counter to grab the phone where I'd plugged it to recharge overnight. Something I forgot to do more times than I remembered. If Ben hadn't been at Julie's, I would've silenced the thing. David left five messages in two hours. Every flash of his number tormented me. Silent pleas I forced myself to ignore so I'd not be taken hostage by loss and pain. How many times could there be a ransom?

This time, it was Julie who called. "Didn't you tell us you were bringing over breakfast?" She already knew the answer, but it was her way of telling me I should've already been at her house.

"Hey, on my way soon. I promise," I answered and tried not to slam cabinet doors as I hunted and wished I'd invested in that label maker Harrison used to bug me about buying.

"In fact . . ." I reached over my head and grabbed a tin on the top shelf of the cabinet. As I pulled it off the shelf, I realized—too late—it actually supported three smaller ones I couldn't spot from my vantage point. I managed an, "Uh oh," and scooted to the left before they hit my head instead of the floor. They crashed against the Mexican tiled floor like cymbals.

Instead of a screech from Julie, I heard a sigh and then, "Let me guess. You didn't use the step stool. Was that your head they landed on?"

If Julie couldn't distinguish between the floor and my head, being late was the least of my troubles. "Step stool. No. Head. No. I'll be there in a few. Bye."

I found a pair of jeans on my bedroom floor and a sleeveless tee that passed the sniff test, clipped a barrette around my cranky curls, arranged the biscotti in the newly dented tin and headed out of the house.

The street was so deserted it could have been a stage set for one of those cowboy showdowns. Not a surprise considering the three-digit heat index. In late spring, the lawns of St. Augustine grass stretched down the street, monster-sized emerald patches made square by the bands of concrete dividing one from another. But a few weeks into June, the fringes of the grass that met the street had already been scorched black. Just crossing the street felt like fighting my way from under a wet blanket.

Julie opened the door before I knocked. The plus side of having glass doors is being able to see company before it knocks. "Come on in, fast." She left a space wide enough for me to squeeze through, then shut the door as if the humidity morphed into a stranger who tried to sneak in with me. "I don't know why you bothered with the oven. With the temperature outside, you could've baked those on the sidewalk on your way over," she said as she followed me into the kitchen.

"If it's this blistering now, we're going to need ice baths by August." I handed her the biscotti, then peeled the front of my T-shirt away from my neck. White may not have been the best choice. "It's scary quiet. What did you do with the boys?"

"Well," she said, arranging the biscotti on the plate like wagon spokes, "the biggest boy is on the golf course. I sent him out with a frozen Gatorade, and told him not to blame me if he died out—" She looked at me, the arch of her chestnut eyebrows lifted over her round hazel eyes. An "oops" washed over her face.

Julie's face softened, her cheekbones more pronounced by the wisp of color that floated underneath the surface of her skin. "And the other two boys were still sleeping when I last checked. They stayed awake late, I'm sure. I found Nick asleep on his bedspread with his Wii control still in his hands, and Ben curled up on the other end of the bed instead of on the top bunk." She pushed the Sunday paper aside and set the plate on her distressed oak kitchen table. Distressed, she'd told me when they bought it, because it already knew it'd be holding frozen meals.

I pulled two coffee mugs from an overhead cabinet. "Guess maybe the trick is taking the controls away before bedtime," I said, and cringed as soon as the last syllable of the ghost of my Mother spilled out of my mouth.

"I'll remember that next time." Julie's sarcasm confirmed what I heard in my voice.

"Okay, my oops this time," I said, filled the mugs with coffee and brought them to the table.

She smiled, glanced at the grandfather clock in the corner, and said, "I'll wake up the boys. Trey's going to be home in time for us to make the noon service."

I watched her walk down the hall while I waved away the lingering steam rising from the coffee. She took a few steps, then turned to face me. "You know, you and Ben are welcome to come with us."

Julie's frequent invitations had dulled the razor of guilt-tinged anxiety that once sliced my spirit. She didn't sense the sharpness any more either, but like an actress in a never-ending play, she continued to rehearse the line. But my response was equally scripted, "No, not today. Maybe another time."

I never revealed that some Sundays, while I rinsed leftover breakfast dishes, I'd watch as their SUV eased out of their driveway on their way to church. When it pulled away from their house, it was as if my unfulfilled dreams left with them, crashing against the concrete like empty cans tied to the bumper. Sometimes I wondered if God could ever fill that emptiness. An emptiness not even my sweet son sliding his way down the wood floors into the kitchen could fill.

---

When Nick said, "Ben, look. Your mom made those stick things," Julie headed straight for the pantry and emerged with three different cereal options.

The boys amused themselves swiveling around on the kitchen counter stools between cereal bites. I refilled my coffee mug while Julie rummaged through the kitchen junk drawer for a needle and thread so she could sew a button on Nick's khakis. "Why are buttons sewn on like the kid's only going to wear the pants once?" She shuffled and reshuffled clutter and produced what looked like a designer matchbook, holding it like a mirror in front of her face. "There you are."

"I know you didn't start smoking. What is that?"

Julie plopped into the chair across from mine. "This is a sewing kit from the Grand Hotel. Remember?" she said and lifted the cover to reveal a needle and six different colored threads.

She turned to the boys. "Nick, stop picking the raisins out of your cereal and bring me your pants." Nick spooned his outcast raisins into Ben's bowl, slid off the stool, and headed to his bedroom.

"That was a fun place." Ben's words sounded as if they'd traveled for a year to arrive in this moment.

We vacationed in Gulf Shores last summer. Our two families plus David and Lori. Trey wanted someone to play golf with. Told Julie and me he needed male bonding. Guess that didn't work out so well for either one of them.

"It was fun, wasn't it?" Julie licked her thumb and forefinger and slid one end of the beige thread between them. "Ben, do you remember when your Uncle David tried to get your mom to parasail?"

Ben looked at me, his shy grin so much like Harrison's. "He kept telling her he'd catch her if she fell. She didn't think he was funny."

He was right. Later that night, I'd told David that Ben had already lost a father, he didn't need to lose a mother too. What I didn't tell him was the truth. That the idea of being 500 feet in the air hanging from a parachute terrified me. I'd faced enough fears by then. I didn't want to wrestle another one.

Nick zoomed in, tossed his pants in his mother's lap, and challenged Ben to one more game before he left. Ben hopped off his stool, dashed after Nick, then put on his foot brakes right in front of me as if he'd hit a wall. "Mom, when are we going to see Uncle David?"

I glanced at Julie. She jabbed the needle through the button without so much as a peek in my direction. Strange. Julie more often pounced into conversations, not engaged in stealth approach.

Ben scratched the top of his head and waited, his eyes wide, as if they could tug the answer from me.

Ice clattered into the bin in the freezer. I finished my coffee and leaned against the cross-back chair. "I'm not sure, Ben," I said and hoped being subdued meant the words would land softly. "He's—"

"Okay," he said, his voice echoed the dullness in his eyes. He pulled his shorts up from his hips where they'd settled and walked off, leaving a trail of quiet.

My heart followed him, but it couldn't stretch across the void my words had caused.

"So, what are you going to do about David?" Julie snipped the thread, folded Nick's pants, and set them on the table. "More coffee?"

I shook my head. She emptied the carafe into her mug, then set the microwave timer. "To remind myself to tell Nick to take a bath before church," she said and sat down at the table.

"Why do I have to do anything? Shouldn't David do something?" Like go back to the one I knew. I reached for a biscotti, but drew my hand back as if it'd been slapped. If food would anchor these emotional waves, I'd need more than an Italian cookie. I'd hold out for the pecan pie cupcakes with caramel cream cheese icing I planned to bake this afternoon.

"He did. He told you the truth." She dunked what was left of her biscotti in her coffee. "And you're punishing him for that."

"Well, now we're even."

# 5

"Mom, don'tcha think I'm too old for these?"

I looked up from my desk where I'd been flipping through Emeril's latest cookbook when I heard Ben's voice. He must have just stepped out of the bathtub. He stood just inside the door to my office, his hair plastered to the back of his neck. In the front, where he'd probably pushed it off his forehead, it stood like a brown fence. Fat drops of water rolled down the sides of his face. With one hand, Ben pinched closed the Disney beach towel he'd wrapped around his body and locked under his arms. It seems Mickey might have made two trips around Ben's pretzel-thin body.

Water glistened in the hollows between his collarbone and shoulder. Ben and Snowball, our neighbors' lab, shared a post-bath philosophy. Why use a towel when you can just shake?

He stretched out his arm to show me the Ironman pajamas clutched in his hand. "So, whaddya think?" He waved them up and down, then brought the bundle to his chest and sniffled, wiping the edge of his nose with his bent forefinger.

My brain started to download an answer. I opened my mouth to speak, when something almost imperceptible, a whisper of time between child and boy, settled in the back of my throat. I stopped. He wasn't asking the question because he thought he was too old. He was asking because he didn't want to think he was too old.

I stood and opened the door to the bathroom off the office. My answer tiptoed out. "Why don't you pop in here? Just throw them on so you can stop shivering, and we'll talk about it."

His entire body sighed. He blinked those wet killer eyelashes my friends threatened to hijack and eased a smile from his lips. "Good idea. I don't want to get sick before school." He walked over, grabbed the door handle, and turned to me. "We can talk about this when you tuck me in bed tonight. Okay?"

That space in the back of my throat opened again and slid right into my heart. "Sure. We'll have time."

I paper-clipped the page with the Eggplant and Shrimp Beignets recipe and shut the cookbook. Emeril could wait. Ben couldn't.

But when he stepped out of the bathroom sporting his Ironman pjs, I wished Ben could wait a few more years. If only I could freeze him at this age until I caught up.

I bumbled my way through mothering. How was I supposed to be a father too?

⚬≈⚬

"What would Dad think about me wearing Ironman? I know he's in heaven and all. I mean if he was still here. With us."

Ben picked at the blanket fuzz. Like his shoes, the blankets also showed signs of wear. Maybe I should have bought bed linens instead of baking pans. Even more reason to make sure the business could support us.

"Mom, are you listening? You're not even looking at me," said Ben.

He was right. I tousled his damp hair. "Sorry, dude."

38

"Are you okay?" He slid from under his covers and propped himself on his elbows.

His eyebrows almost reached for one another in that way they did when math problems perplexed him or his mother's spells of emptiness worried him.

Harrison's eyes peered at me through his son's. Could I continue to tuck the truth under my heart long enough to answer?

"I'm better than okay. I'm here with you, right?"

"I guess," he said and plopped his head on his pillow. "So, what about Dad? Would he think I'm being a baby?"

Ben *was* a baby when Harrison last saw him.

"Your dad would tell you what you wear isn't important. He'd say what matters is who you are inside." I kissed his warm forehead and tucked the blanket around him. I hoped Harrison couldn't see who I was inside.

"Well, I could be an Ironman inside too," he said and grinned. "G'night, Mom."

"Good night, sweet Ben. I love you. Sleep tight."

"Don't let the bedbugs bite." His sleep-soft voice followed me as I walked out of his bedroom.

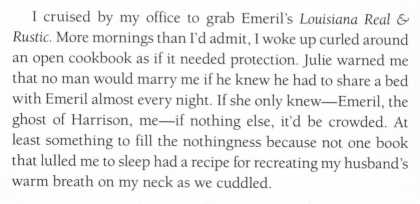

I cruised by my office to grab Emeril's *Louisiana Real & Rustic*. More mornings than I'd admit, I woke up curled around an open cookbook as if it needed protection. Julie warned me that no man would marry me if he knew he had to share a bed with Emeril almost every night. If she only knew—Emeril, the ghost of Harrison, me—if nothing else, it'd be crowded. At least something to fill the nothingness because not one book that lulled me to sleep had a recipe for recreating my husband's warm breath on my neck as we cuddled.

Even after all these years, nights were like walking into a cave blindfolded. The same cave, every night. The cave where, if I stretched my arms straight out from my sides making myself a human T, my fingertips became my eyes as they brushed along the cold, but now familiar walls of loneliness. I was less likely to bump into memories of Harrison as I did in the beginning when I could barely stand as I entered the hollowness of my life. When grief and guilt hung on me like wet wool sweaters.

Eventually I learned balance. Learned not to sprawl across the glimpses of Harrison that appeared in my mind's eye, as if I could hold them hostage.

On my way to brush my teeth, I tossed the book on my side of the bed. My side of the bed. Every side was my side now on a bed docked like an ivory chenille barge in the middle of the room. I was years past turning down the covers on Harrison's side. Sometimes when Ben, transported by thunder cracks, crawled in next to me, I'd wake up to a familiar tangle of sheets. Otherwise, the flat space screamed Harrison's absence.

I scrunched my pillow behind my back and leaned against the headboard, propping the cookbook against my bent knees. Finding the page I'd paper-clipped earlier, I reread the beignet recipe. I'd only recently started including recipes with seafood. Harrison had an allergy to all things shellfish, so severe that everything about his neck swelled to twice its size. All those years spent in seafood exile, but still Harrison found a way to die.

The beignets, if I could find a way to make them bite-sized, would make an appealing addition to my luncheon and reception offerings. Targeting food snobs became my new strategy. They never seemed to mind doling out money for food that was less pronounceable, smaller proportioned, and more unfamiliar.

The curse, I discovered, was if the item became too popular, then they wanted something else.

Tomorrow I'd add a trip to Whole Foods to my school supply shopping. Ben would start second grade in two weeks, which meant if I didn't want to battle dozens of mothers for pencil boxes, construction paper, and clunky erasers I needed to knock out his list. I grabbed the pen and steno pad I kept on the nightstand for all those ideas that wiped their feet on the doormat to my brain right before it drifted off to sleep.

The last thing I scribbled before dreaming of Harrison and Ben pulling up nets of glistening translucent shrimp while I cheered them on was . . .

. . . Brunoise red peppers????

# 6

I'm the mother. I'm the mother. I'm the mother.

I reminded myself of this, despite the feeling that I stood on the edge of a high dive looking into a shallow pool. My son started school today. Not me. Wasn't there a statute of limitations on the first day of school anxiety? First *I* had to deal with it, now it's déjà vu through Ben. First day of kindergarten, then first grade, then middle school, then high school, then college . . .

My mother seemed to handle this so much better. The first day would be like any other that summer, except we woke up earlier and left the house for almost seven hours. David and I each carried a brown lunch bag with our names in my mother's no-nonsense handwriting. None of these curly or bubble fonts for her. We ate a sensible breakfast of eggs and toast, two slices of bacon and a glass of whole milk. We dressed in our uniforms, waited for her kiss on the forehead, and off we went to the bus stop. Now the first day required more than a brown bag could hold.

Julie parked across the street from Cypress Grove Elementary to avoid the bus traffic and the first-day car drop-offs that twisted around the neighborhood like a conga line, minus the fun.

"Maybe next year the school will add 'one small wheelbarrow' to the supply list." She lifted the Honda's tailgate and dispensed new L.L.Bean backpacks, one red and one blue, to Ben and Nick. She handed me a canvas tote crammed with supplies second graders can't live without, grabbed the other tote, and shut the gate. Already, a scattered symphony of slamming car doors hyphenated by voices seasoned with squeals surrounded us.

Ben shifted to adjust his backpack. Standing behind him, I set my canvas cargo on the ground between my legs. I pulled his shirt collar from underneath the straps and adjusted it around his neck. He turned to face me, his thumbs hooked under the padded red straps that crossed over his shoulders. "Mom," his voice signaled a warning, "I got it, okay?"

You're about to embarrass the kid, Caryn. How is it dead people have all these opinions, Harrison? Not like you've endured the shopping wars.

Julie and I spent the weeks before the first school day outfitting the boys with several pairs of khaki pants and shorts, polo shirts in white and navy, and Nike Zooms. Knowing my son wore shoes with toe-wiggling space and shorts that required a belt, left space in the room in my brain reserved for neuroses. Now I could obsess about other issues. Like would his teacher know he needed to be reminded to tie his shoes or that staring at the ceiling meant a deep-thought moment? What if he waited too long to ask to go to the bathroom? What if none of the other kids talked to him?

"Caryn, aren't you walking Ben to the gym?" Julie's elbow in my waist speared me out of my brain fog. "Let's get moving before this humidity wilts the pleats right out of their shorts."

**43**

We spotted the boys' teacher, Michelle Richmond, who waved a purple clipboard above her head and looked like a human maypole swarmed by backpacks.

"Step it up guys," Julie called over her shoulder as we moved closer to their class section in the bleachers. They'd already adopted that kid-respectable distance between themselves and us. Not too far back so that they couldn't find us, but not so close they looked helpless.

I propped the bag of supplies near a cluster of paper towel rolls and tissue boxes, and watched as Ben and Nick checked in with Michelle. "Ben seems so much more relaxed this year than he did last year," I said.

"Funny," said Julie, her tone serious, "Ben said the same thing about you."

"When did he . . ." My voice trailed off after I saw Julie's smirk.

"Michelle's steering the boys over here. Catch her vest. Remind me to tell her at book club that she's about fifty years too young to be wearing it."

Michelle joined our book club after her friend and our neighbor Franny dropped out after her company transferred her to Houston. None of us could figure out why a twenty-something with a body that didn't jiggle when she walked and a face that rivaled Angelina Jolie's, dressed as if she and her mother shared a closet. Julie wanted to nominate her for TLC's *What Not to Wear*, but I always vetoed the idea. Unless we'd be voting today. The black sweater vest featured dancing red apples trapped by green rulers on one side, a yellow school bus and a fat wooden pencil on the other, and the alphabet along the hem. I looked at it and heard the sound of nails scraping against a chalkboard.

She handed the clipboard to a tall man with a whistle around his neck. "Mine are all here." He nodded. I figured he must be in charge of the student inventory.

"Tell your mothers you'll see them after school," Michelle said. Flanked by Ben and Nick, she gave each one a head pat and smiled at us in the same way the labor room nurse did the night Ben arrived who smiled at me and said, "Okay, Mom, we're going to push now." A smile that conveyed "whatever I said will happen and now, or else I won't be smiling the next time I say it."

"Bye, Mom," said Ben. He took a sliver of a step backwards, a pre-empt in case I might have wanted to bend down and kiss him.

Before I could tell him he was safe, he fled with Nick in the direction of the bleachers.

"Guess we're done here." I hoped I'd masked my surprise at Ben's whiff of independence. One inch of movement. It signified miles.

"Oh, Caryn, wait. I need to ask you a question," said Michelle. She reached out her arm and for a moment I thought she might pat my head. Instead she pulled my business card out of the yellow school bus on her sweater, which—good grief—doubled as a pocket.

"Um, Michelle . . . Caryn has boxes of those sitting on her office floor. You can keep that one," said Julie. I looked at Julie and this time thought the head-patting might reverse itself.

Michelle glanced at Julie, recovered from her hiccup of confusion, and handed me the card.

"Remember that email I sent about cooking meals a few times a week?"

"Sure," I answered and wished I really did remember. Ben was fortunate he wasn't an email or I'd have been charged with willful neglect years ago. Negotiating my real world gobbled up most of my time already. Email was on portion-control. Especially because my spam fascinated me, and generally out-numbered legitimate emails by fifty to one. David used to rev up finger-wagging lectures almost weekly that started with "you own a business now" and ended with "you need to check your email."

"Well, yesterday at inservice I told a few teachers you'd be making meals once or twice a week, and they wanted in. I wrote their emails—"

Whatever she intended to say after that was lost in the sound of a million swarming bees. "Morning bell," she said, almost as an apology. She peered over Julie's shoulder in the direction of the bleachers, then allowed herself enough eye contact to say, "Caryn, call me when you're ready to start."

"Wait. You're cooking for teachers? When did that happen?" Julie sounded a bit shocked.

"Just now. I'll explain on the way to the car. I think Michelle just dismissed us."

We watched her walk toward kids she'd be spending more time with than some of their parents. Ben and Nick laughed as a boy standing behind them played an air guitar. Judging by his intense pinched face and the position of his hands, it must have been an electric air guitar.

I waved, but I didn't get Ben's attention. My lips had just met to say his name when Julie squeezed my upper arm. "No," she said as if I had reached for fire. "You'll embarrass him."

"It's not like I'm going to run over there and hug him." I loved Julie, but sometimes she thought Nick and Ben were clones. I knew my son, and he wouldn't be ashamed if I just told him good-bye.

Michelle had started calling kids out of the bleachers, so Ben was already making his way down to the gym floor. When I called his name, he turned and almost tripped. The snorts and giggles rose from the class like smoke from a fire and burned Ben's face. He steadied himself, stepped down, and stared right past me.

"Ready now?" Julie didn't wait for my answer. She walked off.

I sludged through the muck of "I told you so" she left behind.

# 7

On the way home, I told Julie about the weekly meal idea for teachers. Michelle had mentioned at book club that school starting meant her family would be subjected to microwaved meals and take-out. I figured I could help her. What was one meal a week?

"Did you think this all the way through?"

"Seriously, Julie. It's me you're talking to. How much do I think anything 'all the way through'?"

If I did, I would have understood another one of David's phone calls, the one that came the day our lives turned inside out all those years ago.

I remembered feeling cranky and exhausted that day. Ben, however, had slept between stops at the pediatrician's office, the cleaners, the pharmacy, and the supermarket, and home.

Car seat designer engineers made the top of my hit list that morning. When it was time to do a test run on car seat exit procedures, I was certain said engineer didn't have a squirming one-year-old, hands coated with banana paste, swinging an empty juice bottle, and wearing a diaper suspiciously heavier than it should be. Excited by the pending freedom from his straps and buckles, Ben kicked his little Niked feet against the hard plastic shell of the seat and, unfortunately, my forehead when I couldn't duck in time. So when my cell phone demanded my attention, I yelled, "Not now," and wished I had set those two words in my voice program to stop the insistent shrill.

Before I could finish disentangling Ben's legs from the twisted straps, there was yet another call. "I'm busy," I shouted over the front seat in the direction of my purse. A few less shrills. I hoped the call went to voice mail so I could explain later to mystery caller the logistics of removing a child from a car seat without causing either one of us a major brain injury.

When I lifted Ben out of the seat, the banana peel he'd been flattening with his bottom tagged along with him, but it did nothing to mask the smell emanating from his diaper region. "Ewww, Ben," I held my breath for a moment and hoisted him onto my hip. For some reason, that amused him, and he continued to remind me of the contents of his diaper with chants of "Poo, poo, poo . . ." sprinkled with motorboat sounds with his lips.

I grabbed my purse off the front seat and opened the side door into our kitchen. I threw my purse on the nearest chair, kicked the door closed, and had just released Ben when the house phone started ringing. People we knew rarely called that number. "Get out the vote" pleas, telemarketers, and the occasional wrong number accounted for a majority of the calls. We always let the call go to the answering machine first.

Ben found a Cheerio on the floor under his high chair and almost popped it in his mouth before I scooped him up again and pried it out of his fingers. I pulled off his shoes and socks and set them on the kitchen counter while our recording played in the background. "Hello, you've reached our house. Please leave a message." Generic worked for us. Julie and Trey's was a production number. Background music with voiceovers (theirs), and Nick cooing.

"Caryn? If you're there, please pick up." David's voice. And it sounded un-Davidlike.

Something happened to Dad. The thought pinched my heart. I grabbed the receiver and, with the even stinkier Ben still in my arms, headed to the nursery.

"David. What's going on?" I pulled a clean diaper out of the bag hanging on the closet doorknob and handed it to Ben who waved it in front of my face like he was Second Lining down Bourbon St. I trapped the receiver between my ear and shoulder and switched Ben to my other hip. I really needed a different system. I'd been asking Harrison about getting a BlueTooth device, but we both wondered if it would be just one more thing we'd have to dig out of Ben's mouth.

"I'm on my way to your house. I should be there in a few minutes. I'll explain when I see you."

Then no David. Just the white noise of the dial tone.

Still holding the receiver, I lowered both of us to the floor, pushed by the weight of unanswered questions. I sat Ben on the throw rug next to the crib. He dropped the diaper and pointed to one of the sailboats making its way around the blue wool circle. "Ben, boat!"

The boats never changed and neither did the surprise in his voice each time he noticed one. "Yes, sweetie. Boat. And Mommy wishes she could be sailing far, far away right now." He grinned and raked the rug with his little pudgy fingers.

I cradled his head in my hands and tilted him backwards. Hands attached to arms attached to shoulders moved instinctively changing Ben's diaper as my brain tapped its anxious foot. Waiting. Where was David? What happened? What happened? I should have answered the phone. I should have answered the phone.

If only there was some armor, something to shield myself from whatever news David would soon deliver. Even hurricanes had warnings. You could prepare. Bottled water. Generator. An ax in every attic.

I grabbed a clean polo bodysuit out of the dresser and wrestled Ben out of the foul clothes and into the fresh. As soon as I released him, he flopped on his belly, pushed himself to standing, then wobbled away like he was walking on the deck of a ship in a storm.

"Caryn?" My name called from the back of the house. "Caryn?"

David's voice. Why didn't I hear the door open? I reminded myself to tell Harrison the time had arrived for the wireless door alarms. What if Ben decided to roam the streets?

I wanted to answer David. I really did. But I knew he'd find us anyway. In those few seconds before he did, I wanted to sit in the in-between place. The place between what was and what will be. Because whatever David was about to tell me would close one of those doors forever. And I knew that pain. Even from a distance it looked familiar. Sometimes it tiptoed into a memory, invited itself into a dream, spilled itself into a conversation.

"What are you doing?" David's voice was equal parts confusion, franticness, and irritation, stirred and poured into the room. He held out his arms to Ben, who sputtered, "Bubba, Bubba," his own little arms stretched forward with expectancy as he propelled himself toward his uncle.

What was I doing? Still sitting on the floor next to a poopy diaper. Worried you'd never get here and afraid you would. "Ben needed a diaper change," I said, but it sounded more like a question than an answer. "What happened, David?"

I shivered with the realization that Harrison, not David, would be here if something had happened to my father. And the panic I willed myself to ignore since David called vibrated under my skin like electric currents.

"It's Harrison. He's on his way to Meadowbrook Hospital. Sam called and said he collapsed at the office—"

Words swayed through the air like confetti falling from the ceiling. Fragments of thoughts. If only my brain could connect the pieces.

"Sam? Who's Sam? What does that mean, 'collapsed'?" I stood, shoved the diaper into the so-not-magical Diaper Genie. "Wait, Harrison's boss? That Sam?"

"Caryn," David paused to still Ben's fingers tap-dancing on his cheek, "I'll explain on the way. We'll take your car so I don't have to move the car seat." His calm voice rode on tracks of urgency.

"My purse. I need my purse. And my cell phone. I think they're in the kitchen," I walked past David, stopped, looked down at my wrinkled linen shorts, brushed petrified banana crud off where earlier Ben had grabbed on to steady himself. I smoothed my hair as if to make sure it was still there. "My face. I need to fix my face. Do I have time?"

"No. We really don't have that kind of time." David handed over Ben, shoved diapers and wipes in the diaper bag, and steered us out of the room, his warm hands on my shoulders.

---

While Ben and I headed home from buying groceries, Harrison's right leg buckled underneath him as he walked into his boss's office. And while we sang along to "Goin' for a Ride" on the Sesame Street CD, Harrison's words traveled through sludge, never quite making their way to understanding.

An aggressive assault by an otherwise puny blood vessel incapacitated my strong husband. A hemorrhagic stroke. One of fifteen cases out of 10,000. That's what Harrison's doctor said was the risk for males ages 15-34.

———⟨∞⟩———

A few months later, Ben almost passed the Mayo Clinic's potty training readiness quiz. The first question, "Does your child seem interested in wearing underwear?" he bombed on a technicality. I never doubted his interest in his Superman briefs. He clapped every time I showed them to him. He simply wasn't interested in wearing underwear. Or his diaper.

After a week of chasing Ben in his au natural freedom, I decided I wasn't so much interested either. I informed Harrison, who had already relocated to the hospital bed by then, that Ben could be naked butt boy until school started.

"He's wearing me out, and I'm just too tired to play tag." If only I could have sucked those words back in before they'd splattered themselves on Harrison's face. As if he'd needed to be reminded that his role as father had been usurped.

I fixed Harrison his latest mushy meal favorite of mashed potatoes laced with sharp cheddar cheese. Like most nights, I pulled Ben's high chair next to Harrison's bed and supervised while they both attempted to feed themselves. Sometimes Ben reached one arm out as far as he could in his father's direction while his other hand grabbed the edge of the high chair tray. The Big Bird spoon Ben wielded looked like a yellow stick sprouted from his palm. Whatever food it started its load with had already been deposited between the bowl and the floor. No matter. He'd focus on Harrison and screech "Da-deeeee" until the last syllable sounded more like a siren. His father usually rewarded him with a lopsided smile.

That night, Harrison scooped a spoonful of mashed potatoes and motioned for me to scoot the high chair closer. With the arm the stroke left behind, he moved his spoon toward Ben, opening his own mouth wider as the food neared Ben's mouth, in that way parents feed their children as if waiting to be fed themselves. Harrison's internal GPS pointed east instead of north, so Ben had tilted to his left like a sailboat listing in the water to meet the spoon.

That one shared moment between them was ordinary, which is precisely what made it so spectacular. In that frame of time, we could have passed for any family.

Dinner ended, mouths and hands wiped, and I rocked our son to sleep while Harrison struggled to squeeze a rubber ball. I'd carried Ben to his bedroom and returned to ours, flipped on the lamp between our two beds, and turned off the ceiling light. I'd just opened the door to our bathroom when Harrison called "KK," my post-stroke name, as if he'd been telling me a secret. The familiar tenderness in his voice. Months ago, that tender voice would have tugged me into his arms, soothed and weakened me like a warm bath. Now, I tugged at the rope of responsibility, scaling a mountain whose peak was obscured by uncertainty.

After we'd come home a few weeks earlier, Julie and Trey brought over the Rocky Anthology DVD collection. Julie pushed aside the comforter on our king-sized bed that hadn't yet been replaced, plopped herself next to Harrison, and asked Trey to hand her the boxed set. She pointed to the American-flag-draped, bruised and sweaty Sylvester Stallone on the cover and said, "Forceps baby. Paralyzed the whole lower left side of his face. You'll be in good company once you start talking again."

I glanced at Trey who looked like he'd just bitten into a chocolate-covered pickle. He provided one of those coughs intended to break the silence of an uncomfortable moment. "Uh, Jules, I think maybe Harrison and Caryn might—"

"Trey, it's okay. Harrison could use a laugh," I said, and I'd meant it. At the time, I didn't know how much I would miss laughing with him. I didn't know how much I'd ache for those nights washing dishes when he'd stand behind me, slide his arms around my waist, and kiss the top of my head. When he bent to whisper, "Let's go to bed," his breath warmed my ear. I didn't know I would miss the smell of pine trees and lemongrass when he reached for me in the middle of the night.

But after months of care-taking, weariness shared my body. That night I'd turned around, one hand on the door knob, which signaled I'm only pausing, not changing direction. Harrison signed, "I love you," his forefinger and pinky like a goalpost, his thumb straight out. His face, still chiseled handsome, but in a perpetual state of that just waking up look. The stroke recast his features, a portrait artist ignoring attention to details, and drew one eyebrow higher, made one eyelid less taut. A remnant of possibility, the seduction of hope flickered between us. I saw myself walk toward him, rest my head on his chest, lift his useless hand and place it on my cheek. But my body sighed and stayed.

"Me too," I said.

I walked into the bathroom.

Millions of Harrison's cells prepared themselves for another assault.

Rivulets of blood rinsed from my aching gums raced one another down the sink and into the drain.

Gathered by a silent alarm, the cells traveled.

I brushed my teeth. 120 seconds. Upper. Lower. Inner. Outer.

The army assembled in Harrison's middle cerebral artery. And when not one more could fit, they exploded through the wall. Flooding the spaces between his skull and brain. Spaces they were never meant to be.

I stepped out of the bathroom, mint fresh, ready for bed. Harrison had already surrendered.

———∞———

I don't remember how many doors had to open before I stopped expecting Harrison to walk through one of them. Months and months and months of them. Grief was the rope in a perpetual tug of war between remembering and forgetting.

It didn't seem at all fair that Harrison's death reduced me to commonality with a spider. For a while, I even busied myself with fact-finding missions about my female counterpart. Ben seemed amused when I'd entertain him during meals with my latest spider news.

"Hey, did you know that there would be at least 299 more of you if Mommy really was a black widow spider?"

He'd take a bite of his grilled cheese sandwich, his mouth churning, and look entirely engaged in the conversation. All eye-focused and solemn-faced.

"And, they don't all kill their boyfriend spiders after mating, so maybe they're not all widows." I rolled a few blueberries on his high chair table.

"Blerries!" He palmed a few and held them out to me as if discovering a treasure.

When would I feel that kind of pure delight again? Not even new flavors of Blue Bell ice cream made my insides smile.

The first year of my official widow-ness, David devoted himself to Ben and me. A week after Harrison's funeral, David dropped in one night on his way home from work. Ben was already in bed, and I sat cross-legged on the den floor in front of the television watching Seinfeld reruns, wearing one of Harrison's white shirts over my sweats and eating pork 'n' beans out of a can. At first David insisted we eat out because that forced me out of my jammies. Other times he'd cook, and my freezer started sprouting plastic containers labeled with meals.

He'd stay until I fell asleep or he'd crash on the other sofa since I still couldn't sleep in my bedroom. One morning, I woke and found a note taped to the Krups coffeemaker, the one appliance he knew I'd never ignore. David's handwriting looked like it could have been designed by *Architectural Digest*:

CARYN,
ADD THIS TO YOUR GROCERY LIST: SOUR CREAM, AVOCADOS, CILANTRO.
NACHO NIGHT!
CALL ME WHEN YOU WAKE UP.

Grocery list? Who needed a list for "buy food"? I could write that on my palm. But after the third note that week, I realized David gave me what I couldn't yet give myself—a reason to brush my teeth, comb my hair, and change my clothes.

He admitted months later he looked for recipes with ingredients voted the most unlikely to be in my pantry. "When I first started cooking at her house," he'd told Lori one night when she joined us for dinner, "salt would have made the list."

One weekend during those early months when I felt marinated in sadness, David mentioned having lunch with a bank loan officer after a recent closing.

"Lori and I ate at Acme Oyster House. We need to go there one night. Great fried shrimp—"

"Whoa. Did you just mention a woman's name?" I stopped shoveling cheesy orzo into Ben's mouth and looked at my brother. Ben took advantage of my moment of distraction and plunged his hands in his bowl. His attempt to grab the little rice noodles didn't work, but he entertained himself finger painting his face with cheese sauce.

"Were you just mentioning spiders again to your son?" David tossed fresh green beans and garlic in olive oil. The beans hissed and spit when they fell into the pan. He wiped his hands on the cotton dish towel draped over his left shoulder, then tossed it to me.

"I asked first." I cleaned Ben's hands and face, and handed him a few green beans David had steamed earlier. He picked up one in each hand, pounded the high chair table, and mumbled mostly consonants. "You actually had a date?"

"Does that surprise you?"

"Of course not. You spend so many nights and weekends with me and Ben, I wondered if you had a social life."

"I'm insulted. We haven't been social?" He grinned and stirred the sizzling beans. "I wouldn't be here unless I wanted to be. And if a better offer came along, I would have let you know."

"True," I said. Even in high school and unlike me, David never felt compelled to go places because his friends were going. "But, you've never really mentioned dating anyone."

"Because," he said and spooned the beans into a serving dish, "I've been busy trying to build my real estate business, and there wasn't anyone worth mentioning."

"Until now."

"Exactly. But I wouldn't call one lunch 'dating.' "

"Ben, honey, eat the beans. Stop mashing them in your hair." I sighed as I scraped green goo from his scalp. "So . . . tell me about this Lori person."

"She's smart, easy to talk to . . ." He handed me the tub of wet wipes, then carried two plates to the table.

"And? She looks like . . . ?" I attacked the sticky stuff on Ben's face and hands, and waited for David to answer.

Instead, he maneuvered Ben out of the high chair and into his lime green baby walker. As soon as Ben's bottom hit the seat, he slammed the bright red button on the tray and squealed with in concert with the siren noise. "Try to stay under the speed limits okay, Ben?" My son rewarded David with a series of "glks" and "brps," kicked his legs and bashed everything else on his tray that beeped and whistled.

"So, are you going to tell me what she looks like?" I eyed Ben's untouched jar of bananas. If he wasn't going to eat it . . .

David picked up the jar and returned it to the pantry. "I saw you sizing that up. Have a real banana. And I'm concerned that you're fixated on Lori's looks. I thought women didn't like being objectified by men. Never considered you women did that to one another." He opened the oven, removed the roasted chicken, and set it on the stove. "I'm not serving you, so if you want to eat, get your butt moving."

"I'm not ob-jec-ti-fy-ing," I said, moving my head with each syllable. "I'm curious."

"Is that a synonym for nosy?" He speared two chicken thighs.

"Give it up already, will you?" I pretended to poke him with the serving fork.

"She's classy, understated, Ann Taylor-ish. Angled bob haircut, hair the shade of a Starbucks café mocha, eyes to match, and she runs. Twenty miles a week."

"Yuck. Is that the best you could do?"

He set his plate on the table, poured us each a glass of iced tea, and handed me one as I sat across from him. "For now," he said, his lips pressed into a smile that didn't quite connect with the seriousness in his eyes.

# 8

David and his mystery man returned from Mexico over a month ago, but I still couldn't make voice contact with him. Julie told me "couldn't" meant "chose not to." Either way, he and I had not spoken since his Saturday phone call. If one degree of separation mattered (Julie said it absolutely did not), I called Lori. I didn't think getting together to mutually mourn over David would be healthy, but I did want to see her. The upcoming book club selection we were charged with conveniently provided a reason for us to see each other.

Walking to my car that morning, I mentally flogged myself for not suggesting Lori meet me at the thermostat-controlled café at Barnes and Nobles. Even though Labor Day and the possibility of slight breezes hovered around the corner, the end of August in New Orleans was like a relentless steam iron pressing the wrinkles right out of our skin.

The line of people waiting for café au lait and beignets at the Morning Call Coffee Stand already stretched past the news stand and the art gallery. Seeing it made me feel a little less guilty about being late. I parked in the shopping mall's lot and walked across the street, making myself later still.

Lori waved when she saw me and spared me the awkwardness of scanning the string of faces in search of hers. For someone who carried the debris of disappointment, she looked fragile, a whisper of herself. Wedding-broken-off-by-a-fiancé-who-announced-he-was-gay exploded her world, but what remained of the rubble she carried in the hollow spaces David once filled. Months ago she fretted her wedding gown wouldn't fit unless we reenacted the scene in *Gone with the Wind* where Scarlett grabbed on to the bedpost while Mammy cinched her waist. Today, the dress would fit if she wore a child's floatie around her waist.

We hugged, and when I wrapped my arms around her shoulders, I prayed she wouldn't break. Lori must have drawn the Dr. Adkins of grief.

I didn't starve my stress. The Italian grandmother of grief moved in with me after Harrison died. Food soothed me. Two months later I broke a zipper when I tried to shimmy into a pair of shorts. I accused Julie of having washed all my clothes in hot water. "Sorry I was late. The teacher dinners have really taken off. Another late night cooking. Even with Julie helping. I crashed on the sofa. Didn't set the alarm," I told her.

"Where's Ben?"

"Since school started, he and Nick haven't had much play time. I dropped him off at Julie's." Ben also asked me to tell Lori he missed her and wanted to know when he'd see her again. I'd tell her that later, when I wanted to open the David conversation. Ben would understand. Yes, Harrison, he would.

"You know you could always ask me if you're that busy," she said. The door yawned and swallowed a party of six ahead of us. "Oh, good. We're almost in."

I counted the bodies in front of us. "Um, ten people are not 'almost.'" Only five minutes out of the car, and I felt like a tea bag plunged in a cup of hot water. My sunglasses were already sliding down my nose. I tossed them in my purse and squinted at Lori. "If you promise to actually eat something, I'll call you. Maybe I should start delivering to you." I pointed to her jeans. "I don't think baggy's in right now . . . or ever."

"Not you too. I'm already hearing that from my mother." Lori rolled her eyes at me, lifted her bangs off her forehead with one hand and fanned with the other using one of the free real estate magazines off the newsstand rack. Her purse slipped into the crook of her arm making her look like the Queen Mother in a royal parade.

"Sorry." I stared at my feet and wondered if this was how Ben felt when I fussed at him yesterday for daring Nick to make farting noises during dinner. A few years ago, I wouldn't have wanted her to comment on the way my jeans looked like the forerunners of body shapers.

"That's your second sorry of the morning," she said, wearing her own mother's voice, just finding it a bit too tight. She swatted me on my shoulder with her makeshift fan. "I'm getting better. I promise. That's why I wanted to come here. I can afford a calorie overdose."

Seats for two opened up, so the door man—who actually looked more like a door kid—waved us in ahead of two families in front of us. He pointed to the empty stools. "Right there, ladies. Enjoy."

In that small moment, just crossing the threshold, the memories of time spent here with Harrison walked through the doors with me. They tugged on the sleeve of my heart like impatient children who beg for their parents' attention, wanting to show them something important. Eager and impatient and afraid what they want might disappear in the waiting. Look, there's the server who carried nine cups at a time. Over there, that table by the mirror. We sat there the night before

Ben was born. Every time I bit into a beignet, powdered sugar floated to the top of my baby bump like sweet snow.

Not now, I whispered to voices from the past waiting their turn. I shooed them back into the room with the door that wouldn't stay closed. I quieted them by listening to the clattering and the clinking, the waves of voices.

"Someone should make this," Lori's hands stirred the air around her, "into a perfume. Coffee, chicory, frying oil. A whiff of hangover breath."

"My nose is closing at just the thought of that, but no doubt some men would be captivated."

I perched on the round wooden seat of the stool remembering why I preferred sitting at a table. Over a century ago, when the Morning Call first opened, did people have smaller butts or more padding? As if the stools weren't uncomfortable enough, the row of stools all faced a wall of mirrors. Each one framed in a continuous walnut wood arch. Awkward. It meant either looking at yourself or trying not to look at yourself looking at yourself or looking at someone else looking at herself.

I saw my roots; they looked like a gray zipper that parted my Garnier Nutrisse #50 Truffle hair. My Revlon Grow Luscious Mascara had not lived up to its name. I pretended to dig glick out of my right eye when I spotted the server headed in our direction.

"What'll it be, ladies?" He reached between us and swiped the white marble countertop with a towel that reactivated the sticky rather than removed it.

"Two coffees, one order?" I asked Lori.

"Make it two orders. I'm hungry enough to eat more than one beignet. Wouldn't want to fight you for the leftover." She turned to the bow-tied young man whose face looked as if it was on pause. "Make it two orders."

He blinked and walked off.

"Do you have your list of books for our next club meeting?" I pulled a used envelope out of my purse where I'd written titles, most of them missing their vowels, to pick from.

Lori picked up her iPhone. "Yep."

"Show off. I suppose you had an app for that." I smoothed over the fold to see what I'd scribbled there.

"Seriously, Caryn, you're trying to run a business and you're using a cell phone you still have to flip open. David would—"

"What? David would, what?" I asked.

Lori's face looked as if I'd just dared her to punch me.

"Whoa. I wasn't about to say anything negative about David." She tucked her phone in her smooshy black leather tote. Beautiful and practical. Almost the same words David used to describe Lori when he first met her.

"I can't believe you're saying anything about David at all. I don't even want to talk to him. Not right now. What am I supposed to say? 'Oh, I've thought about this gay thing. It's all good'?"

I heard "Excuse me," as the white-sleeved arm of our server holding a plate of three pillow-shaped fried beignets appeared between Lori and me. He set our coffees in front of us and was off again.

Seeing the ripple of frustration tighten Lori's expression, I appreciated the pause in the conversation. She grabbed the shaker with the powdered sugar, a dull silver mug with a handle and a screw on top with holes. The random dents reminded me of the ones in Ben's silver baby rattle after he gnawed on it with his toothless mouth and bashed it on the sides of his car seat.

She turned the shaker over and slapped the bottom in a way that made me wonder if she saw my face there. Powdered sugar whooshed out, blanketing the beignets, the plate, and the counter. I pinched a corner of one of the still hot puffy donuts, slid it onto my napkin and considered I should wait for the reaction on Lori's face to work its way out of her mouth. People had been known to inhale layers of powdered sugar mid-bite during comic or chaotic conversations.

"You haven't talked to your brother?" The question stomped out like a hands-on-the-hips accusation.

The three teen girls on the other side of Lori laughed as they created hover clouds of sugar over their trio of plates. I was grateful they were loud. Talking about my gay brother in the middle of The Morning Call made me more uncomfortable than my ever-growing numb rear end. I pushed my beignet aside and sighed. "No. What do David and I need to talk about?"

"I'm the one who fell in love with him. I'm the one who kissed a man who wanted to kiss another man and not me. But I'm the one who talks to him." With each "I'm the one," she'd jabbed her forefinger into the space below the hollow of her throat. When she finished talking, that same finger blotted the wetness in the corners of her eyes.

She wrapped her hands around her coffee cup and the way she stared into the café au lait reminded me of Madame Harrisonia Katarina, the French Quarter mystic who read tea leaves. One Sunday afternoon, pre-Ben, Harrison and I strolled Royal Street, still in that gazing into each other's eyes stage. We almost crashed into the table outside the door of her shop. Madame didn't even lift her head at our "Oops," as we tripped over the sidewalk and into the street to avoid a collision. Harrison joked she knew from the leaves we would miss her, and he had kept walking. I let go of his hand to stand and watch. It was only then she looked up from the cup, slowly turned her head as if it were moving through bread dough, and stared at me. An expectant stare. A stare that said, "Well?" I felt like the intruder I must have been.

I felt like that now. Like I'd barged right into Lori's loss. But I didn't think she understood, and I didn't understand that she wouldn't. Too bad the coffee's almost scalded milk didn't do the same to my tongue. That way I wouldn't risk saying something I'd regret later.

"Lori, here's the thing. You'll eventually find someone else. David will always be my brother. My gay brother. That's not what I bargained for either."

She looked in the mirror and dusted the powdered sugar off her lips. "Caryn, you know I love you. But you talk like you were the woman left with an unused wedding gown." She tore the one leftover beignet in two and handed me half. "Here. People are still waiting in line. We'll talk about David later."

"Okay," I said, but later didn't matter. Later wouldn't make David straight. Wouldn't change what I thought about his life. Wouldn't change what I thought about his soul.

"So," said Lori as she started tapping her iPhone, "here's my list of suggestions for November's pick."

Every time I grabbed the handle of the door leading into the bookstore I'd feel the same shiver of anticipation as if I'd opened a monster box of chocolates. Whatever I nibbled on and didn't like, I could toss out. I savored the caramel chocolates of books. Harrison used to say that if books were calories, his brain would be a candidate for lapband surgery. Instead, it became a brain no surgery could repair.

Lori and I found a spot with two squatty chairs nestled between the cookbook and the gardening shelves. We sat to look at the four novels we'd each narrowed our book club choices to. Lori picked up *Talking to the Dead* and before she could open it, I said, "Nope. I don't like the title."

She looked at me as if she was peering over reading glasses. "Really?" she said, but it sounded like "Oh, you don't, do you?" in disguise. Lori flipped to the first page and spoke directly into the book, "That's right. You're the one who's not so fond of talking to the living either."

# 9

Because of Paul Prudhomme's Artichoke, Potato and Cheese Casserole and the fact that no one invented a remote control for the unrelenting oven timer, I found myself on the phone with David.

The hyper-annoying timer started to ping while I was in, of all places, the bathroom. I rescued the casserole before it became one of those disasters I fed the animals that used our trash cans for their dinner reservations, but not before my cell phone started vibrating in my pocket. In my frenzy, I answered the phone without checking the caller number.

We were both surprised to hear each other's voices.

"Bad time?" David asked.

Even before I realized he was on the other end of the conversation, my hello sounded specially designed for possible political survey takers.

"Um, yes, actually."

"I can call you back." He sounded hopeful.

"No. We can talk now. For a little while." Even that might be a stretch depending on the conversation.

"So, how are you and Ben? I've missed talking."

"Fine. We're both fine." I paced. "Are you okay?"

"Yes, yes. I'm staying busy. But, Caryn, you're not returning my calls, and I hoped we could find time to talk. Maybe meet somewhere."

"David, I can't talk right now. I have to leave soon to pick Ben up from school."

"It doesn't have to be now. Tell me a convenient time, and I'll call back or we could meet for coffee."

"I'll let you know. You just need to give me some time."

I hung up knowing that I had no idea of how long "some time" would be.

———— ∞ ————

Within months, meals for a few teachers sprouted into meals for a few schools. Ben's teacher had passed my business cards around at faculty meetings, then one faculty led to another. Usually, every Friday morning I delivered Ben and ten meals to the front office, then stopped at four more schools before I headed home to collapse on my sofa.

But after today's last delivery, I headed to Regions Bank where Lori works to make a deposit before our mortgage company made its withdrawal. Last year, I'd taken a second mortgage to help float the expenses of starting my business. Still, it seemed most of the time I ran out of money before I ran out of month.

Harrison's life insurance benefits helped, but dying young didn't. We thought we had time to estate plan, to set up trusts, to save for Harrison's retirement. Who knew Harrison would retire from life before he retired from his job? Neither one of us ever thought money would have to stretch like a rubber band over so many years of life.

I turned into the parking lot and headed for the drive-through window, which years ago convinced me that Ben and

I spent too much time driving to our food. The insider teller's voice had chirped "May I help you?" through the speaker and, before I could answer, Ben leaned over in his car seat and said, "French fries and Coke." He'd earned himself two suckers that day when I retrieved my deposit slip from the transaction drawer.

Just before I pulled into the last lane, I spotted Lori's silver Prius in the employee parking area. Mature Caryn, who sometimes terrified me, crossed her arms over her chest and said, "Park this car, go in there, and talk to your almost sister-in-law." Not-so-mature Caryn argued from the bubble she protected herself in, "She'll probably never even know you were here. You don't need to be getting into any more David discussions. Remember how the last one ended?"

I hoped to not find a parking spot but, of course, I did because the good sense gods were conspiring and would not allow me to wallow in my smallness. Opening the glass doors to the bank, I saw Lori had two clients at her desk so I walked to the counter to make my deposit. By the time I finished, the clients were gone, but Lori was on the telephone. She saw me, waved me over, and pointed to one of the chairs in front of her desk.

She mouthed, "Won't be long," and followed it with a polite clothesline of "yes" and "I see" and "of course" responses into the telephone. I didn't need her to tell me that she'd recently seen David. The sweet lemony fragrance that drifted toward me as soon as I sat revealed it. On the corner of her desk behind her nameplate, a fluted cut crystal vase held a bouquet of willowy-stemmed white freesia. David used to bring her a fresh bouquet of the delicate trumpet-shaped flower every week. She'd planned to use them in the wedding. Said their tiny golden throats would be the perfect touch to complement her candlelight gown.

I sat and stared at my unpolished toenails shamelessly exposed in my flip-flops. When did I stop treating myself to girly mani-pedi days? Lori yammered on while I tried to pretend one of us was invisible so I wouldn't feel as if I were eavesdropping, which I most definitely was. A learned skill from the few recent party caterings. I learned eye contact and an animated expression were detrimental to disappearing in plain sight. No harm in listening. I considered it smart business planning. If a party was waiting to happen somewhere, the sooner I knew about it, the better chance I had to book it. People spend time at one party talking about the next party they're either invited to or not. Listening could pay. Literally.

Lori said, "Great. I'll see you next Thursday," and hung up, which meant I could stop being captivated by the bank's recent financial disclosure statement, framed and propped near her file stacks.

"Hey. Do you have time to visit?" I didn't like feeling clunky with Lori, like a ballerina wearing clogs. Our last conversation was as comfortable as tap dancing in wet mud. But I didn't have a template for redefining our relationship as the almost wife of my now gay brother.

"Sure." She stepped around her standard issue official bank officer desk. A quick hug, and then she sat in the chair next to me. "I'm glad you're here."

"I wanted to apologize for being such a snit when we met a few weeks ago. I thought I'd see you at the book club meeting, and I planned to talk to you then. But I just couldn't drag myself out the door after staying up late the night before getting all those teacher dinners ready." I'd folded and refolded the deposit slip in my hands so many times while I talked that I could have designed a piece of origami. "I should have called you." A part of me still blamed David for this mess. His news stormed through our lives like a hurricane, and we were left clearing the debris.

She granted me a forgiving smile as if I'd just apologized for eating cookies before supper. "Julie told me why you weren't there. And, if you were trying to avoid me, I'd come after you." Lori crossed her legs, her hands over the knee of her top leg as it stirred the air between her chair and the desk. Her black silk pants swished in the background.

"The other thing is," my eyes drifted to the ivory flowers, "I talked to David." I looked at her and waited for her "It's about time" to follow.

It didn't. She leaned back in the chair, clasped her hands on her lap, and nodded her head. "And?"

I ran my thumbnail along the long scratches on the wooden chair arm. "And I just wanted you to know that I didn't ignore him the last time he called." I'd run out of tiny trenches to excavate, so I stopped, drummed my thumb on the wood instead, and waited.

Nothing.

Lori's expression matched my dating life—totally blank.

"If you're waiting to hear some happily ever after, well, it wasn't that kind of talk. I asked how he was doing, he said, 'Fine.' I needed to pick Ben up from school, so I didn't have time to stay on the phone." I shifted in the chair, but the weight of my emotional discomfort still pushed against my chest. This didn't sound like I thought it would. When I rehearsed this in my brain, I imagined Lori would be relieved to hear that I—what does she call that?—stepped out in faith and talked to David. So, maybe I only tiptoed, but it was movement in the right direction.

"I guess talking at David instead of to him is better than not talking to him at all," she said to the space in front of her and fingered the double strand pearl necklace she wore. Yet another gift from David.

The buzzing telephone on her desk spared me more David talk. Lori excused herself to answer the call, and I slipped my purse on my shoulder and scooted to the edge of the chair in the ready position.

She hung up, but before I could tell her what she could already see, she said, "Wait. One more thing, and this will be quick because I have an appointment in ten minutes." She opened a file on her desk and handed me a sheet of paper. "I know Trey's been doing your accounting, but I wasn't sure if he'd reminded you about that balloon payment that's going to be coming up on your second mortgage."

My stomach performed one of those tumblesets over itself the way it does on the down slide of a roller coaster. Of course, I knew about the balloon note. I just hadn't remembered how soon it had to be paid. And even though Trey balanced the money, or the lack of it, David always reminded me, sometimes nudged me, about the financial side of the business. Two years ago, he had suggested a second mortgage to fund equipment for my business and for advertising and marketing expenses.

I scanned the columns until I found what I'd owe and the due date. The tumbling in my stomach gave way to trampoline jumping. I spotted the figure on the page and felt like I'd been in an elevator that fell fifty floors.

# 10

If every teacher in every school in the parish starts ordering dinner every week, maybe I'll be able to make that note in four months." I handed Julie another disposable aluminum pan filled with pesto grilled chicken breasts on linguine tossed with olive oil, garlic, and fresh basil.

"Maybe then we could buy a bolt of foil instead of yards of it," Julie said as she crimped another shiny sheet over the top of the pan. "Or, you could expand your holiday business to include Hanukkah, Ramadan, Kwanzaa," she said.

We'd been assembling dinners for hours. I layered the linguine and chicken into the pans, Julie covered them, and Ben wrote the teachers' names and school sites on the foil. Sometimes his handwriting looked more like what I'd see on a prescription. All angles and lines, seemingly minus vowels. Anything totally illegible, Julie corrected later.

He wrote so hunched over the top of the kitchen table that I wondered if he inherited Harrison's farsightedness. I made a mental note to call for an ophthalmologist appointment tomorrow, but even then I knew messages often failed to stick to the bulletin board in my brain. Maybe I did need to consider updating my pink flip phone to one that could keep track of my life for me.

A crooked smile and a plea from my gawky-elbowed son bought him thirty minutes past his bedtime. I relented because the hours he spent in school and the hours I spent cooking or reading about cooking or cleaning up after cooking left us thin wedges of time together.

Watching him tonight, those long ago lyrics about saving time in a bottle didn't define "corny" as I once thought they did. The night Harrison died, I called his doctor, then stumbled through the dark hallway. I kept my pillow clutched to my chest as if it could soften the grief pummeling my heart, which I feared would explode. At the doorway to Ben's room, I stopped, reached out an arm to the doorframe to steady myself, then shuffled to his bed and poured myself next to his sprawled, tangle-sheeted body. I held my breath until I could hear the fluttering of air escape between his little o-shaped mouth.

Now, the oven timer—Ben's bedtime signal—beeped. "Got it," he said, snapped the cap on his marker and pushed the off button. "Going to brush my teeth."

"And floss," I added.

He looked at the oven clock and scratched his head. "It's late. I'll do that tomorrow."

"Nice try, buddy," Julie said. "You and Nick must practice these lines, huh?"

He shrugged and yawned off his expression of defeat.

I pointed my pasta fork in the direction of his bathroom. "I'll be there in a few minutes." This was code since I had been under strict orders from him not to say "tuck you in bed" in front of anyone other than family.

We filled three more orders, then Julie nodded toward Ben's bedroom. "Go do the good night thing. I can handle this alone."

"I'm sure it won't be long before this comes to an end," I said and untied my apron, slipped the neck strap from around my head, and handed it to her.

Ben had already slipped into bed by the time I entered his room and clicked on his overhead fan. He pulled his ear buds out and set them and his iPod on his night table.

When I held his face in my hands and bent to kiss his forehead, he pinched his nose and emitted a nasally, "Yuck."

"Since when is a good night kiss a 'yuck' for you, Mr. Benjamin David Becker?"

He peeled my hands off his cheeks and waved his hand in front of his face like a fan. "You smell like garlic."

I lifted my hands and sniffed. "Yep. Garlic with a hint of little boy."

He granted me a token grin before he turned on his left side. His arm bent, he propped his head in his hand and tugged at his pillowcase with the other. "Mom, when's Thanksgiving?" His voice sounded the way it did when the question I ask isn't really the one I want the answer to. He didn't look at me. Just traced the edges of the red baseball cap design on his sheet with his finger.

"Almost two months from now. September isn't over yet, then there's October, then November." I straightened the shade on his lamp. The one he picked out himself last year when we shopped for a "big boy" room. The base was a wood football with leather stitching. He liked it because it reminded him of the football his Uncle David had given him. David. The dawn of realization just rose in my brain. That was the answer to the question Ben hadn't yet asked.

"Will Uncle David and Lori come over then?" He had moved on to outlining the baseball bats on his sheet.

When I didn't say anything, he leaned back on his pillow and tugged his sheet under his chin, and stared at me with his father's serious eyes. Once again, Harrison, I'm left to explain the unexplainable. How am I supposed to tell him that Lori won't be Aunt Lori? That the Uncle David who threw footballs was now just throwing people curve balls? "Ben, sweetie, it's so far away. I'm just not sure what we'll be doing. This year may be different. Maybe we could go somewhere, just the two of us, since you won't have school that week. Would you like that?"

"I don't know." He turned on his side and faced the wall. "I'm going to sleep now."

His sadness filled the space between us. But I couldn't make it disappear. I didn't have the solution that could transform it to joy. All I could do was cross the bridge over it. "I love you. Thanks for all your help tonight." I kissed my son on the top of his head, his green apple shampoo scent still lingered. "Good night, Ben," I whispered, clicked his lamp off, and carried my guilt back into the kitchen.

<hr />

Barb, the secretary at Tisdale High School, handed me an envelope of cash and checks to cover the meals I dropped off. "I'm not sure who appreciates you more. Me for not having to cook, or my husband for having something to eat that doesn't come out of a box first."

"After months of this, I think Ben might actually be thrilled to zap a Hot Pocket in the microwave." I tucked the envelope under the other orders on my clipboard and handed Barb the flyer with the menus for October. "November's list will have my holiday meals, and I'll include desserts everyone can order separately if they want."

Barb slipped on glasses that hung from a beaded chain that looked like someone had strung together petrified jellybeans of all sorts of colors. "Chicken or Black Bean Enchiladas, Seafood Stuffed Eggplant, White Bean Chili . . ." Her voice slid off the page as she read the month's new offerings.

A triple play of pings reverberated across the office and seconds later teens with backpack humps spilled into the hallway outside the doors of the office. A whiff of memory rose from their animated voices. Seeing David in the cafeteria. He's talking to a guy whose short wavy blond hair and black Ramones T-shirt both look purposely messy. The new guy turned, and his grin made me think someone might be following me. I glanced over my shoulder and, by the time I realized his soft smile was meant for me, I'm close enough to know I like what I see.

David's arm tugged me toward him, and I prayed I didn't look as clumsy as I felt. "So, this is my sister, Caryn." The cute face nodded. "Hey. I'm Harrison. I just transferred here . . ."

Now, outside the office, the crush of bodies and verbal chaos waned as did the flash of Harrison from all those years ago. I pushed my sunglasses on before Barb could see my wet eyes.

"I'll email the staff as usual. See you next week, I'm sure," said Barb. "I guess you'll be really busy soon with your brother's wedding coming up."

My dark glasses shielded what felt like eye-popping awkwardness. Unfortunately, the rest of my face couldn't hide itself. I hugged the clipboard. "No, I won't be doing the catering," I answered. I wanted that to be enough, but I knew it wasn't. "The wedding's been postponed, so . . ." I shrugged my shoulders and tugged my keys out my jeans' pocket.

Barb might have asked more questions, but I mumbled a good-bye and exited before she could.

I tossed my clipboard in the backseat of my car that now smelled like a Mexican restaurant, blasted the air conditioner, and tried to remember what I was supposed to do next. Somewhere, I'd written a list. When I found it, I'd add, "No more questions" and "need answers." Harrison would've had answers. He specialized in them. Even when I told him and only him, about my relationship in college. The one I thought would last forever. The one that changed me forever. The one that left me broken. He answered my pain with, "I choose forgiveness. I choose you. Forever."

Now what, Harrison? Where am I supposed to go? Where's the Magic Eight Ball I can shake for answers?

Even my father proved impossible. He and Loretta were between cruises the last time we spoke. The year after Harrison died, they moved to Village Lakes, a retirement community in Florida, which they spent more time away from than in. For a while after, I wondered if Ben and I should move there since my father's social life outpaced mine by miles.

I called my father one afternoon a few weeks ago before Ben came home from school, so I could talk to him about David. The conversation bordered on absurd and, had we been talking about someone else's brother, might have been funny.

"Loretta and I think it's a stage he's going through," Dad told me. "Wait, Loretta's getting ready to putt," he whispered.

If Loretta took as much time to putt as she did make a decision, I might still have been on the phone when Ben arrived home from school. She must have been within an inch or so that day because in less than a minute I heard him reward her with, "A par shot for the girl."

"Dad, the only stage that men David's age experience is middle-age crazy and being gay isn't one of the crazies. And if it is, it's so far down on the list no one even knows."

"Well, just in case, we're working on a back-up plan. Loretta's looking into one of those programs. You know, the ones like camps gay men go to get straight."

Later on, I told Julie about the phone call while we watched the boys cruise the driveway on their skateboards. As outrageous as it sounded when my father mentioned it, the reform program held out a smidgen of promise. When I asked Julie what she thought about the idea, she stared at me as if I'd just announced I planned to walk to Mars.

She snapped dead branches that poked out of a nearby waxy leaf ligustrum. "Since when does something Loretta advocates make sense to you? Or have you forgotten she wanted you to register for dates on eHarmony three months into your new status as a widow?"

Of course it didn't make sense. I realized that as soon as my father's words flew out of my mouth and landed in my ears. How comforting it would have been, though, to have a solution to a problem. A matching set. Something that worked.

I watched her comb the shrubs free of their brown leaves. They looked so much greener, yet so less full. Not the life lesson I wanted. "I know. I know," I answered in defeat.

"Think about this," Julie wiped her hands on the front of her jeans. "What if David asked you to go to a reform program that would try to convert you from being a straight person to a gay one? What would you tell him?"

I laughed. "That's ridiculous. No program's going to convince me I'm gay."

"Exactly. So why would you think David would be convinced he's straight?"

# 11

For Harrison, a new Thanksgiving meant a new adventure in cooking the turkey. Over the years, he tried smoked, grilled, rotisserie, deep-fried, oven-bagged. The last Thanksgiving we spent as a family, David and Lori brought a turducken, a chicken stuffed inside a duck, which was then stuffed inside a turkey. My father said it was so good he thought he'd "died and gone to heaven."

Instead Harrison went. And every year since, at every holiday, the throbbing pain of loneliness returned to fill that one empty chair at the table.

Whatever memories Ben had of his father, at holidays and otherwise, were stored too far into his baby brain to access. His experiences of family gatherings centered in my dad and Loretta, David and Lori, and sometimes the Pierces. This year, Dad and Loretta spent Thanksgiving Day dining on mangoes and mahi-mahi in the Hawaiian Islands. Trey, Julie and Nick traveled to Gulf Shores to meet Trey's family for their annual turkey weekend of shopping, eating, and beaching.

So, since this year would be different, what would be so wrong in starting a tradition for the two of us?

Julie had been packing for their trip when I announced my plan for Ben and me to perform charitable acts of giving on Thanksgiving Day. I sat on Nick's bed practicing my two-second T-shirt folding technique, but I felt the sting of her glare even before she stopped tossing socks in his suitcase.

"Have you told Ben about this?" She closed the drawer, leaned against the dresser to face me, and crossed her arms over her tank top, the one Trey told her Victoria should have kept a secret.

"Not yet," I said while I tried to flick Nick's shirt into compliance.

"So, I guess that means you're not going to see David."

"No, but that was David's choice." I looked at her now because I knew she would be surprised I'd actually called him. But her expression registered a question mark, not an exclamation point. "I invited him."

Her mouth untwisted itself and her eyebrows relaxed.

So there. See. I'm not the bad sister.

Still, nothing. Then she glanced at the floor and, when she looked at me, it was as if she'd picked up a smirk there. "Emphasis on *him*, right?"

"Of course. I wanted David to spend Thanksgiving with us. I'm not ready to meet . . . whatever his name is. Max, I think. I tried to explain that to David, but he said he wouldn't come without him. So, he made his choice."

"Well, it's not like you gave him much of one. Would you have left Harrison home if David asked you to?"

Julie's question shoved my denial to the wall, and it wanted to come out swinging. I tapped my feet on the braided throw rug by Nick's bed. We're talking Thanksgiving, and I'm still wearing sandals. Nothing's what it's supposed to be about this holiday. Julie just doesn't get it. "That's not fair. You can't compare Harrison to David's . . . I don't even know what to call him . . ."

"No. You're the one who doesn't want to compare them," Julie said softly, like she didn't want her words to bruise me. She sighed, opened the door to Nick's closet, then turned to me.

"Maybe this good Samaritan thing you and Ben are doing will point you in the right direction. I don't know what it's going to take for you to see David for *who* he is, not *how* he is."

---

I stacked three chocolate pancakes from the griddle on a plate, sprinkled them with powdered sugar, and set them in front of Ben.

"Why aren't we eating Thanksgiving dinner at our house like we do every year?" The suspicion in Ben's voice weighed more than he did. He looked at his breakfast as if it were a bribe.

I guess I had to own that, even though I tried to pass it off as a celebration of the first not-having-to-wake-up-early day of the holidays. Nick, Julie and Trey had driven out before dawn that morning, so neither one of us could count on any of the Pierces as places to stow our emotional baggage. Harrison, this is yet another one of those days I could use a backup.

"But we are going to eat here," I said and opened the freezer. "Look, we'll each have our own little turkey." I held up the two Cornish hens I bought. "Cool, huh?"

"No. Those are dumb. I want a real turkey." He eyed his plate.

"How are the pancakes?" Uneaten. That's how they were. And obviously not effective in my campaign to soften the news.

Ben licked his finger and swiped the powdered sugar. "Fine. Can I have some milk?"

I poured his milk and sat across from him at the table. I stopped myself from reminding him not to hold his fork like he was about to club someone over the head. No point in making this more difficult. Maybe the morning wasn't the best time to discuss this. He still had a crease across his left cheek from sleeping, I supposed, on the seam of his blanket. How could he have moved from a blanket in my arms to one in his bed so quickly?

He sawed through his pancakes with the side of his fork, gulped his milk and looked at me. "So?"

I held my breath and dove into the pool of disappointment. "I thought you and I might want to start a tradition this year. Do you know what a 'tradition' is?"

"Like a Christmas tree?"

"Yes. Well, since everyone else has somewhere to go this Thanksgiving—"

"I know where Nick and PaPa are. But where are Uncle David and Lori going?" he said, taking another bite of his pancakes.

I had no idea where Lori would be. David, however, had sent me a terse email after our equally terse phone conversation: "Max and I will be in New York until Sunday visiting his family. Tell Ben I love him."

"Nowhere—" He scrunched his mouth, but before the question could pop out of it, I said, "Not with each other."

He finished his milk, pulled up the neck of his T-shirt, and wiped his mouth. "Why not?"

"Here's the thing, Ben. Uncle David and Lori won't be getting married."

"Why? Are they getting a divorce?"

He stabbed the leftover pieces of pancake with his fork. Each time the tines hit the plate like metal fingernails on a chalkboard. I leaned across the table and stilled Ben's attack on his food.

"No. People who aren't married don't need a divorce. They just don't get married."

"Is that why you're mad at him? 'Cuz he's not marrying Lori? Is Lori mad at him, too?"

"Ben, I'm not mad at Uncle David . . . well, maybe a little bit. I'm upset that he doesn't love Lori in the getting married kind of way. And I don't think Lori's mad at him now. At first she was. They care about each other, but like a brother and sister do."

"You're Uncle David's sister. Why can Lori be like his sister, but you can't?"

Why does Ben make it sound so simple and uncomplicated? "I still love my brother," I said, but I wanted to add that I didn't like or understand him.

"Then why don't we see him? I miss him." His voice trembled and this time he wiped his eyes, not his mouth with his T-shirt.

I walked over to him, and pulled him close. "I miss him too. I miss him too," I said, glad that he'd buried his face in my arms and couldn't see the tears in my eyes.

---

I tucked Ben in, then I settled in my office to organize myself for what I hoped would be a crazy-busy season between Thanksgiving and Christmas. Trey and I had talked briefly about the upcoming balloon note, and we planned to meet next week to crunch the numbers. He reassured me everything would fall into place, but I didn't know where that place would come from.

I wondered if Harrison had experienced the same breath-sucking pressure I felt trying to stretch money over the month. After his first stroke, I was almost too embarrassed to admit to Trey that I hadn't given much attention to our finances. When Harrison and I decided I'd be a full-time mom after Ben was born, I traded money management for baby management. It worked. He gave me money. I spent it. I gave him the baby. He gave me a break. Not complicated.

I never intended to be a working single mom. But then, Harrison never intended to die. But here we both were. Or were not. Most nights I devoted attention to reading celebrity chef cookbooks, investigating whether I should buy a forged or a stamped knife, and deciding if I should make more white chocolate raspberry cakes or more roasted almond truffles. I doubted any of these issues mattered in heaven, where I figured Harrison must be. And where he probably scratched his head every Sunday when Ben and I didn't end up in church.

<hr/>

For two days before Thanksgiving, Ben and I had conversations that mostly consisted of food measurements, egg cracking and butter melting to make desserts for what I hoped would be our annual Thanksgiving visits. I'd sent emails to two local nursing homes and asked them if we could stop by with our goodies. They both responded with "Thanks" and a trail of exclamation points.

The first day we started our baking marathon, he walked into the kitchen wearing one of my aprons. A Jessie Steele retro cherries half-apron with screaming red trim that had been a birthday present from Julie. I didn't recognize it at first because he wore it backside out. Still, his wearing it bothered me. And it bothered me that I was bothered.

I snapped the mixer off. "Hey, buddy. What's up with the outfit?" I said, in a voice more hesitant than I'd planned.

Ben glanced at the apron, then looked at me, and rubbed his forehead like Harrison used to when caught between confusion and surprise. The gesture soaked through my skin.

"Well," he said, and drew out the word one letter at a time, "you're always telling me not to wipe my hands on my clothes. I looked in your office, but I couldn't find a boy thing to wear." He planted his hands at his waist and shrugged his shoulders. "You want me to take it off?"

I opened a fourth box of cream cheese, plopped it in the mixing bowl, and mentally slapped myself in the head. "Nah. Good thinking ahead. This isn't about clothes. It's about cooking." Got it, Harrison. Follow my own advice. "Wash your hands, then grab a carton of eggs out the fridge."

He headed to the sink, and I mixed the cream cheese, thankful that my feelings didn't magically transfer into my food. Definitely not an effective marketing ploy if every bite of my cheesecakes evoked feelings of parental inadequacy. Therapy. I needed therapy, that's what Julie suggested. In fact, she mentioned the name of a therapist before they'd left for the beach. I needed to find where I shoved that business card.

Four cheesecakes, two pecan pies, and one pound cake later, a flour-dusted and sugar-coated Ben fell asleep as he sat at the table. His head pillowed by his folded arms, his mouth opened, and his feet tucked under his legs. I dispensed with making him take a bath. One night going to bed a sticky mess wasn't nearly as hazardous as waking him up.

He weighed too much now for me to cradle him in my arms to carry him to his room. I missed the warm bundle of him snuggled against my chest. I wondered, is this parenting? Longing for your children to grow and then feeling aching sadness when they do?

I managed to steer him into his room in his semi-consciousness, removed the now gooey apron, and helped him roll between his sheets. He squirmed, sighed, and opened his eyes for a flicker of time. "Night, Mom. We had fun."

My inner mommy cartwheeled at the word "we." I wanted to find something that Ben and I could share. Something that would be our thing. Something that would pave a road, a road that could always lead us back to one another. I didn't care that it reeked of selfishness sprinkled with a bit of sweetness. And if we found it in cooking, then what a blessing that would be. Unlike a sport or a hobby or a game that might shift or disappear at any point, there would always be food.

"Good night, sweet Ben," I whispered, kissed his forehead, and headed to my office. While I'd been cleaning the kitchen, I remembered Lori telling me about an Etsy shop online where I could find aprons for boys. When I started catering, she and David wanted to buy one for Ben. I think my response then was something along the lines of, "As if Ben would wear an apron." All these months later, I cringed just recycling the conversation in my brain.

I found the shop and ordered Ben a chef's apron in navy blue fabric decorated with bats, balls, caps, and catchers' mitts. After another ten minutes of mindless clicking from one link to another, I checked my email. School didn't start until next week, so I didn't expect any meal orders, but Joyce, one of our book club members, promised she'd refer me to her sister Kirby who belonged to Junior League.

Every year, the week before Christmas, the League—a charitable nonprofit—hosted Book Du Jour, a luncheon to raise money for literacy. Instead of having the event at a local restaurant, the planning committee elected to use the new library and serve catered food instead of a seated luncheon. Joyce told me the original caterer backed out on them, and they didn't know if they'd be able to find anyone this late. I didn't care if they considered me the caterer of last resort. The opportunity for contacts and publicity mattered most. In fact, it would be worth having to donate a percentage of my profit to their campaign to secure the contract.

I scrolled slowly, my hope shrinking along with the list of unread emails. I didn't realize I'd been holding my breath until I saw the subject line: "Upcoming Junior League Event" and exhaled. The committee wanted to arrange a meeting one day next week to discuss a catering contract.

"Yes!" I followed with a fist pump so energetic I almost shattered my elbow on my desk. I grabbed my cell phone to text Julie, but it was almost midnight. Too late. My enthusiasm sputtered. Another instance of the collateral damage of being alone. Good news is meant to be shared. Like boiled crawfish. Without the mess.

I answered the email, turned off the office lights and headed to my bedroom. My relief over the good news tonight trailed behind me like a new puppy. Maybe there was something at work here bigger than Joyce or Kirby. Or someone. Could God really be conducting this orchestra that was my life? So much of me was out of tune, out of time, out of tempo. Could He really wave that baton enough to create music instead of mayhem?

I mumbled to my reflection in the bathroom mirror as I brushed my teeth. "If Ben can have a reprieve from a bath, so can you." Talking to myself and skipping a shower. Two more wonders of widowhood. Widowhood which, like my apathetic hair, was entirely too long.

Julie would have said, "Stop whining. They're both your fault. You won't date. You won't even commit to a hair salon." I tried dating. Twice. The first time I met a friend of Lori's sister for coffee at Starbucks. He drank decaf. And he talked too much like Billy Bob Thornton in *Sling Blade*. A hoarse voice that grunted. A lot.

Leonard Nimoy, the Star Trek Vulcan years, was my second date. Not the real one, of course, but definitely a double. A doctor Trey met playing golf, Barry, was a proctologist who informed me he'd prefer to be called a colorectal surgeon. Nice man, obviously intelligent. I didn't ask him about his work, but he told me anyway. More than I wanted to know. Ever.

I guess I knew Julie too well or spent too much time with her or both to be able to have a conversation when she was two states away. Doubtful that she talked to me when I wasn't around. She had Trey. And tonight I had Chase and Bianca, who were somewhere on a beach in Mexico when I last opened the pages of *Forever in the Heat of Love*. Definitely not literary fiction, but when I realized Harrison and I might never share a bed again, I wasn't looking for high concept. I was looking for something I could curl up with at the end of an emotionally exhausting day.

Over the last few years, the book club fed my brain. My romance books fed my body.

And then there were the times when I wondered what fed my soul.

# 12

Baking in November should be happening inside the house. Not outside of it.

But by the afternoon of day two of the great Ben and Mommy Bake-a-thon, the two of us almost changed into bathing suits just to tolerate the heat in and out of the kitchen. Only in the Deep South could the weather on the day before Thanksgiving make you long for a built-in swimming pool.

The scent of pure vanilla and burnt crumbs swelled in the oven heat that was making the kitchen walls sweat. And me. We'd measured, mixed, and mashed since after breakfast. I wanted to cheer when the timer buzzed to signal the last cake was ready. But when I took it out of the oven, it resembled a cream cheese relief version of the Grand Canyon.

Ben stared at the gaping cracks in the cheesecake. "I didn't know these could break," he said. "Can we fix it?"

"Let's see." I tugged the springform pan closer. The crack looked like an open mouth laughing at me. "It's pretty deep. I don't think the sour cream topping's going to fill that."

"We need cheesecake glue, huh?"

"You know, Ben, you might be onto something there," I said and laughed. "Let's put that on our list of things to invent."

The two of us gazed at the cheesecake as if it would soon be revealing the secrets of the universe—or at least tell us why it always rained the week of Jazz Fest—then Ben darted into the pantry and walked out with a box of chocolate graham crackers. "We could put these on top."

My face must have morphed into a question mark.

"Mom," he said as he opened the box, "we can bash these up and make an upside-down cheesecake. Like when you do those things with the pineapples on top."

I opened my mouth to tell him why I didn't think it would work, but as I watched him shimmy himself onto the kitchen stool and sample a graham cracker, I stopped. I weighed the options: Cheesecake. Child. Cheesecake. Child. Not a brain buster, Caryn.

"Hey, you know what? That's a clever idea," I said. "I'll see if I can do some crack repair, and you," I handed him the wooden roller, "can start bashing those cookies into crumbs."

"Cool." He grabbed the handles of the roller and lifted it over his head like winning prize fighters hold the belts they're awarded. "I'm the cheesecake hero!" He opened a clear plastic bag and dumped in a pack of cookies. "Wait'll Nick hears I'm almost like a chef now. He's gonna ask if he can be here next time, huh, Mom?"

"You betcha," I answered as I searched for another carton of sour cream in the refrigerator, glad that Ben wouldn't see that conviction in my voice belied the doubt on my face.

---

Ben asked if we could have our Thanksgiving meal for dinner instead of lunch since we'd be driving around and delivering during the day.

"Sounds like a perfect new tradition," I said, and I meant it. Making desserts exhausted more than meals. A chance to sleep in promised to be as delicious as anything we'd be delivering.

That morning we ate thick slices of toasted pumpkin pound cake slathered with butter for breakfast. We called the Pierces to tell them Happy Thanksgiving, but it was mostly so Nick and Ben could continue their tradition of lame turkey jokes. Ben found, "What smells the best at a Thanksgiving dinner? Your nose!" I handed him the phone before I talked to Julie to spare myself watching him writhe about, a victim of his own impatience. He usually roamed around the house when he and Nick talked, but finishing breakfast kept him anchored to the kitchen table.

After their joke exchange, a "cool" and two "wow" responses, Ben shared that he and I had baked desserts for the past two days. His enthusiasm jumped ship and defensiveness boarded. Now he was the one not making eye contact with me. He answered "no" twice, each time a frown followed. The last word he mumbled before he handed me the phone was an uncharacteristic "whatever."

I asked Julie to wait a bit while I told Ben to brush his teeth and straighten his room before we left. I put my hand on his chin, lifted his face up, so he could see my lips as they moved to say, "I love you." He nodded once, then slumped into himself, and plodded off toward his bedroom. A piece of me plodded along with him.

"Hey, happy turkey day and all that stuffing," I said, ratcheting up the happy in my voice.

"Funny. You too," said Julie and then she dropped to a whisper, "When we get home, remind me why I subject myself to this torture." One of her in-laws probably hovered nearby. And probably a gaggle of others based on the background noise.

I told her about the Junior League appointment, and after the celebratory "wahoo," she said that she'd tell Trey. "Did you ever get back in touch with Pastor Vince about his daughter's wedding?"

Midway between the table and the sink, dirty breakfast plates in one hand, cell phone in the other, I stopped as if I'd just crashed into a wall. I had. The wall of my forgetfulness.

"Caryn?" Julie's voice reminded me to breathe.

"I'm here," I said, sounding as flat as the floor. I made it to the sink, let go of the dishes, and opened the refrigerator. It might be too late to call Pastor Vince, but it wasn't too early for chocolate therapy.

"Well?"

The question burned my ear as I checked the freezer. Sometimes I'd toss tempting junk food in there under the delusion I'd forget about it. I spied a half-bag of Double Stuff Oreos peeking out from between two bags of fries.

"Still here." I popped a handful of cookies in the microwave, and seconds later, I was feeding my anxiety monster.

"You're not answering me, so that means you didn't call him. Right?"

My brain processed the words, but my heart processed their implication. "I'm such an idiot. I meant to call him. Maybe it's not too late. I could give him a big discount. I'll figure out—"

"Stop. I don't know why you forgot to call. But it doesn't matter. Just make it right. Call him and apologize, even if it is too late."

When "forgot" dropped out of her mouth, I translated it as, "you purposely chose not to remember." I headed to my bedroom and stretched out on my still unmade bed. The pumpkin bread and the Oreos battled one another in my stomach. Maybe if I lay down, they'd declare a cease fire.

"I will. I'll call him. I promise." I stared at the ceiling and thought that would be an ideal place for reminders. Some gizmo could flash notes up there. Steve Jobs needed to create an app for that. Maybe I'll call him, too.

"I don't even know why I'm asking this, but maybe you'll surprise me. Have you talked to your brother yet?"

The war waged on in my gut. "Technically, no. But I'm going to send him a text message. He's not here anyway. He went with that guy Max to New York."

"That guy?" Julie laughed. "Reminds me of high school when I seriously dated this guy my mother didn't like. At all. She'd tell people he was 'Julie's little friend.' Really effective way of distancing herself from the truth. I knew she approved of Trey because she never introduced him that way."

"Can we not talk about this right now? Ben and I need to leave soon—"

"No, we don't have to talk now," she broke in, as abrupt as I was anxious. "We're doing the turkey thing for late lunch."

Before we hung up, I invited them over for an early dinner when they arrived home Sunday. I wanted Ben to have a chance to hang out with Nick before school started Monday. And, once again, I'd try to explain myself to Julie. She didn't get it, and I didn't get her. She's the one who's churchy, not me. Why was she the one on David's side, and I'm guilted because I'm not?

I closed my eyes and hoped the rest of the day wouldn't be as emotionally exhausting. On Thanksgiving, I'd be thankful for that.

———— ∞∞ ————

That night, I picked up my book and opened to Chase and Bianca exploring their beach house and one another. Then, a tsunami of exhaustion washed over all of us, and swept away their universe.

I blinked a few times, not sure if the hand on my arm steadied me or made me sway.

"Mom. Mom. Wake up."

Ben's pleas jolted me upright.

"What time is it? Did we miss our deliveries? Why aren't you dressed?" I'm out of bed, and I'm not confused any more. I'm panicked.

Ben picked my phone up off the floor. It must have slipped out of my hand when I fell asleep. "It's 10:06." He turned the screen around and showed me the display.

A wave of relief diluted my franticness. I took a deep breath, gave the careening thoughts in my head time to settle. Ben sat cross-legged at the foot of my bed, pushing buttons on my phone.

"Game time's over. Time to change into the clothes we picked out for you last night."

"Okay." He hopped off the bed. "Can I wear another shirt? Like my Saints T-shirt or something?"

"First, stop biting your nail. Second, wear the shirt we already decided on."

He frowned, but only slightly rolled his eyes before he turned to leave.

"Ben, wait."

He stopped, but barely turned around.

"I forgot third. Thanks for waking me up."

# 13

Acool front passed through overnight. For at least today, the air was crisp. It was exactly the kind of golfing day Harrison used to wait for. As long as it didn't happen on Thanksgiving Day when he'd crash on the sofa after lunch and doze on and off during football games. While he snoozed, Ben and I would go for a toddle since he was too young to walk any more than one or two houses beyond our own. Sometimes David would join us, and he and I would sit on the deck outside while Ben busied himself with leaves and bugs and dirt.

Today, dressed in long khaki pants, a navy Perlis crawfish polo shirt and loafers, Ben wouldn't be chasing leaves or bugs.

I wanted to talk to Ben about his conversation with Nick this morning, but he didn't bring it up. I figured I'd wait until we finished our dessert visits, when Ben would have had a chance to witness the payoff of the past two days.

I tried to prepare him for the experience of going to these centers. While they both were by no means shabby, the fact was Ben hadn't ever been around anyone over the age of sixty. I didn't want him to be afraid of residents who might have signs of early dementia or who were so starved for guests or attention that they sometimes clung to people who visited.

As we drove to our first stop, I told Ben he needed to be very patient. "If you feel uncomfortable, just let me know. Maybe we could have a sign. Like you could scratch your head or pretend to tie your shoe or something."

"I'm not wearing tie shoes, Mom." He already sounded uncomfortable. "Like are these old people crazy?"

"No, Ben. Of course they're not crazy. Some of them are a little lonely because they don't see their families. A few might not be able to remember things like they used to. They may seem confused and not know what year we're in or where they are."

The conversation began to both scare and depress me. Lately, I didn't seem to be in full control of my own faculties. And some nights I wondered if I never remarried or never had another child, what would happen to me when I reached this season in my life? Who would take care of me? Julie joked that having more than one child was insurance that a parent wouldn't be abandoned. But if that was true, there wouldn't be so many homeless elderly people or ones in nursing homes just waiting to die.

I drove past the new synagogue and pulled into the parking lot of the Ethan Goldstein Life Center. Instead of one large facility, there were several smaller buildings that looked like doubles and others seemed to be apartments. The sprawling building in the middle of these units resembled a country club. The property backed up to the Madisonville River, so a high wrought iron fence surrounded the area.

We were buzzed in and greeted at the door by a young woman who looked like she could have graduated from college the day before. Her loose blonde ponytail, manicured nails, and heather gray cowl neck sweater dress didn't at all fit the profile of someone who directed a retirement home. I expected someone on the verge of grandmother. Or someone like me who was generically nonthreatening. Especially today with my black slacks and cinnamon sweater. I looked and felt like a pumpkin on a stick.

"Hi, Mrs. Becker. I'm Zoe Arnold. We spoke on the phone last week. We are so happy you're doing this for our residents." She shook my hand, then glanced at Ben. "And, you're Ben. Right?"

Ben nodded. "Yes, ma'am." He slipped his hands in his pockets and edged closer to me.

Zoe peered around Ben, probably wondering if we'd forgotten the reason we were there since we were both empty-handed. "Did you need some help bringing the desserts inside?"

"That would be great. Thanks," I said.

"Sure. I'll get Sam and Eli to help you."

I reached for Ben's hand, but he gave me enough of a head shake to know his hands weren't leaving his pockets.

We stepped into a wide reception area designed to look more like a foyer than a lobby. Three oak church pews flanked the wall across from the reception desk, which was really an antique door laid flat on top of stained bead board. Sitting behind the desk was Zoe's mother. I knew she had to be because she looked like her daughter plus forty years.

"Mom, where are Sam and Eli? I need them to help carry the goodies in."

"Check the sunroom. I think they were showing the Bensons how to bowl on that new thing they just set up."

"A Wii?" Ben may have tried to hide the surprise in his voice, but he couldn't mask his expression. "They play Wii here?"

Zoe's mom smiled and handed Ben and me two name tags. "I know. Isn't that crazy?"

Ben looked at me with the "uh oh" face, and then I remembered our conversation in the car. "She means crazy like it's a surprise," I said.

"Got it," he said.

"Do you play, Ben? You might be a better teacher than the twins. Let's see if we can find them," said Zoe.

We walked through a pair of paneled doors into a spacious area that looked like a ballroom, except for the round tables and chairs scattered around. But nothing compared to the view that an entire back wall of glass provided. The space between the wall and the lake had been transformed into an outdoor oasis filled with paved walkways, an outdoor kitchen area, two lap pools nestled alongside a rock wall, and a meditation area with a fountain. Such an abundance of colors, it was as if someone planted dozens of crayons capable of sprouting flowers. I felt like I'd been transported to the set of an HGTV program.

"This is our multi-purpose area," Zoe said. "We use it for meals, when we have speakers or presentations, exercise classes." She pointed to four ladies sitting at a table outside playing Mahjong. "That group asked if we could have Zumba workouts."

I laughed. "Seriously? I can't keep up with Latin music."

"Oh, they're serious," she said as we walked through another set of doors off the main area. "Class starts next week."

Most everyone we passed on our way to the sunroom was socializing, playing cards or a board game, or reading. A few were on the computers grouped in two corners of the area.

Zoe walked us past a small library. "We're still trying to build our collection of large-print books. But since we just opened a few months ago, we're focusing first on bigger needs. Like more residents. That's my husband's job. He's our marketing man."

We could hear the thundering crash of bowling pins before we entered the sunroom, a smaller, more upholstered and comfy version of the main area. She opened the French doors and led us in. "We intended this to be the theatre room, which explains all the televisions. Then Sam read this article for his senior research paper about Wiis being used as therapy and exercise for senior citizens. After that—"

"Hey, Zoe," a man on the other side of the room waved her over. "Come get these useless brothers of yours and find something for them to do. Legos maybe."

The six or so people around him laughed, including the two young men sitting on the couch, clearly Sam and Eli because the only difference between the two was the color of their shirts. They both leaned forward,

"So, guys, what's the story?" Zoe asked.

Sam or Eli started to explain setting up the game, then the other one talked between his sentences, and soon the other people took turns chiming in. Ben watched, his head moved as if he was following a tennis ball at Wimbledon. Apparently he understood the conversation because he'd nod at Sensor Bar, co-axial cables, A/V cables.

It wasn't until we were within conversation range that I noticed that not all the residents were elderly. At a distance, some of them appeared to be so because of their baldness or frailty or age spots. The men in the circle talking to Zoe couldn't have been much older than fifty or sixty. And, as I looked out into the garden, I noticed other men obviously not here because of their age. But there wasn't any doubt that they weren't in good health.

"Mrs. Becker," Zoe's voice broke through my people-gazing, "if you give Ben your keys, the boys can follow him to your car and carry those desserts in."

They headed outside, while Zoe and I walked back to the dining room.

"I'm so impressed with this facility. I knew it was family-owned, but I didn't expect to really find you here," I said. "I'm sorry. That was supposed to be a compliment."

Zoe stopped and turned to face me. "It's okay. We didn't plan to be here. This," she looked from one end of the room to the other, "all this was my brother's dream. He always had such a heart for the elderly." She tucked a few stray hairs behind her ear, and crossed her arms, her hands resting lightly on her upper arms. "We used to joke that he was born an old man."

A quiet sadness surrounded her. I waited before I spoke, hoping she might tell me what happened to her brother. She didn't. I looked past her and saw the boys nearing the door.

"So, he's not working with you?"

"Ethan died of AIDS four years ago."

# 14

Ben left The Goldstein Center with cheeks the color of strawberries from incessant pinching by sweet little blue-haired Bubbes. I left with confusion and sadness roiling in me, imagining myself in Zoe's place.

We stayed at the center longer than I'd planned. Between the attention from Sam and Eli and the adoration from the residents for his baking skills and his Wii prowess, Ben perked up. In fact, I think he was actually enjoying himself.

I passed up the road twice on our way to The Holy Redeemer Senior Center. Trying to locate a gravel road marked only by a rural mailbox proved almost as mystifying as producing a glossy smooth cheesecake top. When we finally made the right turn, the road snaked through stands of pine trees so dense, I made a mental note to never make a night visit.

The gravel road didn't actually come to an end. It looped all the way around the center, a French Acadian style home with a wraparound porch lined with rocking chairs. Not as spacious or as new as the other center, but nestled between two massive oak trees and rings of magnolia trees, Holy Redeemer had a genteel, easy charm.

This center didn't have a buzzer to announce visitors. Instead, it had two chocolate Labrador Retrievers—one I'd bet Ben could have saddled and rode to the door—that barked and bounced and bounded around our car.

"We could go back to the other place," Ben offered, his forehead pressed against his window.

"Those are friendly barks, I'm sure. Labs are sweet. They're just overgrown puppies." I dug for my cell phone to call Sister Pam. No way were we getting desserts past this rambunctious canine tag team.

"Hey, Mom, that lady with the weird thing on her head is calling the dogs." He unbuckled his seat belt. "Can we go in now?"

The dogs trotted away and disappeared behind the back of the house.

"That must be Sister Pam, and that 'weird thing' is part of her religious habit. Meaning it's part of what nuns wear. Like their uniform." I dropped my cell phone back in my purse. "I'm glad you're so excited to be here."

He squirmed in the seat. "Yeah, me too. But I need to go to the bathroom."

---

"Honey, some of us have the diabetes, you know. A sugar-free apple pie might be a nice idea for Christmas," said Teeney as she sliced herself a slab of praline cheesecake with one hand and clutched her aluminum frame walker in the other. She tapped Ben on his shoulder. "Baby, you wouldn't mind putting that little slice of cheesecake on a plate and carrying it right over to the table now would you?"

Halfway to the table, she planted her four-legged walker in the shag carpet, and twisted the top half of her body around so she could see the sofa. "Percy, I might want a little, little piece of that pound cake when you get up off it and get over here by me."

Teeney's husband, Percy, just shook his head from side to side. A matchstick of a man, his face a collection of wrinkles and furrows, like the inside of a well-worn baseball glove. He didn't take his eyes off his wife until she commandeered the nearest chair at the table. "Ain't she somethin' else?"

"Yes, she sure is, Mr. Percy," I said, but likely not for the same reasons.

"We married almost seventy years next month. Some peoples don't even live that long." His voice faded toward the end and, though he stared at the space in front of him, it seemed his eyes saw something else entirely.

"No, you're right again," I said. "Some people don't live that long." Some people don't even live half that long.

He eased himself off the couch. "You want something?"

You bet. Lots of somethings. "Kind of you to ask. But, you know, it's funny. After I bake all those desserts, I can't bring myself to eat any."

Percy's eyebrows stood at attention. "They that bad?"

"Oh, no, of course not. I just meant desserts are better when you don't have them all the time. If you're around them almost every day like I am, they don't seem that special anymore."

He looked at Teeney, then back at me. "I sure am glad my marriage ain't dessert," he said and shuffled off in the direction of the pound cake.

---

Sister Pam stood by the kitchen stool where Ben perched, his head propped on his hands as he leaned on the island and looked out the bay window. I sat across from him arranging pound cakes slices on a pewter serving tray.

"Ben, would you like to go outside and watch the boys play catch?"

He looked at Pam as if she'd just asked him if he wanted to swim in a pool of pudding. "Um, no, that's okay. I can just watch them from here."

"You know, I used to be really afraid of big dogs, and I never wanted to play at my best friend's house because she had one. In fact, it was a lab just like Moses and Noah, only Thelma was the color of sand." She walked over to the pantry and came out with two new chew toys the size of small fireplace logs.

Ben eyed the dog treats. "What are those for?"

"Dinner," she answered, smiled, and lightly tapped him on the shoulder with a rawhide bone. "Well, for the boys, they're like a snack." She opened one and handed it to Ben. "Here, hold on to this while I open the other one."

"Sister, will you be making coffee?" The question sounded more like an accusation, especially coming from a woman who had the height and the body type to have played center on a basketball team. She carried several empty plates with both hands, the spoons tremoring on the top plate until she set the stack in the sink. I noticed, then, the arthritic curves of her fingers, mostly because of her long fingernails, painted as if she'd dipped them in a ripe cantaloupe.

"Now, Marsha, you're standing right there by the coffee-maker. I know you don't see anything in there." Pam smiled, crumpled the plastic packaging, and tossed it in the cabinet waste basket. "If you want coffee, I'll be happy to get it started."

Marsha yanked her long-sleeve cardigan around her waist. The heather brown shade matched her eyes, though the cashmere sweater itself was much softer. "Well, then, I'd like that hazelnut should you still have it," she said as if she'd just given Pam permission. "I'm going to settle Daniel in for the evening."

"Then you and the coffee should be finished at the same time," Pam announced as she scooped coffee beans into a grinder.

Marsha walked to the island where Ben and I sat, eyed my son who looked like he would start playing drums with the chew toys, and said to me. "Oh, and I thank you for providing us with these delicious desserts. You can stop by anytime with those." She reached out her hand, not to shake mine, but to pat me on the shoulder, and then headed to the den.

Pam pushed a button on the front of the coffeemaker and filled the kitchen with the jolting whirring noise of pulverized beans that released a sweet, rich, and nutty aroma. She sniffed the air, "Doesn't that smell delicious?"

Ben spun around on the stool and asked Pam, "Do I have to keep holding these?"

"No. Since I finished making coffee for Miss Marsha, I'm going to surprise the dogs with them in just a bit."

"That lady smelled like peppermint sticks." Ben put the dog bones on the counter. He leaned toward me. "She talked kinda mean, too."

Overbearing, I thought, but not mean. I leaned back on the stool to peer into the den to make sure Marsha and her husband weren't in earshot. "Ben, we can't always judge people by the way they talk." I needed to file that one away in my unwritten rule book of parenting. A book Ben added pages to every year. Funny how children made me confront my own issues.

"Your mom's right." Pam served herself a slice of pound cake, broke off a piece and ate it. "Sometimes the people who are the hardest for us to be nice to are the ones who need it the most. We can't always look at people and know what's happened in their lives." Pam paused to finish the rest of her pound cake. "Miss Marsha and her husband moved here to live close to Bethany, their daughter. The weekend after they settled in, Bethany flew to Boston to attend a sales meeting. She died in a car accident the day before she was supposed to come home. She was their only child."

"I'm sorry for saying she was mean," Ben said to Pam, his voice solemn and soft.

"Ben, Sister Pam didn't tell you that about Marsha and her husband for you to feel like you did something wrong. She wanted us to know because it helps us understand better why people might act a certain way. And that's a good lesson to learn. To not judge people too quickly."

Pam held Ben's hand in hers. "Your mom's right again. And you know what I learned from Miss Marsha's story? To be very grateful for all the people God's placed in my life, and to let them know I care for them while we're still here together." She picked up the chew toys and eyed Ben. "Remember what your mom said about not judging people too fast?"

Ben looked confused, but nodded anyway.

"Well, mister, we're going to go practice that lesson with Moses and Noah."

"Uh, but," he turned around on the stool and peered out the window, "but they're dogs."

"Works the same way," she said. "I'm just going to introduce you to the boys, and let you learn a little bit about each other. I'll be with you the whole time. I don't want you to be afraid of them, and the only way to get over that is to get to know them. And how could they not like someone as cool as you, right?"

He shrugged. "Right."

"You trust me?"

"Yep." He slid off the stool. "You're going to watch, huh, Mom?"

"Of course," I said. "I'm proud of you. It's a very big deal to do what you weren't sure you could do."

My words made a round-trip flight and crash-landed in my gut. I'd just commended my son for doing something I was unwilling to do myself.

# 15

By the time Saturday arrived, Ben couldn't stop himself from looking out the window of his bedroom every hour waiting to see the Pierces' car in their driveway.

"You're sure they're coming home today?"

"Yes. Remember, Miss Julie sent me a text message that they were an hour away?"

"But that was a long time ago."

I looked at my cell phone. "No, Ben. It was less than fifteen minutes ago."

He scratched his head. "How come time goes so slow when you're waiting for something good to happen?'

And that's why, for me, time was supersonic.

"We could play a game. Or you could sweep the porch. Or you could . . ."

He stared at the ceiling, then at the floor and kicked an invisible something with the toe of his shoe. Probably one of those microscopic bugs. "You're just giving me things you know I don't want to do so I'll think of something to do. Right?"

Smart kid. "You mean you're going to pass up a chance to beat me at checkers?" I pretended to be insulted.

He looked suspicious. "You let me win."

"Truth is, buddy, I don't." And I didn't. The game required more focus than my brain could summon when I sat for that long.

"Okay," he said and pulled up his shorts. "I'll go find the game."

He walked away, but I heard him mumble, "Maybe Nick will get home by the time I find it."

Several games later, Nick finally saved Ben and me from each other.

When Ben heard the doorbell, he leapt out of the chair and bolted to open the door. Of course, he opened it and the only thing jumping up and down was the excitement in his voice. He was already entering the "cool factor zone" where it wouldn't be too cool to act like he really felt.

What a shame.

<hr />

On Sunday, Julie invited Ben and me over for a late lunch and so Ben could watch the Saints game with Nick and Trey. "Plus," she said, "I'm craving your potato salad."

While Trey grilled chicken and hamburgers, and the boys disappeared into Nick's room, Julie and I caught up.

I told her about the Junior League meeting and asked if she'd go with me. "I could use the moral support." I tossed the last of the chopped egg whites into the bowl. "Where's your olive oil?"

She handed me the bottle and laughed. "Come on. You know you want me there because if they try to charm you, I'll open my big mouth."

"I don't expect them to do that. They're the ones with no caterer and a splashy event about to happen," I said. Not that Julie was wrong. I don't handle negotiations well. But it did bruise me a bit to know that she thought I couldn't take up for myself. I certainly couldn't the way she did.

"Of course I'll go. And I promise not to blow it for you." She peered into the bowl filled with potatoes, shallots, eggs, olives and a shower of Tony's Seasoning. "Do you need a taste test?"

"No. I need the mayo. And I'm waiting for you to tell me about your lovely vacation."

Julie walked out of the pantry with a new jar of Blue Plate. "Did I hear you say vacation? Did someone go on a vacation?"

While I stirred, Julie reeled off tales of the terrible. Minor mother-in-law mishaps like forgetting she drank only decaf. "The woman did not go to bed until two o' clock in the morning. And guess whose fault that was?" She pointed to herself. "Yep. Heard about that one for the rest of the day. Fortunately, she woke up late because she went to bed so late."

Trey walked in and the charcoal grill scent traveled right on in with him. "Julie, the pit's hot. Got that meat ready?" He pulled out a bottle of water from the refrigerator. "Hey, Caryn. Glad you're here."

The smoke wasn't the only fog in the room. Julie and Trey were like two magnets with their poles reversed. Not that they never fought, but I hadn't seen this level of tension between them since—well, never.

"The chicken was right there under the water bottles. How could you miss it?" This time, Julie opened the refrigerator, slid the tray out and handed it to Trey.

He shrugged. "I didn't see it. Just proves even when things are right in front of you, you can miss them." He gulped down half the water, closed the top, and shoved the bottle in his front pocket. "I'll let you know when I need the barbecue sauce."

"Please do," she answered, but he was already out the door. Probably fortunate for both of them.

"Whoa. What's going on? Brought home the evil twin and left the nice one at the beach?"

She answered me with a chorus of slamming cabinet doors. "I know I bought a new bottle of that sauce he uses . . ."

"Are you ignoring me?" I twisted fresh cilantro and parsley and clipped them with her kitchen shears. Little green leaves rained on top of the salad.

"Found it," she said with relief rather than triumph. "And, no, I'm not ignoring you." She nodded toward the backyard where Trey stood in a cloud of smoke. "He thinks I'm ignoring him."

"Are you?" I pulled on disposable gloves and dove in to mix the salad. Besides the fact that mixing with my hands was so much easier, I liked that mushy feeling as I rolled the potatoes and eggs over one another. It made me think of playing in mud pies. Not that I ever did, but it must have been a lot like this. But cleaner. And this was edible.

"The first night in Florida, he had this delusion we were going to make love. Right. With his awake parents in the next room. The next day, we made an excuse to stay in the condo while everyone else walked over to the beach. I thought it would be the perfect opportunity." She poured the sauce into a bowl and added a glop of honey.

"You might want to squeeze half a lemon in that," I tossed the gloves in the garbage.

"Are you sure you're not related to my husband? He never stops giving me tips either."

"Hey. Lighten up. I'm not used to you being hypersensitive. So, go on, but I don't need all the details."

She wiped her forehead with the back of her hand. "Anyway . . . mission accomplished. I'm thinking we're good. We met the crowd at the beach, did the play in the sand thing with the kids. I laughed at his dad's feeble jokes. I didn't even go off on his brother when he started bashing my politics."

"I'm already impressed. So, what went wrong?"

"Victoria's Secret and Anthropologie and Pottery Barn. He found the credit card receipts in the car console when he drove the kids to the Marble Slab for ice cream that night. When he gets home, he tells me he wants to talk. I could tell by the tone of his voice he meant talk and not 'let's pretend we're talking,' you know?"

I nodded, but I really didn't know. Harrison and I never used code words. When his father died, Ben could barely speak himself. There you go, Harrison. You didn't live long enough for us to have experienced a new way to signal an impending fight or an impending frolic.

The backdoor swung open and the smell of slightly burning chicken skin filtered through.

"Hey. Ready for the sauce." The door closed. The smell stayed.

The promise of food must have enticed the boys to abandon their latest session of Madden football. They dashed into the kitchen, both of their faces expecting what wasn't there. Nick looked at the empty table. "Mom, when's lunch gonna be ready?"

"As soon as you and Ben go outside and give this sauce to your dad." She handed the bowl to Nick and a long barbecue sauce brush to Ben. "Get going, guys. The chef's waiting."

After the door closed, Julie continued. "Here's the microwave version. Trey asked me about the charges and accused me of trying to hide them from him. As if I could hide the monthly Visa bill. We pay everything online." She grabbed placemats out of a drawer and handed them to me. "You ever try to have a fight when you can't scream? I think it makes everything seem worse."

That I knew. I remembered those kinds of fun times in front of my own father when Harrison and I would be engaged in verbal warfare through clenched teeth and smiles.

"So, after the 'haven't we talked about trying to cut back on the credit cards' talk and the lecture on the state of the economy as it pertains to the Pierce household, we get ready to go to bed. He thinks," she looked through the kitchen window as if to remind me who the guilty party is, "we're going to have a repeat performance of our earlier sheet music."

I didn't need to hear the rest of the story. I could fill in the blanks just by the expression on Julie's face.

"No way was that going to happen. Not that night or the next or the next." Every "next" was punctuated by the thud of a plate hitting the table as Julie made her way around. "And that's the problem. Well, more like that's his problem because I'm sure I can hold out a lot longer."

I followed behind her with the silverware. She didn't ask for my opinion, so I didn't offer it. Besides, what did I know? My books kept me company at night; they didn't talk back or worry about credit card bills either.

---

The first day the boys returned to school, Julie and I met with Kirby about the Junior League event. Julie suggested I not bring an a la carte menu. "Narrow their choices. It'll make things easier on you. Plus, the pricing when you present a package doesn't seem as negotiable."

I'd worked out three plans for the committee to consider. We met the four committee members for a sushi lunch. Their choice. I ordered shrimp tempura. Years earlier, I tried to join the trendy crowd of raw fish consumers, but I never made it past the first bite.

After spicy tuna rolls, sashimi, and pieces of salmon, they selected the priciest package. I'd not left myself too much wiggle room in any of the pricings because the League considered this a charity event, and I considered it an opportunity to get my foot in their door. Even if I was the only one whose foot wasn't in a Jimmy Choo shoe.

I spent the next few days making lists of food orders, pulling together recipes, and working out a schedule for the Junior League event. As grateful as I was to get the contract, the job was going to be worth more for the referrals than for the spike in my bank account.

A week later the owner of Suzie's, a local café, called and asked if I'd consider supplying a few of their desserts. Susan Weigand happened to be one of Zoe Arnold's friends. "After you delivered those desserts, Zoe called and raved about your cheesecake. I asked her to save me a bite. That's all I needed." She referred to the "delish" praline cheesecake and wondered if I could make a coffee flavored one and a peanut butter and chocolate version. She wanted me to deliver them in a week.

School meals, Junior League, Suzie. Tight schedule, but I'd rather be stressed doing catering jobs than stressed because I couldn't pay the mortgage.

As I reviewed the plan with Julie the afternoon of Susan's call, she pulled up her phone calendar, made a few swipes across the screen. "Did you forget about Ben's class party? Didn't you promise you'd make those fancy cookies you dip in chocolate for his class?"

I didn't remember, but since Julie carried half my brain in that calendar of hers, I figured she had to be right. I just had to push myself through the next few weeks, and I could rest after Christmas.

"Here." I handed her my planner. "Can you write those dates in here for me while I look up a few more killer cheesecake recipes?"

"It's a primitive system, but sure." Julie poured herself another cup of coffee, then stretched out on the sofa in my office. "Brilliant idea moving this coffeepot in here. Surprised I didn't think of it first."

"You would be. But this is a new coffeemaker. The other one's still in the kitchen."

"Oooh. Living on the edge, are you?"

"Only if joining an online coffee club to get the free coffeemaker, then canceling the membership is considered edgy." I clicked to the *Southern Living* website to check out their new recipes.

"Edgy? No. Borderline dishonest, maybe." She eyed me as she sipped her Pecan Torte flavored coffee that came with the maker.

"The agreement says 'no obligation.' " *Okay, so maybe I'll order one more month of coffee.* I scrolled through dessert options. "If we're going to talk edgy, you're the one sleeping on the edge of the bed."

She laughed. "I'm back in the middle. Trey sent me a dozen roses. Hand signed the card, which meant he actually made the effort to walk into a florist shop." She set her mug on the lamp table and picked up my planner. "Of course. I ended the cold war in our bedroom, and I rewarded him for good behavior."

"Sounds like Trey's catching on to you."

Silence. Uh-oh. That meant Julie was processing, and I wasn't going to back out of this one without explaining myself.

"Since your face was hiding behind that monitor, I couldn't tell if you were joking." She tilted her head to make eye contact.

The tie-dyed cheesecake recipe would have to wait because Julie's stare said she wasn't about to. In our color-coded trauma advisory, this qualified as a flashing yellow proceed with caution. "Maybe Trey's beginning to get, you know, what he needs to do." Real brave, Caryn.

She propped her feet on my desk, settled back on the sofa. "You're right. He needs to give, and then he'll get."

I opened my mouth to explain myself, but Julie had already moved on to checking her email. Maybe I wasn't giving Trey enough credit. Maybe he understood the rules more than I understood the game.

---

Seafood cheesecake. Julie should have kicked me under the table when I suggested that as a substitute for shrimp mold for the Junior League event. My first attempt that day resulted in a puddle of cream cheese in the middle of my springform pan. I'd started my second try after dinner, which meant hitting the sheets before midnight would be a miracle.

Standing at the stove pouring crab boil into a pot of water before I added shrimp, I heard the soft splat, splat of Ben's feet as he crossed the kitchen. "Finished your bath already?"

"Yep." His arms wrapped around my waist before I turned around, but they felt strangely cold. The front of my T-shirt where his hands met was damp, and I felt water soak through the back where his head must have landed.

As I turned around, he unclasped his hands, and what I saw—on any other day—might have been funny. Water dripped from his hair and his pajamas stuck to his body as if they'd been taped on. "Did you wear your pajamas to take your bath? Why are you so wet?"

His eyes opened wider as my impatience turned up the volume of my voice. He tugged on his ears and then pulled his shirt away from his body.

"Ben, I don't have time for this right now. What happened? If I walk in your bathroom and find a mess, I'm going to be very upset."

Behind me, the pot of water started to rumble and the pungent, peppery, nose-burning smell of the liquid seasoning stung my eyes. I blinked several times to dilute the pain.

"Mom, don't cry. I'm sorry. I'm sorry . . ." He shifted from one foot to another. "I couldn't find a towel when I got out the bathtub, so I just put my pajamas on." He bit his lower lip and stared at me as though waiting to hear his sentence.

I wanted to pull him toward me, laugh and plant a kiss on his head and send him to bed. But the pressure of the upcoming weeks steamrolled the kindness and cleared the path for the irate mother to take center stage.

"You're supposed to get your towel before your bath, Ben. If you'd do what you're supposed to do, you wouldn't have this problem. I don't have time to clean up the messes we already have, and you're going to make new ones?"

He dragged a hand across each eye. "I won't do it again," he whispered. "I'm going to bed now. G'night, Mom." He reached his arms around me, like I would break if he hugged too hard.

"Goodnight, Ben. I love you." But the words escaped like a sigh, and I turned around to the angry boil that demanded my attention.

---

A trip to Ben's bathroom while I waited for what I hoped would be a real cheesecake this time, solved the mystery of the disappearing towels. The laundry basket in his closet was filled with dirty towels. We obviously needed to have the "what happens when wet towels live together too long" talk or next time I'd be fighting stinky mildew.

I stopped on the way out, and set the laundry basket on the floor. I knelt near Ben's bed and laid my head on the mattress, to feel the soft rhythm of his breathing. To stroke his hair, and to ask myself why I allowed him to be the brunt of my frustration. He clutched a Wii controller, so I knew he'd gone to his room and played a game before he slept. I imagined him alone after I'd sent him away, and my heart ached. I thought about times when all I wanted was a few seconds more with Harrison to ask forgiveness for all the stupid things I did or said. Things that, after he died, I realized didn't matter. They didn't matter in life either, but I didn't have the perspective of time. With Ben, I had no excuse.

Sometime later between the seafood cheesecake success and matching socks, David sent me a text message. Technology today made not contacting someone impossible. Call. Text. Instant message. Email. Twitter. Facebook. He asked me to call him. Wanted Ben and me over for the holidays.

He wasn't going to give up, that much was obvious. At least this time, I had a legitimate excuse. I replied, by text of course, that I had more jobs than I could handle, and I couldn't take time away. He called two minutes later. Twice. If I didn't relent, the ringing might not either. I picked up the phone.

"Caryn, you must have picked up a lot of holiday business. Do you need some help?'

"No. I'm fine," I said and hoped I sounded as if I truly was. "Julie's been giving me a hand." Well, that much was true.

"I really miss you and Ben. Is there anyway we can get together?"

Ben's face from the other night flashed before me. Those sad, pleading eyes. And I heard that in David's voice. "I don't know, David. I just don't know." I waved my hand around the kitchen as if it was a video camera that could send a feed of the clutter. Maybe next time I would Skype him. Then I could walk around with my laptop and prove I was overwhelmed. "There's just so much going on right now . . ."

"Okay, I understand. If you change your mind let me know. We're going to Christmas Eve service, so we'll be home all Christmas Day."

Maybe because I was already tired or annoyed or overwhelmed, but when I heard David mention going to a service, I felt a burr in my brain. "David, I don't get how you can go to church. I mean, it's not like your lifestyle is, well, church approved."

"Max and I go to a service every Sunday, but my relationship with Jesus isn't on trial here. And, even if it was, Jesus would be my judge."

He responded without a hint of anger or irritation or defensiveness. And, as I said good-bye I realized the person questioning his church attendance was the very person who didn't attend church herself.

# 16

I managed to finish Suzie's orders, but only because I slept less than ever before. The preparation for the Junior League charity event involved more than I anticipated. Days passed, and I couldn't remember if I'd eaten. At least Ben was eating because he stayed at Julie's almost every school night. When the guilt monster started chomping at my insecurities, I fed it with the thought I was investing in our financial security.

"It's not like you're abandoning your son because you're whooping it up on Bourbon Street," Julie said when she'd called to tell me Ben would be spending the night.

"I don't know if that's the good news or the bad news," I said. The wildest side of my life took place between the pages of books, reading about somebody else's lovemaking life. But I wouldn't have told Julie that.

"Nick has a dentist appointment Saturday morning, so I doubt if Ben wants to hang out with us. I'll send him home before we leave," she said. "Now, go cook or bake or broil, or whatever it is you're doing."

"Thanks, Julie. I don't know what I'd do without you."

"Come to think of it, I don't either," she laughed.

"Just don't let me find out, okay? And tell Ben I'll call him after dinner."

⸺ ❧ ⸺

I wandered into the office while I waited for cheesecakes to cool. I wanted to find a source for new business cards and to check my email, which I hadn't done in days. I scrolled through the usual smatterings of advertising, occasional spam, and book club announcements, but stopped when I spotted an email from Sidney Washington. All I knew about Sidney was he would be running as a third party candidate for state representative for our district. But if rumor was true, he didn't intend to stop there. Some talked about his ambition to run for governor.

Ordinarily, I deleted political junk mail without even reading beyond the subject line. Except, this time, my name was the subject line. Both my stomach and my jaw dropped when I read the email. Mrs. Washington belonged, of course, to the Junior League and heard Caryn's Canapés would be catering. I'd come highly recommended from friends of theirs who were either teachers or married to teachers who had ordered my meals. The Washingtons wanted to discuss a menu for a party the night of the elections.

For almost two years, I struggled and wondered if there would ever be a payoff. And, in the past two months, the offers were not only astoundingly profitable, but amazingly connected. And this could be big. This could mean space to breathe. This could mean time out of the kitchen. This could mean saying "yes" to something Ben wanted instead of watching the shade of disappointment on his face hearing "no."

The election was at least six months away, which meant sufficient time to plan, but I needed to start meeting with them soon. I breathed deeply to still the wiggling in my gut, wiped my hands on my sweatpants, and clicked "reply."

I wrote I would be honored to be a part of the celebration. I hoped a celebration. I honestly didn't know enough about politics to know if he'd be a cinch winner, but I did know the incumbent had been involved in a few indiscretions that didn't make him popular. At least not with female voters.

The buzzer for the cheesecakes sounded. I covered them in foil, put them in the refrigerator and went back to the office. I remembered thinking that I needed to log off and get some sleep, but I wanted to check out one more website designer before shutting down.

My left arm felt numb when I woke up. I must have fallen asleep with my head propped on my arm and my hand somewhere in the vicinity of the mouse. I wiped the crusty remnants of drool off my arm. The monitor had timed out and flashed photos of Harrison and Ben and me. Still in that in-between state, I tried to shake off the sleep like it was a design on an Etch-a-Sketch. I checked the time. 9:00 a.m. Something I needed to do—what was that? Then I remembered. Ben. Ben was supposed to be home.

I slapped around my desk to locate my cell phone to call Julie. I'd just started to punch in her number when I heard the front door slam, and Ben and Julie appeared at my office door. Both of them wore faces that might have worked for a horror movie audition, but not for a Saturday morning.

"Mom!" Ben shouted, his face an upside down version of what it was seconds before. He ran to me and threw his arms around my neck. "I was so scared."

If I didn't already know I was awake, I would have thought I was still sleeping. I hugged Ben. "I'm fine. I'm fine." When he released me, I looked at Julie. "What's going on?"

I couldn't read Julie's expression. She was either relieved or annoyed or a mixture of the two, but with an overdose of annoyed. She strolled in, shoved aside a pile of papers I'd thrown on the sofa, and sat. "Just a minute." She called Trey. "She's fine. Asleep. Call you later."

"I thought Nick had a dentist appointment?" I yawned, felt the early morning slime that coated my mouth, and wished I had a bottle of water nearby. I peered in the mug by my keyboard. A half cup of murky coffee. Thankfully, it was far enough away that I didn't knock it over in my comatose state.

Julie cleared her throat. But in a way that let me know it was for effect not for need. "I sent Ben home before we left for Nick's appointment. He came back within a few minutes. I heard him screaming my name while he was still outside." Ben sat on the sofa next to her and nodded. Julie patted him on his knee and smiled. A gracious smile.

"Wait. Ben came home before I woke up? Why did he leave? I'm confused." I pulled my hair off my neck, found a rubber band in the drawer and yanked my hair into a ponytail. It felt like damp mop strings on my neck.

Julie turned to Ben, "Can you get your mom a glass of water? I'll bet she's thirsty."

"Sure. Be right back."

As soon as his body cleared the door frame, Julie scooted to the edge of the sofa and her calm demeanor scooted away at the same time. "The reason he left," she said, with a long emphasis on re-son, "was he walked in here and when he saw you, he thought you had died." She closed her eyes a moment, and I felt like the sludge in my coffee cup.

"Caryn, I probably could describe what I saw on your son's face and heard in his voice, but I don't think you really want me to."

At that moment, I knew exactly what he looked and sounded like and, for Julie, it was a rerun of earlier years when I ran to her door, Ben in my arms, to tell her Harrison had died. I buried my face in my hands. How could I have done this to my child?

"I didn't know I was going to fall asleep on my desk." I sounded more defensive than I meant to.

"I get that. I'm not suggesting you did this on purpose. "

Ben stepped into the room with a water bottle and a glass of ice. "I didn't want to spill the water, so I brought this." He set them both on the desk next to me. I pulled him close and kissed him on his cheek.

"Ben, I am so sorry. I never meant to scare you. I feel terrible."

"I felt my heart go like this." He put his hand under his shirt and patted his chest as if his heart pounded through it "That's when I ran back to Nick's house."

I rolled the desk chair out so he could perch on my lap, but Julie wasn't finished with me yet.

"Ben, sweetie, could you do one more favor for me? See if your mom has a Diet Coke, would you? And can you bring me a glass of ice just like you brought your mom?"

He wiggled away from the chair, but leaned over to kiss me on the cheek. No matter how many baths he took, he still smelled like freshly mown grass. I expected him to pout at another request, but he didn't see it as a diversion tactic. He saw it as a way to do something for Julie.

"You bet. I'll be glad to serve you, ma'am." He grinned and bowed as if he had just addressed the Queen of England.

"What a great server you are," said Julie. "I'll be sure to pass that on to the head waiter."

"Okay, what now?" I asked, opened the water bottle and took a sip to swish in my mouth. "I must have terrible morning breath."

"You know, for someone who just scared the crap out of your son, you're taking this all quite casually."

"What do you want me to do now? Promise I'll never fall asleep at my computer again so my son won't be terrified and think I died?" I took a second noisy gulp. "Okay. I promise."

"You have to get a grip on your life and your business. I know you need the money. But you're taking on too much. It's already a problem for Ben. He spends more time at my house lately than his own."

"I thought you wanted to help. If Ben being there is a problem, let me know."

"No. Ben's not the problem. You're hearing me, but you're not listening. You're the problem. Or at least your total 'overwhelmingness' is."

"I just need to make it through the holidays." I knew this was not the time to reveal I'd just taken on another job, even if it was months in the future.

"You can't keep doing this on your own. Did you already forget that you had someone to call when you needed to?"

"Give it up, Julie. I'm capable of doing this without David's help."

"If I didn't know better, I'd wonder if you worked like a maniac because in some cosmic redemption it would either make David straight or make you forget he wasn't."

I wanted to tell her how stupid I thought that was, but Ben walked in with her Diet Coke.

"Here," he handed Julie her drink and glass. "Mom, since you're okay and everything, can I go watch TV?"

"No problem. Not too loud, though."

"Can I get something to eat? We ate breakfast a looooong time ago."

"Sure, just be careful you're not picking through food I'm cooking with."

"I won't," he said as he sprinted out the room.

I stood, pulled my sweatpants away from where they'd bunched around my hips, and slipped my feet back into my flip-flops. I relocated the stack of papers on the sofa to an empty spot on the floor, and sat in the empty space with my feet propped up on my desk.

"Trey brought Nick, so I guess that means you're stuck with me until they get back," Julie said.

"You can stay as long as you stop beating me up."

"Is that what you think? I'm Caryn-bashing?" She emptied her can in her glass and paused to sip the carbonated mountain of fizz before it all bubbled over. "How long have we known each other? You know I'm going to tell you the truth. And the truth is you've stretched yourself so thin, I could slip you between the pages of one of those cookbooks piled on your desk."

I stared at my hands. Thin. My fingernail polish was thin. My savings account was thin. My patience was thin. Everything except my body. My tired body. I wished Ben knew how to make coffee because a cup of fresh ground Southern Pecan would be a treat.

I loved having coffee in bed with Harrison on Sunday mornings. I loved having Harrison in bed on Sunday mornings. Tomorrow was Sunday, but only the memories would be in bed with me.

"Hey . . . are you still here?" Julie waved her hand near my face as if cleaning a smudged window.

Maybe it was the memory of Harrison that set me off. Or the lack of caffeine. Or needing a pedicure. "Do you know what it's like to be a single mother? No. You have no idea what my life is like. I'm responsible for Ben every minute of every hour of every day. Physically, emotionally, financially. Everything depends on me. When your husband dies, a lot of your choices die with him."

"I'm not sure what you mean," Julie said.

"That's exactly my point. You can choose to ignore or pay attention to your husband, in and out of the bedroom. You can choose to work or stay home. You can choose between being lonely and alone."

"I didn't come here to fight with you, remember? Your son thought you'd died. Why do you persist in being so stubborn and controlling? Why don't you ask for help when you need it? You hardly asked for help taking care of Harrison. If you didn't have Ben to take care of, you probably would have sat here suffering in silence."

"What happened to 'I'm not Caryn-bashing'?"

"I'm not bashing. I'm asking. Let me—let somebody—help you. Stop thinking that asking for help is a sign of weakness."

"If we're going to be honest, after that day in the bowling alley when you obviously didn't want me to say anything about David in front of Trey, I'd been waiting for you to explain what happened. You never have. I don't know if I can talk about my brother in front of Trey or not."

"I didn't plan to not tell you. Sometimes I think I'm protecting people from being hurt, but it happens anyway." She sank back on the sofa. "Trey had the same college roommate for two years. A few months after graduation, the guy tells him he's gay. Trey hasn't been in contact with him since. Not because Jonah's gay . . . well, maybe partly . . . but he couldn't believe he lied to him for so many years. He trusted Jonah, and he thought Jonah trusted him. But if he couldn't tell him the truth, then Trey figured he didn't. Anyway, I wanted to tell Trey myself. Not have him hear in a bowling alley that someone he's considered a friend for years came out."

"And you told him since then?"

Julie looked away, then back. "Yes. I told him. I don't think he wants to see David anytime soon."

# 17

Go to sleep an hour later; wake up an hour earlier. A few more days of this, and I'd meet myself in the middle. Julie helped me assemble the last of the school lunches, and she volunteered to deliver them while I learned how to let go.

Well, maybe loosen my grip.

I learned Ben and I could survive on peanut butter and jelly, while I finished a tomato-caper-black olive sauce for stuffed ravioli with artichokes, feta cheese, and fresh herbs. I learned the vacuum cleaner didn't require weekly exercise, especially if the clutter covering the floors made navigating it seem like an episode from The Great Race.

I learned I didn't want to be the person my mother would have looked at, made the sign of the Cross, and said, "There, but for the grace of God, go I." According to my mother, had God not been watching over her, she would have been the homeless person begging at a corner, the woman who died in surgery, the mother who lost a child, or the abandoned wife who gained fifty pounds. God's grace was her tragedy-proof vest. I don't think I inherited the vest. According to Julie, I've already inherited God's blessings, no charge. I didn't get this

God of give-aways, especially since lately He seemed the God of take away.

The past few Sundays, Ben attended church with the Pierces, and this Sunday he came home revved about the children's choir. "The songs are fun. We sang one called 'Walk in Jerusalem.' And you get to clap. Loud. In church." Still wearing his new jeans and button-down polo shirt, he smiled from the inside out. "It's cool, Mom. When you stop cooking, can you come with us?"

I reached in the bottom cabinet for more plastic containers, relieved he couldn't see me say, "Sure," because he would have known that it really meant, "We'll see."

"Aw-right! Can't wait to tell Nick," he said.

"One more thing to feel guilty about," I told the smoked oysters under my breath as I mashed them for a pâté. They ignored me.

"I'm gonna change my clothes." He sniffed the air in the kitchen, then peered into the bowl in front of me. "That's people food? Yuk. It smells like dirty feet."

The kid was two for two, and it wasn't even lunch yet.

The Junior League luncheon was two days away when Sidney Washington called me as I seasoned three dozen petite crab cakes with tarragon and mango sauce. I'd forgotten I'd mentioned in my email he could contact me if he had questions before we met.

"Caryn Becker?"

I answered, "Yes," and almost launched into a blathering of thanks when the voice spoke again.

"Hold on for Mr. Washington, please."

If the oven heat in the kitchen hadn't already wilted me, that abruptness would have.

I hit the "speaker" button and started to wrap the finished cakes in foil. But when I moved the first batch to make room for the second, I slid the box of foil over too far. The box batted the telephone receiver off the island, and Sidney's hello sailed through the air with it. I leaned over to grab the phone, mashed my elbow in the unwrapped batch of crab cakes, and sent them crashing to the floor. His second hello came as the phone scuttled across the tile like a turtle on its shell and crashed landed into the baseboard. The crab cakes splatted on the floor near my toes.

I dragged my hands across my apron, reached for the phone, and managed to answer before Sidney spoke again.

"Did I catch you at a bad time?"

In the summer, a frosty voice like his would be appreciated. No, you didn't catch me at a bad time. You caused the bad time. "Absolutely not. What can I do for you Mr. Washington?" I squatted on the floor and picked up the ruined crab cakes.

"My campaign manager neglected to consult my calendar before she scheduled me into yet another meeting."

He paused. I opened a roll of paper towels to finish wiping up the mess.

"So," he said, "We need to reschedule our appointment."

I wet an arm's length of paper towels, sat on the floor, and wiped a few tears and hours of work away. "No problem at all. What did you have in mind?"

"I can meet you the same day and time the following week. Can you be there then?"

I hadn't seen my planner in days, and I didn't have time to find it now. "That date is fine," I answered as I tossed a dozen crab cakes and a mess of paper towels in the garbage can.

"Well, then, we're set."

"Yes, I—"

"I'm sorry. Lurlene just informed me a conference call is waiting. I'm looking forward to meeting you. Good-bye." And the phone went dead.

The mattress disappeared beneath me, and I rocked as if laying on the deck of a sailboat, the waves gently taking turns lifting me up and then down and then up and down. I felt myself surrendering to the quiet rhythms when a blast of noise broke through and shoved me back into my bedroom.

I must have set the alarm volume to its highest because when Steven Tyler hit a high note, I shot up from the mattress like someone had doused me with ice.

I fumbled around in the darkness, hoping to find the reset button before Aerosmith launched into its screeching chorus again. Two hours of sleep. But today was the day. The Junior League luncheon would be over. I could redeem my life.

For a while last night, I considered not even trying to sleep, but my legs refused to support me, and I wasn't sure my brain did either.

Determined to make myself as efficient as possible, I had typed and printed two "TO DO" lists. One for my purse and one taped to the back of the front door to remind me of everything I needed to walk out with.

I'd even ironed my new Jillie Willie Girlfriends in the Kitchen apron, my black linen skirt and made sure the new emerald cashmere sweater from Banana Republic still fit.

I showered, not bothering to wash my hair since I'd braid it. I didn't want there to be even a suggestion of hair in the food.

The kitchen looked as if the pantry and refrigerator had packed for a long trip. Whatever wouldn't spoil was packed and labeled in plastic containers. Everything else was in the refrigerator until it was time to leave.

I zapped a mug of leftover coffee in the microwave. It hardly seemed fair to even call it leftover since I'd just made it not so many hours earlier.

I woke Ben and had breakfast waiting for him on the table. "You made pancakes this morning?" Even in his barely awake stage he was shocked.

"Well, sort of. I made some a few days ago, then I froze them. Now you can just pop a few in the toaster and, bingo, pancakes."

He sat and eyed the stack like he was waiting for it to make the first move. "They're like regular pancakes?" He lifted the top one with his fork and peered underneath.

"Ben, they are pancakes. This was supposed to be a surprise. A good one." I slammed the bottle of syrup on the table. "If you don't want them, find something else. But eat. You have to be ready when Julie gets here."

"I was just asking. Sheesh." He squeezed the bottle with both hands and made smaller and smaller circles of syrup until there wasn't a dry spot on the top pancake.

We made it through breakfast without any major catastrophes, so I sent him off to get dressed. He had to make two return trips. One to brush his teeth, and the other to brush his hair.

I straightened his shirt collar while he stared out the back window. "I thought we had somebody to cut the grass? What happened?"

"That somebody is me for now. The man who used to do it moved, and I haven't found anyone else." Plus, I can save money.

"I think I could help you do that." He narrowed his eyes, and looked like he was assessing the situation to give me a quote. "Or maybe you could buy one of those lawnmowers you drive around the yard."

"You know, I hadn't thought of that. I'll check it out." With my driving record, it could end up being more costly than another yard service.

"If you get one, could I drive it?"

"Probably not. At least not right now." I checked behind his ears.

"I'm not two." He tilted his head away from me. "They're clean."

Julie's horn saved him from a neck inspection. I walked him to the door.

"You remembered your bug project?"

"Yes, Mom." Ben slipped his backpack on and scrunched his face when I wiped the corner of his mouth with my thumb. "Eww. That's gross."

"Not as gross as showing up at school with toothpaste crust on your face," I said. "Have a great day, and by the time you're home from school, I'll be finished with the luncheon."

"And I'll be finished with school till next year!"

"That's right. Today's your last day before the holidays." I hugged him. "It's a big day for both of us."

# 18

Of course the one morning I needed the interstate to be accident free, the other drivers didn't cooperate. Twenty minutes behind schedule. I called Kirby and explained what was going on.

"I'm probably just a few minutes in front of you, so we should arrive close to the same time," she said. "And if this is one of those endless delays, I know where to find food."

Whew. At least she had a sense of humor. "And I won't be hard to locate. You'll just follow the smell of shrimp and smoked oysters."

"Oh, that should make you popular with the cars around you. Don't worry. I can already spot flashing red lights ahead, so it's getting cleared. I'll see you soon."

I closed my cell phone and readjusted my earring that had mashed into the side of my cheek. It was time for me to buy one of those Bluetooth jobs, but it would be so much more exciting to buy a car already Bluetooth enabled. Of course, then I'd need to retire the primitive cell phone, which would mean I'd need a different cell phone plan. Good grief. Technology was a lot like that book I used to read to Ben about giving a mouse a cookie, then he would want a glass of milk, then a mirror to check for a milk moustache, and on and on and on until he ended up exactly where he started.

If only Smart phones were priced like cookies . . .

The milk mustache reminded me to check my smile in the rearview mirror to make sure my two front teeth weren't edged in lipstick. A social mortification second to coming home after an event to discover broccoli, popcorn kernels, or pepper wedged between my teeth. Yet another bonding experience for Julie and me. In public, we'd be human mirrors for any teeth-related issues. After a meal we'd give each other a quick dentist office smile, code for "make sure my teeth aren't holding food bits hostage." And if one of us said "lipstick," the other knew that called for an immediate teeth wipe. Bizarre the things that bonded friends. The small acts that said we watched each other's back, or in this case, front to protect one another from embarrassment. Today, though, I was on my own.

---

Satisfied my teeth passed the test, I settled into my seat, and picked up my travel mug, a stainless steel one monogrammed with my initials. A gift from David not long after Ben started school because, as he said, "You're spending more time in the car than home." And since it eliminated drive-thrus, it saved me time and money. And David knew better than anyone that I lacked both of those. The lid disappeared months later, but as long as I didn't fill it, it wasn't a problem. Until today, when the truck in front of me stopped sooner than I expected, which caused me to stomp on the brake pedal, which caused coffee to spill over the edges of the mug, which landed on my skirt, which caused me to want to say words I learned not to say since the day Ben explained to his pre-school teacher that a "d$%# accident made us late."

I hoped this didn't predict a give-a-mouse-a-cookie kind of day. I blotted coffee with the MickeyD napkins I found on the passenger side floorboard. Finally, I arrived and probably not long after Kirby and her crew.

The house sat on lakefront property and had undergone an extensive remodel last year. When I drove up, I remembered it from the before and after pictures when it had been featured in our local magazine. The six columns of the plantation style house soared to the second story. Porches and galleries ran along all four sides. The stucco at the ground level and the wood at the upper were painted a creamy butter color. Above the oversized cypress doors was a cut class transom.

I just pulled out the tray of skewered artichoke and garlic shrimp when my cell phone rang. The phone slipped out of my hands. I tried to balance the tray I held and forgot about the tray of crab stuffed mushroom perched on the tailgate. One tray clobbered another, and dozens of mushrooms slid down and landed on the street.

I'd already pressed answer, so I could hear Ben's voice. "Mom, are you there? It's me. Ben."

I snatched the phone from where it had landed on the street. "I can't believe you're calling me right now. Is this an emergency?" "Not really," he said. I stepped away from the glop near my feet. You know I'm right in the middle of this important job. I don't have time to talk. If you forgot something at home, I can't help you today. You'll have to figure out what to do. I have to go because I have a huge mess to clean up."

I snapped the phone closed and tossed it on the seat of my car. That's it. I've been too protective. I've babied that kid too much. He needs to learn this lesson. I'll apologize later for being so loud when I talked to him.

But right now, Kirby and Lizette walked to the car to see if I needed any more help. But unless the three of us could throw together another appetizer, the entire tray was unsalvageable.

A lesson learned for my next event. Make an extra tray of something—anything.

⸻

As I garnished the black bean and corn salad with cilantro, my cell phone vibrated in my pocket. The school phone number flashed, and my aggravation right along with it. I almost didn't answer, but I'm listed on Nick's emergency card, so I didn't want to risk that it might be about him.

"Mom?" Ben again. His voice crept out, and I could see him on the other side with his head down and his eyes round. Probably scuffing the toe of his shoe on the carpet.

"Ben. I'm very busy. What do you want?"

"My teacher said I could call you back. I wanted you to know that I didn't forget my project. I called because, well, you didn't bring the cookies for the party. I was afraid something happened because I knew you wouldn't forget because you promised."

I looked around to see if there was a hole deep enough for me to fling myself into. My shame, though, nailed my feet to the hardwood floors beneath me. I looked at the clock. No way could I make cookies happen. I could make a catered luncheon for seventy-five happen, but not a few dozen chocolate-dipped sugar cookies. With icing and sprinkles.

"Oh, no. Ben. I'm so . . ." Stupid? Selfish? Inconsiderate? His silence intensified my pain. It's as if he knew I searched for the right word, and he waited for me to find it so he could hear the truth. "Sorry. I'm so sorry."

"Okay." I heard acknowledgment, not forgiveness in his voice.

"Ben, is Ms. Richmond there?"

"Yes. She's right here."

"Can you hand her the phone for me, please?"

I heard him tell Michelle I wanted to talk to her, but then he came back. "Are you still picking me up from school? Ms. Richmond wants to know."

Made an outstanding impression on, not only Ben's teacher, but the friend who helped me launch the teacher meals that reached almost a dozen schools. "Yes. I will most definitely be there. In fact, don't wait in car line. I'll park and walk to the classroom. Okay?" Oh, generous me.

I felt as if I was about to be assigned detention, maybe worse, as I waited for Michelle to talk to me.

"Hi, Caryn." She wore her 'I'm the cleaner, and I'm here to tidy up this mess' voice. "Ben asked if he could call one more time. I hope you didn't mind."

"No. No, of course not." I stared out the kitchen windows. The backyard sloped to the lake where a gazebo-covered pier deck had been built. It looked like an inviting place to be right now. "I apologize for letting Ben and the kids down. I'm in the middle of catering a luncheon today, and I honestly forgot. I feel like an idiot. Is there any way I can help make this up to them?"

"Actually, Ben figured out a plan. The class was treated to those magnificent cupcakes from Babycakes, that new bakery in town. It couldn't have turned out better," she said. I could tell she meant it, but I didn't understand.

"How did that happen?"

I wandered into the study or if it wasn't, it should have been. I opened the blinds to see the wall color. It looked like cinnamon. The large room had been divided into two distinct areas. In one area was the actual office itself, which was shaped like a U. The office overlooked a second area centered on a flat screen TV. It could have served as a small apartment.

"Ben remembered his Uncle David was listed on his emergency card, so he asked if he could call him. I think he hoped he would know where you were. When Ben explained to him what happened, he told Ben he'd be at the school before the party ended. And he was. Came in carrying those three dozen cupcakes. Ben was so proud, he introduced him to everyone in the class."

∞∞∞

Kirby and Nan didn't mind my leaving a half-hour early so as not to be late getting Ben. I opened my car door and willed myself behind the steering wheel. What I wanted to do was kick off my heels, stretch out on the backseat, and sleep until I could wake up a whole person.

I didn't remember that David was on Ben's emergency card, so the fact that Ben did stunned me. As grateful as I felt for David having rescued Ben, he just tipped the scales in his favor. Since neither Ben nor Michelle mentioned anyone being with David, I supposed he arrived alone. At least I didn't have *that* to explain. As it is, before we hung up, his teacher said, "You didn't tell me your brother was so attractive." I surely wouldn't now.

I drove to Ben's school, and felt like I was headed to the punishment phase of my trial. Today, I would've opted for a long jail sentence since I wouldn't have to cook, clean, or worry about what to wear. A simplified life.

Ben didn't see me at first. He leaned against the brick wall, his backpack at his feet, and held a red box covered with green polka dots that could have held a ten-gallon hat. Next to him stood a girl wearing a white ribbon woven through her French braids. Compared to Ben, she seemed all arms and legs. The kind of gawky that in ten years will bloom into beautiful. Did Ben even notice her? Should he notice her? What do kids these days and this age do about the opposite sex? I wondered if David leaned against walls and tried to figure himself out when he was Ben's age.

My exhaustion was leading me down unmarked and untraveled roads. Some of them needed "Trespassers will be Shot" signs.

What if Michelle asked me about David? She knew he'd been engaged, and by now, like everyone else in a twenty mile radius of the central traffic signal in town, also knew the wedding had been canceled. What should I say? "David's just not ready to date yet" or "David's dating. He's just not dating women"? How come there was no handbook for this? Would I have bought it anyway? I might have, like I buy all things that I think people would use to judge me. I would order it online, and it would come in the mail, and no one would know.

David had an unfair advantage. He knew people on both sides. I didn't know any gay men or women that I could confide in. Or maybe I did know them. Maybe I just didn't know they were gay. No, that couldn't be. Surely, I'd know. But then, I didn't know about David.

When Ben spotted me, he turned to French Braid, said something that made her laugh, and walked toward me. But the grin that usually rewarded me on afternoons like today was missing. Probably in that red box somewhere.

"See, I made it," I smiled, sounded happy, and didn't attempt more than a one shoulder hug in front of his friends. "Where's Ms. Richmond? I want her to know you're with me."

"She went in the office."

"Well, let's go tell her we're leaving."

He shrugged. "Sure."

"Do you need some help with that box?"

"No. I saved cupcakes for the Pierces." He opened the top. "And you."

# 19

It was just a matter of time before you self-combusted." Julie opened another box of Christmas ornaments. "You're just lucky the Junior League luncheon went so well."

"Yes, despite the fact that an entire tray of stuffed mushrooms filled with expensive crabmeat fell in the street." She handed me strands of twinkle lights begging to be unraveled. "Are you sure you want to start this while Nick and Trey are gone?"

Julie pulled pieces of last year's tinsel off the hat of a wooden snowman. "Last year Trey made sure the lights worked, put a few ornaments on, then snored on the sofa. After Nick hung all the ornaments that he made over the years, he kept asking when we could quit for the hot chocolate and cookies. Not quite the Hallmark moment I expected." She unrolled and shook out their needlepoint Christmas stockings. "I wouldn't be surprised if he's looking for a totally decorated tree that folds, ornaments, garlands and all. Don't think either one of them will mind if we get a head start."

I handed her their stocking holders, three gold fleur-de-lis, for the fireplace mantel. "Do you ever think about how things would be different having a daughter?" I wondered, more often than I should have, if I had missed my chance. But then I might have missed Harrison and Ben.

She hooked Nick's stocking, his name embroidered in white against forest green velvet with a train loaded with presents headed toward the toe, then rearranged the other two holders. "I'd like to have a daughter," she said and her voice sounded as if she'd climbed on Santa's lap herself with her Christmas list. "My mom and I went through a few rough years. She tells people I went in a tunnel until I was twenty. But, by the time I came out, we were friends."

I nodded remembering a time when my mother was the only person I wanted to talk to, the only person who could have comforted me, and the only person whose disappointment I feared. If heaven didn't have secrets, then what I couldn't tell her then, she knew now. But whatever comfort that brought me subsided when I realized that Harrison knew as well.

Maybe if Julie ever did have a daughter, they could learn something from my experience even if it was too late for me. "I doubt Trey would mind practicing for a girl," I teased and handed her his Santa trimming the tree stocking.

"Are you kidding? He'd train like it was an Olympic event."

"You don't make that sound positive."

"Do you know how long it took to convince him that once a week meant normal frequency?" She grabbed a handful of red and green peanut M&M's, and popped one at a time into her mouth between hanging her own cotton white angel stocking on the other side of Nick's and making sure the three were evenly spaced on the mantel. "You and Harrison quadrupled that on a weekly basis. I used to hope they didn't compare normals."

"That's one less thing you have to worry about," I said and, before what I suspected would be an apology about to roll out her open mouth, I added, "And don't knock it until you've actually tried it."

—◯◯◯—

After Julie's fifth "I'm such an idiot" apology and a fresh cup of Toasted Almond coffee, I declared her sufficiently mortified and the discussion about former and present relationships with former and present husbands officially over.

We sorted through their ornament collection to find small ones for the top branches of the tree. I volunteered for ladder duty and just as I reached to hang a Baby's First Christmas ornament, a blue bassinet with 'Nicholas' engraved on it, my cell phone rang.

"Do you need to get that?"

"No. If it's Sidney Washington, it's really just someone calling for him. Lurlene," I said with a feigned sophistication, "would certainly leave a message. Otherwise, I don't think I'd be getting too many calls the week before Christmas for catering. "

"Here, hang this one front and center so Trey's mother won't have to dance around the tree pretending like she's not looking for it."

I almost fell into the Douglas fir when I saw the ornament. "Penguins? With Santa hats and little matching scarves. I'm speechless."

"Yeah, yeah. Go ahead and laugh. When we start on your tree, I'm going to find that treasure of yours with the two bears paddling a canoe. I may even take a picture, and post it on Facebook."

"You didn't just stick your tongue out at me, did you?" I laughed and climbed off the ladder and pushed it to another section of the tree. "Truce. Let's get at least the top finished before the guys return."

Five ornaments later the phone vibrated again, but this time it also pinged that someone sent a text message. "Got to hand it to Sidney. The man's persistent." I patted my pocket.

"Maybe you ought to check. It might not be Sidney. Isn't your dad still on his cruise or hike or whatever they're doing?"

"Cruise. Mediterranean, I think. They're supposed to be home for New Year's Eve. It's their wedding anniversary, remember?"

"Of course. I don't think I've been to any other wedding reception until midnight and sent the bride and groom away with party hats and horn tooters."

"Or it could be the Christmas tree hunters we sent out. I have a feeling they're going to come back with the Charlie Brown Christmas tree. Ben's attracted to all the trees no one else wants. He thinks they should be adopted. Set up a table at the Christmas tree lot. Let people pay for them, and then plant them in the woods."

"You know, he may have something there."

"Just what I need. Another investment."

Again the phone vibrated.

"Caryn, maybe it's Ben sending you a picture of the Christmas tree he wants. Or Trey warning you about the one on its way home."

"Well, by now, I think somebody would have thought to call you, huh?"

I slipped my phone out of my pocket. The call and the texts came from David's number. I scrolled to the message:

"David in Mercy Hospital. Seriously injured. Please call."

# 20

The phone shivered in my hand. I shivered with it. I heard Julie, but I couldn't make words come out of my mouth to answer her. They seemed trapped in a hollow tunnel between us.

"What? What happened? Oh, dear God. Please, please not the guys." Julie grabbed my phone. She gasped. "Who sent this message? This is David's phone number? Right?"

I nodded and grabbed the top of the ladder as if it prevented me from falling off a ten- story building. The movie played. A rerun. The glass doors of the ER. Harrison's face.

"Let go, Caryn," her voice as soft as her hands over mine. Julie steadied the ladder as I made it down. "Come sit down. I'll call for you and find out what's going on." She wedged herself on the chair next to me, and patted my knee. She hit call and the speaker button. It rang twice. The voice that said, "Hello, is this Caryn?" belonged to a man. A man not David.

"No, this is Julie, her friend. She was at my house when she read the message."

She wiggled off the chair and took the phone off speaker.

"Who are you talking to? Is that his doctor?"

She shushed me. "I understand. I won't. We'll leave here in the next five minutes. Okay. Bye." She stood and walked to the key rack by the backdoor.

I followed behind her. "What happened to him? What's wrong? Was he in an accident?"

She grabbed her car keys. "I don't know. Max said he'd explain when he saw us."

"Why couldn't he just tell you? I don't understand."

"Caryn," she put her hands on my shoulders. "Stop. You don't have to understand right now. You just have to go to the hospital."

"I have to get my purse. Call Ben." I darted to the front door. Another train, loaded with disaster and sorrow and fear hurtled down the tracks. Impact was inevitable. But maybe I could outrun it, buy myself time.

"We're going, we're going. Help me find my cell phone so I can call Trey. And you're not driving. I told Max, I'd get you there. He didn't want you to be alone."

---

"I can't find my purse. Where did I leave it? How can I be so stupid? I can't find it!" I darted from room to room, bouncing off targets like a ball in a pinball machine. I lifted stacks of newspapers, shoved towers of unfolded clothes aside, and checked the knobs of every door I passed.

What if David asked for me? What if he needed me to be there?

In the foyer, Julie pressed her cell phone to her left ear with one hand and held the other hand over her right ear as if to block out noise. An oversized clip holding her hair off her neck looked like a white butterfly landed on the back of her head. She stood hunched over in that body language people on cell phones used that said "back off, I'm trying to have a private conversation."

I wanted her off the phone. I needed her to tell me what to do. I didn't want to be forced to remember how I walked through here years ago. On my way to the same hospital, then to see my husband, today to see my brother. My brother who sacrificed a night with his high school friends to chauffeur Danny, my first date, and me to dinner and then to the Sweetheart Dance in junior high and spared me the awkwardness of Mom and Dad driving. My brother who visited me and my roommates in college and always arrived with a trunk full of groceries and rolls of quarters for the laundromat. My brother who, when he held Ben for the first time, whispered, "Hi, Ben. I'm your Uncle David. I will love you always and forever."

My feet moved forward, but my insides lurched and stumbled and crashed into one another. The clock on the microwave showed 11:57. Maybe if I ate something. Something portable. Like a bagel. But the wheat one I found in the refrigerator doubled in size when I chewed it. I gagged and leaned over the kitchen trash and spit it out. Enough time wasted, Caryn.

On the way to my bedroom, I pulled off my tennis shoes and abandoned them in the hall. I walked to the closet where I hid the laundry basket, which was filled with dirty clothes. I dumped the basket on the carpet and burrowed through the pile. Black skirt. Black skirt. Where was it? Not there. I scanned the hangers. No. Not there. Then I remembered. I'd worn it to the luncheon, came home and tossed it in the basket of clothes I needed to drop off at the dry cleaners. The coffee blot had been joined by a number of now unidentifiable spills.

When I finally found it, I shook as many wrinkles out as I humanly could.

Julie appeared at my closet door. "What in heaven's name are you doing? Nobody cares what you look like."

"I care. I care." My voice verged on hysterical. I unzipped my jeans, wiggled out of them, and pulled on the skirt. I smoothed it over my legs and slipped my feet into a pair of plain black flats.

"Are you ready?" Julie tapped her cell phone against her leg.

"My purse. I still can't find it." By then, I'd launched so far out of our Sanity Advisory Zone, even my voice sounded as if it traveled through space. My tears seemed stuck in my throat instead of my eyes.

"Calm down, Caryn. Don't hit the panic button over your purse. We have time," said Julie, a yoga-like calmness in her voice.

Move with the breath. Flow with the breath. Be with the breath. I quit yoga after Harrison died. Every time she told us to breathe deeply, I closed my eyes and saw Harrison not breathing at all.

"Time? No. We don't have time." I walked out of the closet and kicked aside a hill of sheets. Had I not replaced my clunky tennis shoes with soft leather flats, my toes would have been spared the shock of meeting one of the four bed posters. The pain pushed the tears, the anger and the fear out. "Harrison died in the time it took me to brush and floss my teeth. All those months of not wanting to be away from home for long. Days of going to bed late, waking up early. For what? So he could die fifty feet away from me? In the few minutes I spent brushing my teeth? How does that happen?" I picked up a pillow case, swiped it down my wet cheeks and under my nose, and threw it on the floor. "So, don't think David can't die while I'm looking for my purse."

"Okay. Thirty seconds, and then we'll leave." Julie scanned the room, then walked to my dresser, where my pink shoulder

**151**

bag parked itself. It looked at me as if to say, "What? I've been here all the time." When Julie reached for it, I saw her glance at the books stacked nearby. The covers didn't need titles for her to figure out they weren't book club fodder. She handed me the purse. "What are . . . never mind. Not important. Not now."

The question in her eyes didn't disappear. It just hid behind the urgency of getting to the hospital.

―◦◦◦―

"I talked to Trey. He and the boys were on their way home. I told him to tell them we had to make a last minute Christmas run." Julie merged into the I-10 traffic, which always moved slower the week before Christmas. As if the entire town decided to do a group shop at the same time.

"But I need to talk to Ben—" I twisted a paper towel in my hand from the roll I snatched from the kitchen on our way out when I couldn't find facial tissues. But I didn't need them for tears. I used them to have something to hold on to because my gulping sobs had been replaced by stillness. A stillness that had returned from a place faraway. A stillness that scared me more than the tears.

"You're not calling Ben. Not right now. Wait until we know something."

Something like, "Ben, your Uncle David died without your mom ever telling him she loved him. Your uncle died thinking his only sister hated him."

Saturday afternoon. Family day in traffic. An SUV passed with a mom, dad, two children. A truck. A convertible. Like individual pods moving in one direction, but only look like they're together.

"I should call Lori. She needs to know." I scrolled to find her number.

"No. Not yet. Wait until we . . . you have something definite to tell her."

"You're right. Plus, if she wanted to meet us at the hospital, it'd be hard to tell her not to. She probably would want to, but how awkward would that be?"

Julie nodded. I could tell there was a conversation going on in her head she wasn't sharing because she did this weird almost pucker thing with her lips and her forehead wrinkled. When we played Monopoly, and we saw that look, we knew to start saving our cash because the girl would be soon putting up houses and hotels.

"What? I know there's something you're not telling me."

"It wasn't a big deal, just thought of something funny. But you probably won't think so, and I don't want to upset you."

"Upset me? Past that. Go ahead . . . what?"

"I thought of Max, Lori, me all in waiting room—like a gay version of while you were sleeping—we could call it While You Were Awake."

When I tilted my head against the passenger side window, I saw my face reflected in the rearview mirror. It needed blush. And lipstick. "I should have started going back to church. I wanted to. But then David called and everything changed."

"David's not gay because you didn't go back to church." She glanced at me. "And are you saying you didn't go to church because David came out? You're going to have to explain that one to me."

Julie exited and stopped for the red light at the four-way intersection. Gas stations anchored three of the four corners. On the other corner, Starbuck's and Babycakes, where David had picked up those designer cupcakes for Ben's party, peeked out from between Ane's Art Gallery and TipToes Shoe Boutique.

"Well, David's changed to another church now. And he was the one who tried to get me to go there. And now he's not there, and I have no idea what the pastor thinks . . ."

"Church isn't an AA meeting. You don't stand and say, 'Hi, my name is Caryn, and my brother's gay.' And I've not heard too many stories of people saying things like, 'By the way, is it true you have a gay brother?' Sometimes I think you worry that David being gay says more about you than it does about him."

"I wanted to get back to church. Especially now that Ben's older. But then I worried that Ben would get confused hearing, you know, how some people can talk about gays. And I'm already confused."

"You didn't give anyone a chance to help you feel comfortable. You're assuming things about people in that church just like you think they're assuming things about you." She turned at the hospital sign that pointed to the Emergency Room. "Plus, going to church isn't about you and David. It's about you and God. He's the one you focus on when you're there."

She turned into a parking spot, and when I looked at the Emergency Room doors, a beehive exploded in me. I saw myself, tap dancing on the rubber mat in front of the electric doors as if it would make them open faster, walking in breathless, even though David had dropped me off at the entrance. I remembered scanning the faces of people in the waiting room, as if I expected Harrison to be waiting for me, telling me that everything was okay. But he wasn't okay. And he wouldn't be okay. Ever.

Today, I didn't search the room looking for David's face. Today, the man who all those years ago, followed me into the ER was the man whose name I repeated at the front desk. "David Collins. I'm here to see David Collins. I'm his sister."

The receptionist wore a red Christmas scrub jacket decorated with red-hatted, white bearded, smiling Santas. Patsy
(according to her name tag) looked like she could have been
Mrs. Claus. Or Santa's sister. She reminded me of Aunt Bea,
from Mayberry reruns, and her face was kind. "Wait one minute, honey," she said as she flipped pages on a clipboard. "He's
in surgery." I felt Julie's hand squeeze my shoulder. "If you follow the green stripe down that hallway . . ." She pointed to the
one directly across from her desk, ". . . it'll take you to the elevators to the family waiting room on the third floor. When you
get there, check in with the volunteer so they'll know someone
is here from his family."

Except for the occasional doctor paging and the measured
clapping of our shoes, we walked in silence.

"It's not that difficult to locate the elevators." Julie looked
back down the hall. "People really need a green stripe? Maybe
I should paint one of those from Nick's room to the laundry
room."

We stepped in the elevator, Julie pressed the button for the
third floor, and elbowed me as we both faced the door. "Great
idea. That can be our post-Christmas mission."

"Sure. You first. Let me know how it works, and then I'll
start painting." Assuming enough paint existed for what I
wanted. A green stripe that would lead from my life to a normal one. Or maybe I had a green stripe for normal, but someone forgot to mark the detours. Today was definitely a detour
and, I hoped, not a roadblock.

We followed the signs and, this time, a red stripe to the
Surgical Waiting Room. Julie turned to walk in, and I clutched
her arm. "What do I say to him? To Max?"

"Why don't you start with 'Hello'."

# 21

Several years ago, the family of a high school cheerleader severely injured in a car accident involving a drunk driver, donated a generous sum of money to renovate the hospital's surgical waiting room. Her parents told the local news that Haley survived three surgeries, but they almost didn't survive the boredom of reading the same two-year-old magazines and the anxiety of not leaving for long stretches of time for fear the doctors would come out and find no family there.

The room could have been featured in *Southern Living*. Two plasma televisions hung on opposite sides of the room on sand colored walls. Each had a seating area with a caramel brown leather recliner, upholstered chairs, and floral chenille sofas. An aquarium on the opposite wall separated a children's play area with game stations from computer stations on the other side. In the middle, a granite island held beverages, coffeemakers, and trays of cookies and fruit.

So entranced by the unexpected serenity of the room, neither one of us realized we were standing in front of the check-in desk. I heard the receptionist before I saw her.

"Welcome. May I ask the patient's name?" To my right, a woman sat behind a desk, her face barely visible behind the computer monitor until she rolled her chair away. Mrs. Samuels. A royal blue ribbon stamped "20 Years of Patient Service" hung from her name tag.

I wanted to ask if *patient* described her or the people in the hospital but I gave her my brother's name instead.

She lifted her zebra-striped reading glasses away from her round face, folded them before she freed them to dangle from her beaded neck chain, and peered at us. "The gentleman here earlier also checked in for Mr. Collins. He said he was going to the cafeteria. He left about an hour ago, so he should be back soon." She handed me a digital pager. "If you need to leave, we'll be sure to page you if the doctor needs to speak to you."

I handed the pager to Julie. "Here. You're in charge of this thing. No telling where it might end up if I am."

"One more thing, ladies," Mrs. Samuels handed us a Welcome to the Meredith Robichaux Surgical Waiting Area brochure. "Please silence your cell phones."

A beat of silence later, Julie pulled her cell phone out of her purse, hit the screen twice, then showed it to the receptionist. "Silent," she said.

"Mine too," I said as I adjusted the volume.

Mrs. Samuels nodded, clasped her hands and, in her soothing, inside voice, said, "Please let me know if there's anything you need. As soon as I have some information about your brother, I'll let you know."

"Let's go sit over there," Julie said and pointed to the seating group that faced the entry. "That way, we can see Max when he comes in."

We sat in two barrel chairs that faced a small round coffee table. Julie tugged her chair closer to the table, propped her feet on it, and found her cell phone. "I'm going to send Trey a message to let him know we're here."

I ran my palms along the soft chenille of the chair arms. "This is so smooth. Like velvet." The movement calmed me, though, the weight of the silence in the room, between me and Julie, pressed itself against me.

Julie stopped texting, looked at me and raised an eyebrow. "You, okay?"

I almost went for the easy answer. The, "Of course, I'm fine." I moved my hands to my knees to still the shivering. Maybe with a little pressure I could push it down my legs and through the bottom of my feet. I talked to my shoes. "No. I feel like I'm going through life on a train that keeps stopping at the wrong stations. First, it's the 'your husband has had a stroke' stop and then the 'your husband died' stop. And just when I think I've gone through the tunnel, it's the 'David is gay and is in surgery' stop. This isn't the trip I planned. When—"

"I think this might be Max," Julie slipped her feet off the table and leaned toward me. "Remember, he's meeting you for the first time, too."

<hr />

I don't know if Max, or at least the man we assumed to be Max, saw us before he stopped by Mrs. Samuels' desk. But in the seconds before she pointed in our direction, I had already decided that Max was not what I expected him to be. Maybe I watched *Will & Grace* too much and thought he'd be more Jack than Will. Maybe I expected to be able to pick him out of a lineup of straight men. And, maybe, I tossed every gay stereotype I knew into my brain blender and added a pink boa. The real truth was I wanted to not like him.

When he looked our way, I saw a look of relief and of recognition that softened his otherwise square face. He shortened the distance between us in long strides, reached out his hand,

and said, "Caryn, I'm so glad you're here." He didn't shake my hand so much as hold it between both of his.

"You must be Julie," he said. "Thanks for making sure she got here safely."

"Of course."

At that moment, I wished I had a freeze-frame button. I couldn't process everything that bombarded my head and my heart. Sensory overload. This man, this stranger, took Lori's place in my brother's life. I don't even know how they met. I don't even know his last name. All I knew was he lived with and loved David. And because of that, I distanced myself from my brother. And now, this tall, brown-eyed, black-haired man who I only knew by his first name, knew more about David than I did.

"Let's sit down. I'll fill you in," Max said, and as he moved to sit on the sofa, I noticed dark blotchy stains covered the bottom of his sweater. Stains too dry to have happened at lunch.

"What happened to your clothes?" I regretted the question as soon as it left my mouth.

Julie looked at Max's sweater. She gasped. "Oh, dear God, no," she said and blinked as tears filled her eyes.

Max inhaled deeply, and when he exhaled I heard David's name.

I let my purse drop to the floor as I sunk into the chair next to Julie's and covered my face with both hands.

"I found him on the porch. He must have pulled himself there. So much blood. I thought he might be dead. I called 911 and waited . . ."

Max didn't need to finish the story for me to know what happened to his sweater. The movie unfolded in my mind's eye. Max sitting on the porch. Cradling my brother's head in his arms until the ambulance arrived.

Max told us a friend of theirs, an orthopedic surgeon, met him in the emergency room. "I called Walter right away. It was obvious that David would need him."

He didn't go into detail, and I didn't ask him to. I just wanted to know that he would survive, regardless of the injuries.

"I thought you said he was in an accident?" Julie looked as confused as I felt.

"I did. It was just too much to explain on the phone. But, no. His car was at the house. The keys still in his pocket. His credit cards and cash were in his wallet. The Tag Heuer was still on his wrist. They didn't take his iPhone or his Macbook." He counted off, on one hand, each piece of evidence he presented. "Hey," he added with a hint of a smile, "he's going to be so excited when I tell him that his Apple toys are safe."

That Max already understood David's obsession with all things techie surprised me, yet made me uncomfortable. If someone had written Max's words, and handed them to me without my knowing the source, I would have been pleased that someone not only knew what my brother enjoyed, but who delighted in making that happiness possible. Had Lori just spoken those words, I would have been glad that she connected to David this way. But, of course, it wasn't Lori. Was the burr in my sensibilities that I couldn't deny my own hypocrisy?

The sound of Mrs. Samuels' voice accompanied by a murmur of unfamiliar ones caught our attention. I was certain the see-saw of expectancy followed by a thud of disappointment reflected in Julie's and Max's faces was mirrored in my own. No white coats with news from surgery. A family, or maybe two, with toddlers and parents and grandparents staked out a spot at one of the plasma televisions. The low rumbling voices hummed behind us. I welcomed the noise. Anything to crack the overwhelming stillness.

I waited for Max to continue, to answer the question that tugged at me like an impatient child who needed attention. But he didn't, and I needed to understand. "I don't get it. If the intention wasn't to steal from David, then what was it?" I couldn't sit one more minute. Maybe I could pace to soothe the two-headed beast of frustration and anxiety that now roamed my world. I walked the length of the sofa and back again. Seven steps. Seven small steps. Seven small quiet steps. The rug underneath my feet felt as hard as the floor. I paused in front of Max. "Why would anyone want to hurt him? He's one of the kindest, most laid-back people I know."

"Caryn, here's the thing," Max said as he leaned forward, his elbows on his knees, his hands clasped between his legs.

I stopped pacing, perched on the edge of the chair, and drummed my fingers softly on the armrests.

Max bent his head, cleared his throat, and then looked up at me. "I can't prove it. Yet. But based on what we—Walter and I—can tell, this wasn't random. Whoever attacked David, and it's likely that it wasn't just one person, targeted him."

"Wait, wait." I held my hands up in front of my face as if my palms could have trapped the words in the space between us. Each sentence Max spoke became a wire that wound itself around my heart. The harder it pounded, the deeper the words sliced into it. "You're telling me," my voice shoved its way past the tightness in my throat, "somebody . . . some people . . . meant to hurt David because . . ."

When Max looked at me, the sadness in his eyes belied the anger that hardened his face. "Because he's gay."

In college, when I arrived home "over-served" and topped off with a Waffle House breakfast, I'd go to the bathroom and force myself to vomit. At least it was pre-Facebook, which saved me the indignity of being tagged in photos that could brand me for life. Shoving your finger down your throat is nothing to be proud of and clearly not a pretty sight. But I learned that unless I purged all the wretched and toxic substances out of my body myself, I would be forced to suffer hours of torture as my stomach orchestrated its revenge.

College ended and, with it, my episodes of post-partying, self-prescribed wellness. The last time I experienced that sour milk, smelly feet taste that coated the inside of my mouth, the culprit wasn't Jack Daniels. It was Ben. And that was it.

Until today. Except the hatred that sickened me belonged to someone else. People capable of this level of violence thrived on the toxin of prejudice in their bellies. And even if a quick fix existed, this group wasn't looking for it. History proved that.

"I'm going to find some tissues and a bathroom." Julie unwedged her phone from between two sofa cushions and left.

The initial wave of nausea had subsided, and even if it returned, my rumbling stomach had nothing to offer. At some point, soon, I needed real food, but so did Julie. I decided that while I waited for her, I'd look for something to drink that contained caffeine, then grab a few cookies. I stood at the other end of the sofa and debated if I should ask Max if he wanted anything from the kitchen.

Max leaned into the sofa, his hands rested above the dark red and rust brown stain on his sweater, and his head propped on the low back of the sofa so that he could have counted the ceiling tiles if he wanted to. Which I'm sure he didn't because his eyes were closed.

He looked younger when he slept. But that rule applied to everyone, at least everyone I ever saw both asleep and awake. My dad called it our "heaven face" because when we're sleeping we're letting God take over. At bedtime, he'd ask David and me, "Who's ready for 'peaceful and fancy free'?" We jumped up and down in our pajamas, one or both hands raised straight up in the air, and screeched, "Me! Me! I am, Daddy! Pick me! Pick me!" Some nights my toes felt sticky from the kitchen floor. Even when Dad picked David first, David always told him to let me go first instead. I'd try to reward him with a kiss, but he'd back up and cover his cheeks with both hands and he'd say, "No, thanks."

Dad would hoist me up on his shoulders, and I'd tell him, "I have the best big brother ever!" It took awhile, but eventually I realized that David let me go first every time Dad picked him because that meant he stayed up later. And, of course, he was also a co-conspirator at one point because he knew the game was designed to get me in bed whine-free. Now I'm older, still not whine-free, but I'd volunteer to be first if we still played "peaceful and fancy free."

I decided to let Max sleep, and as I walked away, the family in the waiting room with us gathered in a tight circle and held hands. When I heard, "Dear Heavenly Jesus," I stopped. I didn't know if moving around would be a sign of disrespect, as it was during the Pledge of Allegiance. They bowed their heads, so I did too, even though I didn't want to eavesdrop on their prayers. Since they already brought up the subject of Jesus, I figured I'd open the door a bit for my own talk.

*Jesus, it's been a very long time . . . I was on my way back to you, and then this happened to David . . . on your watch, by the way. I don't get it. But don't blink and lose my brother. And this Max and David thing. I don't get that either. Some people think men like Max and David won't get the secret password and won't ever have* "heaven faces." I think your Father is a lot like mine. I'll bet he plays "peaceful and fancy free" with his children too. And what daddy, when he asks his kids, "Who's ready?" when he sees them dressed up and laughing with their arms high, shouting, "Pick me! I am! Pick me!" . . . what daddy wouldn't scoop them up and take them with him?

I lifted my head.

The family was gone.

# 22

Julie sent me a text that she'd been outside talking to Trey, her parents, and her pastor. She said the boys were fine, and Ben was going to send me a photo of the tree he picked out.

I asked her if she'd pick up a pizza or hamburgers on her way back because I was so hungry even cafeteria food sounded good.

"Lucky you," she sent back, "I found cash in these jeans. On it."

"Get lg. piza or 3 brgrs in case Max hungry." My texting skills qualified me for a remedial learners class. I had to shorten where I could or Julie would have already been out the cafeteria door before I finished.

I found a Diet Coke and a bottle of water in the mini refrigerator. I must not have set off any alarms because Mrs. Samuels flipped through the pages of a magazine and didn't even glance in my direction.

I walked over to let Max know I was back. "You're awake." *Brilliant assessment, Caryn. He's checking his messages. Impressive.*

"Yeah, I guess you could call it that," he said, and put his phone on the table. He massaged the back of his neck, stretched his head back, side, front, side. "Leaning my head back on that couch to rest seemed like a good idea at the time. Now, not so much."

"I brought water. Wasn't sure which one you wanted, but I can grab another Diet Coke if you'd rather have that."

"Thanks, water's great," he said. He did waist turns, then stopped and surveyed the room. "That's what this place is missing. A weight room." He pointed to the other wall. "If they dumped that television and seating area, there'd be room. Maybe not weights. Maybe an elliptical and a treadmill."

"Or a yoga studio," I said, "with a massage therapist." I played along to be polite because I still spied a perfectly fine television and a not too ugly, not too grand sofa grouping.

He tipped his water bottle toward me. "Hey, I like how you think."

My cell phone vibrated. A message from Julie: "Got food. Found cool patio. 5$^{th}$ fl. Meet me."

"That was Julie. I asked her to pick up food for the three of us. She planned to bring it here, but she just said she found an outdoor spot."

Max twisted the cap on the half-full bottle and glanced at his watch. "I think I'll just hang out here. He's been in surgery a long time. We should be hearing something soon."

"We'd probably be back in thirty minutes." I might as well have said, "If you're good, we'll buy you a toy." The two sentences would have sounded alike. This time, I made a conscious effort to shut down the "Ben take your medicine, it's good for you" Mom talk. "Max. Seriously. We have a pager. It's not like we're leaving the hospital. You need fresh air. Sun. Vitamin D."

He took a deep breath. "Yeah. I guess you're right. I can make a few phone calls while we're there," he said. "Plus, we have this." He picked up the digital pager and waved it in the direction of Mrs. Samuels.

I nodded, then grabbed my purse and Julie's. "Let's go tell our house mother our plans."

"You have David's sense of humor." He smiled. "You're exactly the way I imagined."

So, we're one out of two.

———— ∞ ————

Hospitals should post signs that read "Reality Optional" so those who aren't patients can dispense with the confusion that comes from attempting to apply outside the hospital rules, inside the hospital. The disconnect reminded me of that joke David told ADD does it take to change a light bulb? Answer: Want to go ride bikes?"

For everyone in hospital universe, we were two women and a man who shared a cheese pizza on a December day the week before Christmas in which we could sit outside and roll up our long sleeves. Growing up in Louisiana, I spent most holidays singing "dashing through the snow" while I played outside wearing shorts and polo shirt. Today was one of those almost sticky days and we're listening to "I'm Dreaming of a White Christmas" playing on the patio. The ebb and flow of conversations around us made talking difficult at times. At the table next to us, a dozen or so white lab coats and scrubs played "musical present exchange," switching gifts every few minutes in the songs. In the center of the outdoor dining area, a Christmas tree looked as if it sprouted from the dozens of red and white poinsettias that surrounded it.

And there we were. My best friend Julie and I, sharing a pizza with a man whose last name we still didn't know, whom we just met that morning, and who had been living and sleeping with my brother for months. And while the three of us debated the pros and cons of Mellow Mushroom Kosmic

**167**

Karma pizza, a team of doctors worked over that same brother in a surgical room two floors above.

Between text messages to and from friends and family, Max related the timeline of events from breakfast that morning to his knowing where to find David.

"David and I planned to Christmas shop this afternoon. His office called early, eight o'clock, to ask if he could show a house . . ." Max shook his head, swept his hands down the sides of his face as if he could drag away the regret written there. "I couldn't believe somebody would be house-hunting this close to Christmas. But the office told him it was a relocation, that the guy passed the house the day before and really wanted to see it before he left today to go home for Christmas. I should have gone with him . . . I had already scheduled someone to help at my store." Max pushed his plate with two uneaten pizza crusts to the side. "You know that feeling you get when one plus one is not equaling two?"

Julie and I nodded. "We both know that one well," she said.

"I didn't listen. It's like you get a dog for protection, then when it barks, you tell it to shut up. What's the point of the dog, right?"

His cell phone rang for what seemed like the fiftieth time since we started eating. This one, he let go to voice mail. Did they have that many friends or were the same friends constantly calling? Either way, there were people in their lives who cared about them and let them know. And before today, not one of those people included his sister.

"I think those feelings we get in our guts are the barking dogs God gives us. I need to learn to pay attention, and to honor whatever it is He's trying to tell me," Max said. The words settled on the  table between us. I looked at Julie, but she was nodding in Max's direction. He drummed his fingers on the table, then checked his watch, and gave in to his obvious anxiety. "I'm going to head back." He slid his chair away from the table. "Thanks for lunch. I'll see you later, okay?"

Even though David told me he and Max attended church, Max's honesty and conviction proved my well of expectations was far too shallow. His sincerity and passion weren't performances, weren't practiced Christianese. His faith ran deep and felt real.

*Gay Christians?* Those words, from just a few weeks ago ran through my head. When Julie told me about the hundreds of online resources she found, I scoffed. Called it a contradiction of terms. Repeated, "It's impossible to be gay and a Christian."

Christmas seemed equally as impossible. Surrounded by silk magnolia garlands and pinecone wreaths, I wondered how the joy of the season would make its way to our house.

We finished eating and headed back to the waiting room.

Julie slipped her arm around my waist.

"You okay?"

"Not really. Am I supposed to be?"

When we reached Mrs. Samuels' desk, Julie hugged me. "Just know, we're praying for you. All of us. For all of you."

"Ladies," she cleared her throat. "Mr. Trahan is in the first consultation room on the right. Your brother's doctor should be there in just a few minutes."

"So, that's his last name." Julie said to me and flashed a confused Mrs. Samuels her cell phone again to prove her compliance."

Max leaned against the door of the room, his arms folded over his chest, his right leg bent at the knee over his left. Seeing him framed there, calmer than when we met, it was as if I saw him for the first time. Even with my limited fashion sense, I smelled expensive. If the clothes wore you, generally not expensive. If you wear the clothes, generally yes. From the jeans with the horseshoe embroidered flapped back pockets to the charcoal leather moccasins with contrast stitching, the stainless steel Tag Heuer, to hair meant to look like it naturally grew that way and stayed that length, Max invested considerable money to appear as if he didn't. He resembled Ben Affleck, the later years, and the bags under his eyes notwithstanding. And though I considered myself so far out of his league I didn't even play on a team, I'd not only accept a date with him, but I'd take pictures as proof it actually happened.

Whumpf. There it was. That huge elephant in the room I didn't want to or need to discuss refused to stay invisible. It was now entirely possible, because I just proved it to myself, that my brother and I would find the same man attractive. One of us would lose, of course. But is it really competition when you're playing the same game on different fields?

I valued my relationship with my brother because I trusted him. But, when he said that he was gay, our relationship became awkward for me. Just the fact that I felt this uneasiness introduced something I never experienced with David. And, when I considered what that attraction meant, in real-life situations, I felt uncomfortable. Like the story Angie, in our book club, told about the times she, her ex-husband and his new wife attended the same function for the kids. At the volunteer luncheon, when the speaker wanted to recognize Mrs. Jordan, both women stood.

But only one of them went home with Mr. Jordan.

# 23

A box of facial tissues, a Bible, four or five nondescript chairs. All in a room with as much space as an elevator. A get in and get out kind of room whose bare and windowless walls suggested not much good news happened there. All of which served to explain why none of us sat when David and Max's friend, also their physician, Dr. Armstrong—a short man, not much taller than Julie—arrived.

Max pointed to me, "David's sister," and Julie, "David's sister's friend," then rolled out questions as if he'd been winding them on a spool all day. "How is he? Can I . . . can we see him? How long will he have to stay? Will he—"

"Slow down." Dr. Armstrong gently patted Max's arm. "Let me give you my doctor talk, and whatever I don't answer, you can ask."

The three of us nodded as if he asked for our approval.

"Excuse me." The doctor placed his hand on the chair next to where I stood. "I'm going to sit for a few minutes." He had one of those fifteen-to-twenty-year faces. He could have been in his forties or sixties, but right now he looked like he could use a long nap.

"Okay, let's start at the top with the concussion. He lost consciousness; we're just not sure for how long because we don't know the time between the attack and Max finding him. The MRI showed swelling, which we expected, and a golf-ball sized hematoma, which should resolve itself." He went on to explain that David needed continued monitoring over the next few days for any signs of more serious symptoms such as nausea and vomiting, double vision, slurred speech. "If all he had was this concussion, we'd be talking severe headaches. I think the pain meds for his other injuries will help with those."

Julie shifted beside me, and then asked Dr. Armstrong, "Would you like something to drink? Water? Coffee?" She generously offered to be hostess because of her low tolerance for medical discussions. I've seen her dash out of a room where someone's talking about a child throwing up to avoid providing her own live demonstration.

"Thank you. Yes. I would appreciate if you could locate a bottle of water. It doesn't even have to be cold."

"Anyone else?" she asked as she squeezed past the doctor. "No? Okay, I'll be back."

The door closed and Dr. Armstrong continued. "Next, he had a severely displaced fracture of his right elbow." He shifted in the chair, made a cup with one hand, bent his arm and placed his cupped hand at the elbow. "Where those two long bones in your arm meet, there's a part that cups around the end, makes rotation possible. That bony part of your elbow."

"How did that happen?" Max asked the question, but I don't think either one of us wanted to know the answer. At least not now.

Dr. Armstrong took a breath, looked away for a moment, then focused on Max. "Some things we won't know for sure until David can tell us. This kind of fracture can happen indirectly, for instance, when somebody's attempting to break a fall. The tendency is to stretch the arm out straight, but the elbow locks, so if a person lands on the wrist, it results in this fracture. Or it can happen directly. An unexpected fall or being hit by a hard object."

Max pulled out a chair, motioned for me to sit down, then moved another chair close to mine, and sat down himself.

My eyes dripped, my nose dripped. Where were those stupid tissues? Dr. Armstrong sensed my distraction, reached across to a table, and extended the box. I took it with a "thank you" before telling myself to just listen and not think. To try to focus on the clinical part, so I could understand and ask questions.

Dr. Armstrong continued and a few words broke through my self-induced fog . . . "tricep muscles" and "incision" and "plates and screws." We were still on David's elbow. How was I going to make it through the rest of his body?

All the king's horses and all the king's men, couldn't put Humpty together again.

"We'll remove the stitches in ten to fourteen days, but he won't be able to lift anything for at least six weeks. The good news is we can start the range of motion exercises soon. Most patients, with physical therapy, recover their strength in around six months. To heal fully, a year. Even then, a full range of motion may not be possible."

"Just me." Julie knocked as she opened the door. "Sorry for the delay. I went to the cafeteria." She handed Dr. Armstrong the bottled water. "I have a few calls to return. But I'll be right outside if anyone needs me, okay?"

"One more major, then we'll go the minors." The doctor drank half the water, poured a little in his hand, and splashed his face. "Not very sophisticated, but it feels good."

By the time he finished—and it seemed as if he never would—I felt like we'd stumbled onto the medical injuries aisle at Wal-Mart, and we were trying to load up our cart. Except it wasn't a cart. It was David with a fractured patella, that small bone in front of the knee joint where the thigh and shin bones met, that Walter pinned, and wired and sewed together. And a cast, knee brace, physical therapy, and one or two years later, removing the wires and pins.

Julie slipped back in just in time for what Dr. Armstrong called "the performance."

"You're going to see David today, but not for an extended time. By now, David's not the only person who needs rest. And I'd make that an order if I could . . ."

He finished his water, pulled his chair closer, and leaned forward. "David came through long hours in surgery, but you're not going to see any of that. Those incisions are covered with bandages. But there are other effects of this attack that bandages won't cover. His torso is badly bruised, so much so that we fully expected internal injuries. But, so far, there's no evidence of any."

Max pulled tissues from my box. He hadn't wiped his eyes for a while, but he'd become so pale, he was almost translucent. His hands shook as if his teeth were chattering, and he attempted to mimic the rhythm.

Julie leaned over and stilled Max's hands when she held them in her own. A simple gesture that left me humbled and ashamed.

Dr. Armstrong continued. "David's nose is broken and bruised, he has two black eyes, a cut on his upper lip, scratches on his forehead . . . his face is swollen . . . when you look at David, please try not to let him see himself in your reaction. He'll see himself soon enough."

We were told David would be in the recovery room for another hour, so Max went home to change. Julie and I cruised through the gift shop, found a walking trail that circled the hospital, and finally migrated back to food.

"How long have we been here? I feel like I need two showers."

"We've been here long enough for a shift change. Long enough to not feel guilty that we're drinking coffee and eating a mediocre fudge brownie with a scoop of ice cream. And," she checked the time on her phone, "almost long enough for you to see your brother."

I mashed the remains of my brownie into the ice cream. There's a better dessert here waiting to happen. Brownie beignet stuffed with ice cream? "What has Trey been telling the boys? If Ben thinks we're Christmas shopping, after being gone this long, he's going to wonder why fifty presents aren't sitting under the tree on Christmas morning."

"Tell you the truth, I don't have a clue what he told them. We spend more time worrying about how not to worry them than they spend worrying. Who knows . . . maybe they're out somewhere shopping for us." She ate the last piece of her brownie. "Want the rest of my ice cream now that you made brownie soup with yours?"

"Hey, that could be it!" I squealed, much louder than intended. "Are people still staring at us?" I shoveled through my purse to find paper and a pen. I kept my head down, and tried to stare up. Not comfortable and not working.

"They were over it before you stuck your head in your mini-suitcase of your pretending to be looking for something."

"That was no pretend." I held up a pen and my checkbook.

"You're writing me a check for saying 'brownie soup'?"

"Only if the idea makes it big." I turned the checkbook over, folded the back away from the checks, and wrote myself notes on the blank sides. "When I can't find paper, I just use my checkbook as a jotter," I explained

"Well, now I understand how you drove Lori a few miles into crazy."

I jerked my head up at Lori's name. "Good grief. We still haven't called her." I tapped my pen on the edge of the dessert plate. "And this would have been the perfect time to call."

"We? There's no 'we.' She's your ex-almost-sister-in-law. And this is the perfect time? Why, because Max isn't here?" She swept her arm around the cafeteria. "Lot of space for phone calls."

"Look, I just didn't want the situation with Max and Lori to be awkward, that's all." I wrote down an ingredient I didn't want to forget, then put everything back in my purse. "It's been a rough day. What's wrong with my wanting to protect their feelings?"

"Um, let's see. Because it's not their feelings you're protecting. You haven't seen your brother in months. Talked to him maybe a handful of times. This awful thing happens to him, and you're forced to meet Max. You spend most of your time around him like Goldilocks, trying to get it 'just right.' You haven't been the Ice Queen, but you're not buckets of sunshine either. You're protecting you."

"I keep saying this, and you don't seem to get it. It's different when it's your brother. I'm trying to figure out how this is all supposed to work with this man. Is this supposed to last forever? He could be gone in a month or a year. Somebody else could take his place."

"And what if he's not gone? What if he stays? I'm your best friend, and every time I try to talk to you about it, you tell me 'not now'?"

"I just didn't feel comfortable talking."

"Y'know, that, my sweet friend, is a lesson to be learned from Jesus. He did his best work among the uncomfortable."

# 24

He's in the fifth bed on the right."

What the receptionist at the desk didn't mention was that, in the post-recovery room, you don't actually see the beds. You see curtained areas on both sides of the room that looked like round green pods with legs. The privacy curtains prevented visitors from seeing people, but definitely not from hearing them. It reminded me of the dressing rooms in Macys when all you knew was the person in the room next to you "never could wear these blouses."

"Four . . . five. This is it." Julie stopped, looked up and down the curtain. "Can't ever figure out where these things open and close."

I watched Julie, momentarily suspending a conversation with God I'd started when we walked out of the elevator. If he is the God of do-overs, I need a second chance. I'm pathetic and weak, and Julie's probably right; I'm selfish. As much as I dreaded seeing David, I was relieved to not have to say much. The truth was, I didn't know if I could say what David wanted to hear. His body was battered. I didn't want to beat up his spirit. And if I already had, then I hoped God was the God of third chances.

Max must have heard us because, like a magician, he stepped out from the curtains, his finger on his lips in the "shush" position. "He's asleep, but he'll open his eyes again. He's been doing that off and on since I've been here." Max lowered his voice and leaned closer. "The doctor wasn't exaggerating about how he looks. Come in now so you can ditch the shock on your faces before he wakes up."

Julie read a text message, shook her head, and mumbled a few words that could have placed her on the Ladies' Altar Society "least wanted at a meeting" list. "Trey can't find the outdoor Christmas lights. Shocker. Probably because they're in the garage where they're supposed to be." She looked at the ceiling, "Lord, help me," and then at the two of us. "Okay, I'm going to call Mr. Hopelessly Dazed and Confused. Besides, you're the two people David most wants to see. Find me in the waiting room when you're finished."

Julie provided my buffer all morning. I wondered if this might have been her way of telling me I was on my own. Once again, I braced myself for an inconceivable shock and as I slipped through the curtain, everything I thought I knew about hate and forgiveness and love slipped out.

Shock, I knew about.

After Hurricane Katrina, I learned when devastation happens far beyond anything we ever can imagine, our minds and our hearts can't process it all at once. Houses shoved off their foundations, a yellow truck perched between the stripped branches of an oak tree, a neighbor's shed in the middle of a kitchen. Roof rescues and food shortages and months without electricity. In those early days and weeks, numbness was our protection, perhaps even our sanity. As time passed, our brains fed us like infants ready to be weaned. Open wide, here's your grandmother's house after thirteen feet of water moved in for a week. Swallow it until your heart groans from the excess. Then another bite and another and another until the entire banquet of pain and loss were set out before us, and we were strong enough to choose for ourselves.

And so as I stepped beyond the curtain, my brain allowed me to see the broken and bruised body, but my heart—my heart could not reconcile that wounded man, pale and still, with my brother. My brother, who took Ben to his first LSU football game, who lifted my husband out of his hospital bed and into a golf cart so even if Harrison couldn't play the game, he could enjoy the ride. My brother, who bought everything I needed to start a catering business, and said I could pay him back in meals—for the rest of his life.

I wrapped one hand around the cold bedrail and gently placed my other over his fingers, being careful to avoid the back of his hand where the IV had been inserted. One minute, David. I need one minute before you open your eyes. Just one minute to let my rage and grief spill over the floodwalls so calmness can rise and fill their place.

Max stood on the other side of the hospital bed unwinding earplugs from around an iPod. "When I went home to change, I picked up a few of David's gadgets. This," he held up the electric blue Nano, "and his Kindle. I don't know how long he'll be here, but I knew he'd go nuts without entertainment."

"What about his laptop? He's a compulsive email checker." Kind of surprising Max would have left that behind. Maybe there were some things he *didn't* know about David.

"I know. And that's exactly why I didn't bring it. Not that he can't check his email on his phone." He put one of the plugs in his ear, turned on the iPod, and added, "But knowing your brother, if his laptop's here, he'll try to start working."

I didn't understand the problem with David being distracted by work, other than having only one hand for the keyboard.

But Max wasn't asking my opinion and it didn't seem like David being between us would end with this hospital bed.

Max fiddled with the iPod when David started to wake up. His head turned from side to side and when he opened his eyes, it was Max he saw first.

And that's when it hit me.

The realization that this was the first time I saw this David. With Max. As in David and Max. Foreign territory for me, and I didn't have a passport. I wasn't sure I wanted one. But I was sure I was exactly where I didn't want to be all those months ago when David called me.

The same brain that floated me down the river of denial after tragedy, refused to allow me to board the ship as I witnessed the unmistakable tenderness in Max's eyes and the relief I heard, even in David's raspy voice when he said, "You came back."

"I never left," said Max, his voice as tender as the hand he held against David's face.

I felt like an intruder. Like the afternoon I knocked on Julie's backdoor as I opened it and walked into the kitchen to witness her and Trey quickly and awkwardly untangling themselves. I opened my mouth to eliminate any possibility of another affectionate exchange, but Max spoke before I could. "David, Caryn's here."

Dr. Armstrong couldn't have prepared me for this pain. A pain that slammed into me with the sudden shock of a stubbed toe against a coffee table when my brother radiated a smile from a swollen face covered by shades of purple and black. My eyes burned with tears as I stood on tiptoe and reached over the bedrail to attempt an awkward hug. I slipped my face next to his battered one and whispered, "I'm sorry. I'm so sorry."

# 25

I didn't realize I slept on the drive home until the galumph of the tires jolted my head forward. The screeching and squeaking of the garage door opening invaded my dream and left unresolved the conversation between Zoe and Julie, who stood over the bed of someone I didn't know. I shook my head and tried to clear the remnants of memory. It must have been, in dream land, an intense discussion because my aching jaw meant I clenched my teeth for quite a while.

Julie turned off the car, leaned against her forehead on her folded arms on top of the steering wheel. "How many days have we been gone?"

"I know. I feel as if we've experienced a temporal rift—hurled through space and landed at some other place, some other time—and then found our way back." I yawned and stretched my legs out in front of me. "You must be exhausted. Even after my car nap, I'm tired. Hope I didn't snore."

She opened her car door. "Not as much as Trey. At least you're good company for someone who's supposed to be asleep. You even answered some of my questions."

"I don't even want to know." I said and started to haul my body out of the car.

"No. Trust me. You don't."

I detected enough of a smile in her voice to know she was teasing. As close as we were, some parts of my life I wanted to stay buried.

---

"We're here," Julie chanted in her *Poltergeist* imitation as she opened the side door from the garage. The resiny pine scent of the Christmas tree we'd abandoned earlier that day greeted us.

"I'm in the kitchen," Trey called out.

Julie hung her purse on the doorknob and muttered, "It's after nine o'clock. He better not be fixing dinner." She sighed deeply.

I sensed an "or else" but kept that to myself.

We walked into a dark kitchen except for the lights from the bronze pendants hanging over the island where Trey stood measuring scoops of coffee into the brew filter. "Glad you're home. The boys are already asleep." He lifted his eyes, but kept counting. "Thought I'd make coffee, and then you can catch me up on David."

I gave Trey a thumbs-up, then sat on one of the barstools. As if it realized the immediate threat of collapse had passed, my body finally paid the emotional toll of the day. My arms and legs ached, my back tight. I propped my head, my hands on either side of my face and tried to figure out what Julie was up to.

Julie's face looked pleased, but her eyes swept the room as if she searched for the slip-up piece of evidence of a wild party in our absence. She peered in the empty sink, "You fed the kids?"

"Of course not," Trey said as he put the coffee beans into the cabinet above the coffeemaker. "They asked for bread, and I gave them stones." He kissed her forehead. "We ate and cleaned the kitchen." He turned to me. "See what I have to put up with?"

Julie hugged him. "Sorry. Long day. Thanks for entertaining the boys."

"You can reward me later."

"Am I invisible here?" I waved my hand across my face. "Don't think so. Save that talk for later." Based on Julie's past conversations, I didn't have to guess what the payoff would be for good behavior. "Or, better yet. Work it out while I go see Ben."

I wanted to see my son. I *needed* to see him. As if lost in the tangle of sleep and dreams, he could provide an antidote to my sadness. Like Ben's room, Nick's held the familiar lingering smell of wet puppy that not even the hardy Colorado blue spruce Christmas tree could penetrate. With the help of the night light in the hall, I made out Ben and Nick squeezed into the bottom bunk together, more like two pretzels than two peas.

I knelt on the rug in front of Ben, sat back on my heels, and willed myself—for the first time that day—to be still. To allow today's drama to just settle in peace without an autopsy. To just be here with Ben, grateful for the undeserving gift he was, and to ask God to protect Ben and to help us find a way back to Him.

Ben's mouth formed an "o," a slightly larger version of the one from his crib years, and he clutched his pillow as if he just tackled it on a football field. When he breathed, his body melted into the mattress and floated back up again. I didn't want to risk waking him, so instead of kissing him goodnight, I placed my hand on his cheek. How many mothers of how many young sons felt the warm silk softness of their cheeks, watched their fluttery breaths at night and, years later, placed that same hand against that same cheek—battered, bruised and broken?

I couldn't stop the tears.

———∞∞———

"We were about to send out a search party," Julie said as she handed me a white mug. "Be careful. I just zapped it in the microwave to reheat it."

"Santa Claws? These must be from your mother," I smiled at the sight of the Santa-hatted crawfish.

"Oh, you mean the Queen of Kitsch? Of course. But she's carving out new territory for herself. Now she's into 'Southern Kitsch.' "

"Maybe that won't be so terrible. At least you might avoid another lava lamp, or Elvis toilet paper holder singing 'Love Me Tender.' Or wait, I'm forgetting one of my all time favorites . . ." I followed her into the family room, "How could I have forgotten the bacon scented room freshener?"

I shifted my attention to Trey. "Trey, I really appreciate your taking over today."

"Once Julie told me what happened, I figured the two of you would be there for a while. I promised Ben we'd shop for a tree for your house too. Since we had so much time, I got this wild idea to go to the Folsom Christmas Tree Farm. Now, that's an experience. Next time, I'll be sure to pack a lunch. If you think picking out a tree on a lot is a pain, try walking through a forest of them."

"And, let me guess. Ben still picked out the shortest, scrawniest tree there." I smiled thinking of my son's compassion for Christmas trees.

"Yep. He sure did. Even Nick tried to talk him out of it." Trey shook his head. "You know that old show about kids saying, what was it? The darndest thing? Your son looked at me and I gotta tell you, Harrison was written all over the kid's face. He said, 'Mr. Trey, maybe this is the tree we're supposed to have because nobody else took it. It's been waiting here for us this whole time.'"

Julie chimed in. "Ben will never grow up to be a Christmas tree farmer. If he does, you'll need to support him."

"Caryn, I wasn't sure what to tell Ben, but I needed to say something because he was getting upset. So, I just told him his uncle was in a bad accident, and I didn't know the details."

"That's probably the best thing you could have said. How do I tell him his uncle was brutalized because he's gay?"

"I don't know. I really don't know about that one," Trey said.

# 26

Ben and I walked home the next morning after breakfast with the Pierces. I promised him we'd visit David that afternoon.

"I need to make a few phone calls, check up on some of my appointments after Christmas, then I'll shower and we'll go."

"Remember how we brought food to those old people places on Thanksgiving? Can we make something for Uncle David and bring it to him?"

I hadn't factored in food prep time, but I couldn't tell Ben that, especially after he made the connection that what we did made a difference in somebody else's life.

"What if it's something we already made? Would that work?" I always had something extra stashed away. When my customers learned that, they called when they had dessert emergencies. Then I started keeping extras of the extras. Trey said I should be charging more for the last minute dessert deliveries. "Doctors charge extra for after hours calls. Heck, even our plumber's walk-in-the-door charge is higher on weekends." At first, I thought the idea crazy. But in the past six months, my emergencies already jumped from monthly to almost weekly. I told Trey the next time I printed brochures, I'd include an upcharge for orders under 24-hour delivery time.

Ben stood before me and scratched his head. "Well, I guess so. What do you have?"

Since he heard about David, serious was a new look for Ben. Not that eight-year-olds had reasons to be somber beyond what might be taken away from them when they were punished. Since he'd woken up that morning, he looked as if he exchanged bodies with a bank president whose tie was already knotted too tight.

"I don't know. I'd have to look at my inventory to be sure. We'll have time to do that later. In fact, I'll let you pick whatever you want."

"What if I call him and ask him what he wants?"

"That's a great idea for later," I said and unlocked the front door. I followed Ben in and added, "but he's not supposed to be getting phone calls right now."

We walked into our house, and a hill of unfolded clean towels greeted us from the den sofa. The sun plowed through the windows and spotlighted the dust dancing in the air and the layers already gathered on the furniture. Julie and Trey's house may have bordered on Chevy Chase's Christmas Vacation minus a few lights and roof decorations, but our house certainly balanced the neighborhood. There was no evidence of Christmas in the house. I hadn't even hung Ben's stocking. Tonight maybe we could at least set up the scrawny tree. I had to figure out a way to not let my catering business totally control our lives.

I didn't even bother changing my clothes. If I stepped away from this mess, I'd end up in my room, curled on my bed in the fetal position. For a while after Harrison died, folding in on myself provided me a reprieve from reality. But now there would be no David to yank me back into the world. I needed to call my father and Lori, but that could wait. Dad was still on his cruise, and Lori, well, I wasn't sure I had the emotional energy yet for that call.

I closed the blinds, cleared a spot on the sofa, and started folding. Ben disappeared into his bedroom and returned with his Game Boy. He plopped in one of the side chairs and within seconds his thumbs were mashing buttons.

"Ben, if you help, this could go faster," I said.

"Folding clothes is for girls," he said without even pausing to make eye contact.

Serious was one thing. Attitude was something else. Very something else. "Okay, sweetie. Put the Game Boy down and look at me. Now."

He stopped his game, his eyes narrowed, and he said, "Mom, please don't call me 'sweetie' anymore. Especially in front of my friends."

The words pelted me like pieces of ice. The "please" didn't translate to "appreciate." And his tone didn't suggest a request. My son, the little dictator, was about to be told he could rule the country of his bedroom for an undetermined period of time. I let the unfolded towel fall across my lap and looked at Ben, who now stared out the backdoor. And from where I sat, I saw that his demanding pinched-face had morphed into round-eyed confusion. I think he realized he didn't just step across the line; he pole-vaulted across it.

I knew that feeling of going too far, so far that familiar faces and landmarks disappeared. All I wanted then was to be guided back to myself by someone trustworthy and kind. I suspected that was all Ben wanted too, but like me, he didn't know how to ask.

Something wasn't right. I needed to figure out what forest he'd landed in. I knew Julie and Trey hadn't said anything to Ben about David coming out. Even if they had, I didn't think he had a clear definition of that. So this wasn't a reaction related to David. Then, what was it?

Choose the hill you want to die on, Caryn. Okay, Harrison, I've got this one.

"Thanks for telling me you don't want me to call you 'sweetie' anymore. I didn't know that bothered you and I won't use it again. I might forget, at first, but just remind me, okay?"

He squirmed in the chair, but I didn't think it was the chair that was uncomfortable. "Okay. I mean it hasn't been bothering me a long time. It's just, well, you know, I'm getting older . . ."

"Sure. I get it." I got it, but I still didn't understand what drove him there. I understood his labeling clothes folding as a girl thing even less. "But, I'm going to need you to explain something to me that I don't get."

He kicked his bare feet against the chair and nodded.

"What did you mean when you say folding laundry is girls' work? I don't remember the two of us ever talking about boy jobs and girl jobs. At least not around our house."

He bit his lower lip, and I wondered if he'd draw blood soon.

"Ben, why don't you want to explain this to me? Are you afraid I'll be angry?"

He shrugged. "Sort of," he whispered.

I pulled a footstool over to the chair and sat on it facing him. "Ben, I'm glad we're having this talk. I hope we can always talk to each other if we feel confused or worried or angry. I can't read your mind." I tapped his forehead. "I'm just trying to understand."

"Yesterday, Mr. Trey told me I needed to, you know, 'man up.' I kind of started crying when he told me Uncle David had been in an accident." He took a deep shuddering breath as he flipped the Game Boy over and over in his hands. "And he said I needed to get tough, so I don't grow up to be a sissy."

"A sissy? That's what he said?"

He nodded. "Uh huh."

"And did Mr. Trey explain what that meant? To be a sissy, I mean."

"He said a sissy is a boy who acts like a girl."

───※───

After talking to Ben, I was tempted to call Trey and tell him to "man up" and come to my house and watch me "woman up." But I knew children had a way of putting things in absolute terms—like "we always go to McDonalds" or "my mom never spends any time with me"—so I had to give Trey the benefit of the doubt. And if what he told Ben was his bottom line, then I hoped Julie and Nick rose above it.

I explained to Ben that our physical bodies (Mr. Rogers used to say, "Girls are fancy on the inside, and boys are fancy on the outside.") were what made us boys or girls. What we did in those bodies didn't change who we were. "Babies have to crawl on their hands and knees before they walk. So, does that make them puppies?"

"That's silly," he said and allowed himself a partial smile.

"At one time, almost all doctors were men, and all nurses were women. But not anymore. Do you think Dr. Liz is a man because she's doing something only men used to do?"

"No, Dr. Liz is cool. Plus, we saw her at the pool, remember? She's definitely not a man."

"Well, because she works so many hours during the week, her husband Jeffrey helps her cook and clean. He even helps with the laundry, which means," I handed him a towel from the stack, "he probably folds clothes."

"Do you think he cries?"

"Yes, I'm sure he does."

**191**

"Did my dad cry?"

"Yes. But, did that make them sissies? No. No. No." I reached over and held his chin in my hand. "You heard that, right?"

He nodded.

"One day you'll learn in biology that our bodies were made to cry. Not just girl bodies. Boy bodies too. And why would God give boys a body that can make tears and cry, then tell them they weren't allowed to do that?" I handed him a few washcloths.

"Well, we learned in Sunday School that God doesn't make mistakes. So, if God made us that way, why does Nick's dad say not to do it?"

I had a few ideas, but I didn't think Ben needed to hear them. "You know, Ben, I'm not sure. What I do know, though, is Mr. Trey loves you. He'd never hurt you on purpose. Sometimes people grow up thinking things that aren't true. Or maybe they just don't understand the things that are true."

"Maybe Mr. Trey would feel better if I told him God said it was okay for him to cry," Ben said.

Oh, and how I hope I'll be there when you do. "He just might. But, here's the most important thing I want you to always remember: Inside, then out. It's who people are on the inside that matters, not what they are on the outside."

Well, Caryn, hope you were listening.

———

I sent Ben to bathe while I called my dad and Lori. Since Dad and Loretta were on a cruise ship in the middle of some ocean somewhere, I reduced the story to its simplest terms, sanitizing the reason for David's attack and minimizing details about the extent of his injuries. Even with that version, Dad wanted to end their trip at the next port and fly home. Once they arrived home, they'd understand why I didn't disclose the full story. We didn't even have all the details anyway.

"You'll be home in a week. David will be fine, and by that time, I'm sure he'll be ready to ditch me for you if he still needs help," I said, omitting the part that David may be still in the hospital. I knew I needed to seal the deal, so I played the guilt card. "You know David would be incredibly upset if he thought you cut your trip short because of him. Especially one you've waited a lifetime to enjoy."

"That's true. That's true. We'll call David and tell him we decided not to leave the cruise. And first thing after we park this boat, we'll head over to his house."

Sometimes living in a world of instant communication could be exasperating. Now I had to call David, or call Max to tell David the story as Dad knew it, before he called. Or . . .

"Dad, why don't you just let David call you? He could be sleeping or eating and you don't want to disturb him."

Dad agreed that made sense, too.

"Ben and I are going to visit David today. I'll tell him we talked, and I'm sure he'll be excited to talk to you soon."

After the compulsory repeated good-byes, followed by the "I love yous" and "we'll see you soons," I called Lori.

While I waited for her to answer, I checked my email. A few new teacher orders for when the school year started again in January, one from the Junior League saying the check was in the mail, and not surprisingly, yet another email from Mr. Washington. Best to wait on that one, even if I wouldn't be trying to talk to Lori, who seemed to not be answering her phone. It should have gone to voice mail after this many rings.

She answered two rings into my "I'll let it ring three more times" limit.

"Sorry. I expected the call to go to voice mail," Lori explained. "And, anyway, I planned to call you as soon as I hung up."

She sounded out of breath. Maybe I caught her at the gym, though she rarely answered her phone during her workouts. "Hey, if you're at the gym, I can call you later."

"No, I'm home."

Her voice alerted my crisis radar, and my legs started to feel hollow. Please, not something wrong with Lori, too. "Are you okay? You don't sound okay."

"I heard about David." She started crying before she finished the sentence.

I thought I heard her say David's name, but her attempts to breathe between sobs broke it into three syllables. "You know about his attack? How?"

"Max called our friend Beth who works in David's office and asked her to tell me. That's who I was talking to when you called."

Was my crisis radar set on self-destruct? "Back up. You know about Max." I stood up and paced in front of my desk. "I'm confused. How did that happen?"

"We met for dinner a few weeks ago. It was my idea. I just needed to see David and to meet this man. You probably think it sounds ridiculous, but it was closure. David was very happy, and that was obvious. And, honestly, I needed to do it for me too. To know that there was nothing I could do. But, I called yesterday strictly for bank business. I needed some information from clients of his who are financing a house through our bank. Max checked David's messages, so when he heard mine, he had Beth call." She paused. "She thought I already knew." Another pause.

I kicked off my flats, stretched out on the sofa, and saw I desperately needed a pedicure. "At first, all I knew was that he was in the ER, then surgery, then recovery, then post-recovery. Julie and I got back late . . . I wanted to be able to give you as much information as possible when I called . . . so you wouldn't have to wait and wonder like I did." I expected an invitation for my pity party to arrive in my gut anytime now. I should have added that calling her trumped taking off these cruddy clothes and a shower.

"If I'd known sooner, I could've at least had the choice of whether I wanted to go to the hospital. Not having someone make it for me."

"If I'd known sooner that the three of you shared dinner and were BFFs now, I would've called you. And that dinner happened weeks ago, not yesterday."

"I'm sorry I sounded so harsh." A space of quiet, and then she said, "You've had twenty-four hours to think about this. I've had about twenty-four minutes. I know you thought you were doing the right thing."

I picked up my shoes and headed to my bedroom and a shower. It was time to end this conversation. "Yep. I did think I was acting in your best interest, not mine. Listen, I promised Ben we'd visit David, and I still need to shower . . ."

Lori said she planned to see David before he left the hospital, and she hoped she'd see Ben and me there, maybe we could go for an early dinner.

I hung up and played that drama in my head. David, Max, Lori, me. Ben. Awkward. I debated calling her back to ask when she thought for sure she'd be there, so we could be someplace else.

Then again, I might learn more about Max, this stranger in my brother's life.

I decided to take my chances.

# 27

Ben wanted to surprise David with dessert, but he wanted to choose only from desserts he helped make. We looked in the freezer so long, I feared my nose would crack off my face.

As he told me when we were searching in the arctic zone, "That's what made the dessert gifts special."

I loved that he made the connection between sacrificing and giving. That it's not just the value of the gift, but the time and love you invest in it.

Ben couldn't decide between the chocolate cheesecake and the mini pecan pies, so we brought both. He balanced the cheesecake on his lap, and I reassured him the little pies would be fine on the floorboard in front of him. He was so excited about seeing David that I could have plugged our Christmas tree lights into him and had twinkling for days. Assuming our Christmas tree was ready for lights. Which it wasn't. It wasn't ready at all.

Decorating might be a stretch this year. I couldn't decorate, as my mother used to say, "if my name was decorate." Poor Ben would be stuck with me. Last year Lori and David helped and, even though it held our hodge-podge collection of ornaments, the tree was beautiful. They tied ribbons to pinecones, and laced it with cranberries and strings and strings of lights. At night, it looked like a swarm of fireflies landed on the tree.

I wonder if that's where the decorating gene went. I'd have to file this question away in hopes a time would come when I could ask it and maybe find it funny. We weren't there yet or at least I wasn't. Julie wouldn't be amused. She would accuse me of perpetuating a stereotype.

"Mr. Trey said he'd drop off our tree sometime today. You're ready to start decorating tonight?"

"Yes! That'll be so fun."

He assumed his responsibility of Keeper of the Cake, which I dubbed him as I passed it off to him after he settled in his seat, with great seriousness.

"Can we make one of those popcorn things again?"

"A garland? Sure, as long as the popcorn actually goes on the tree and not in your stomach." We both laughed at that one. Last year, David sent him to the kitchen at least five or six times asking for more popcorn. He dashed in with the empty bowl and said, "We're out again!" He'd run in every two and a half minutes. After the last bag I popped, I told him I couldn't wait to see the garland because it must be the longest one ever. Of course, his wide-eyed face told the story before I opened the book. When I surveyed the tree all I saw was one anorexic garland slumped on the bottom branches. I pretended to be horrified. David and Lori took the fall, and named Ben as an innocent bystander. Ben told that story for weeks after Christmas. Even to those of us who'd been there.

"Mom, you'll have to buy lots of boxes of popcorn because Uncle David . . ." The light went out of his face as if someone blew out a candle. "He won't be able to come this year, will he?" He tapped his fingers on the cake holder.

I reached across the seat and patted his hand. "He'll be fine by next Christmas. And that gives us more time to stock up on popcorn."

"Yeah, I guess." He stared out the window and, in less time than it took to listen to "Jingle Bells" on the radio, he turned around and looked as if he'd just discovered oxygen.

"I have a great idea!"

"We're almost to the hospital, dude, so spill it."

"Remember how we went to those two old people places at Thanksgiving? What if we pick a Christmas place?"

I had to ask the question even though I already suspected the answer. "What Christmas place would you pick?"

"That one!" he pointed to the hospital across the street from us as we waited for the traffic signal light to change. "Uncle David's hospital."

Before we left home, I did my best to prepare Ben for seeing his uncle. Even as I explained the bruises and the broken bones, I wondered if I might be setting him up for long-term emotional scarring. But he seemed more upset about not visiting David than scared by how David would look when he saw him. We agreed on a contingency plan, just in case he changed his mind after seeing David. "If you don't want to stay, just ask me to show you where a bathroom is. That way, you won't have to say anything in front of Uncle David, okay?"

"But what if I really do have to go to the bathroom, and I'm not trying to get away from Uncle David?"

I reassured him that I'd be able to tell the difference.

But in the elevator on the way to David's room, I remembered I hadn't mentioned Max's presence to Ben. I assumed Max would be at the hospital, but I'd never asked him directly in any of the text messages we exchanged. I don't know how to navigate this territory. Once again, I'm a visitor in a foreign country without Rosetta stone to learn the language.

But we were just two floors away, so I tapped Ben on the shoulder, partly to pull his attention away from the man standing next to him holding a pink heart-shaped "It's a Girl" balloon, who had a tattooed spider on his elbow that was in the center of web that branched from his lower to his upper arm.

"I forgot to tell you that Max, a friend of Uncle David's, will probably be visiting too," I said. "Or, he may be there already."

"Okay," said Ben, and inched closer to the doors when he saw David's floor number light up. I wasn't sure why I felt compelled to tell Ben about Max, but as we stepped off the elevator, I wondered if it didn't have more to do with me than my son.

The door to David's room was closed. I looked at Ben, "Ready?"

"I'm fine, Mom," he said with a hint of impatience. "Can we go in now?"

I softly knocked as I opened the door "It's Ben and Caryn. Can we come in?"

"Of course!" David said, his voice weak.

Ben pushed a smile out. "Uncle David, look who's here!"

He walked in, then stopped as if with one more step he risked falling from the ledge of a tall building. Standing behind him, I could imagine Ben's face by the look on David's.

"Creepy, huh?"

"Kind of." My son's voice was as hesitant as David's was puny.

I dropped my purse in the chair by David's bed. Ben still hadn't moved, and I was on the verge of using the code question, when he asked David, just above a whisper, "Does it hurt?"

He nodded. "Not as much as it did yesterday."

Ben sighed. "That's good."

"So," said David, "what do you have there?"

Ben smiled. "It's chocolate cheesecake," he said as he placed it on the bed tray table. "Mom and I made it."

"If you move a little closer, I'll give you a one-arm hug."

Ben's eyebrows seemed to shoot up to his hairline.

"Uncle David has two arms. He just meant he can only use one right now," I reassured him.

"Ben, look," David pointed to his cast, "here it is."

I watched them together, and I hated myself for keeping my son away from my brother. They loved each other, and what did Ben know of anything beyond that?

David gave Ben a tour of his arm and knee, and Ben—to my surprise—didn't make any "ewee" noises or close his eyes. Put a lab coat on him, and with his khakis and polo shirt, he could have passed for Doogie Howser, the early years.

"Did it hurt when it happened? Your accident?" Ben leaned against the bed.

"My accident?" David looked at me. "I don't remember too much about my accident." Even with his sandpaper voice, I couldn't miss the emphasis on *accident*."

It was high school all over again. I invented a story to pacify my parents, they'd ask David questions, and I'd feed him the lines. Later, I'd explain why I told Ben he'd been in an accident. I couldn't tell him the real story why David had been attacked, not now. And I didn't want to tell him his uncle was robbed and beaten because then Ben might be afraid any time we were in public. Surely he'd understand I told that story to protect Ben. And, actually, I wasn't the one who told Ben that in the first place. Trey told they boys that story when he run out of reasons for why Julie and I weren't home yet. I just kept the story on life support.

I felt like a wilted flower in a greenhouse. I pulled off my sweater, cleared my throat, but pretense didn't swallow easily. "I told Ben about being on your way to meet clients. Then you got on the interstate, and the car, coming out of nowhere, running you off the road . . ."

"And that's when you crashed into that cement wall." Ben finished the story as he knew it.

David glanced from me to Ben. "Oh, that wall. Guess my pain medicine makes it hard for me to remember things."

"You have company!"

Words I never expected to say to myself: "Thank goodness Max is here."

Max walked in with a basket of fruit, which he set on the dresser, and what looked like a laptop case, which he set on the corner of David's bed.

He held out his hand to Ben, "Let me guess. I'll bet your name is Ben."

Ben shook his hand. "Yes, and this is my Uncle David. Are you his doctor?"

"No," Max smiled, "I wish I was. Then maybe he could leave here sooner."

"Well, you're not a nurse or else you'd be wearing a uniform," Ben said. "Hey, you must be Uncle David's friend. You're Max."

"Yes. You're right. Pleased to meet you, Ben."

Max opened the portfolio and set the laptop on David's tray table. "I can't believe I let you talk me into this." He shook his head as he plugged the charger in and attached it to the computer. "Ben, did you know your Uncle David has a very hard head?"

"Is that why he didn't break it in the accident?"

Max, David, and I exchanged glances like we'd just made a silent "we'll laugh on the inside" pact.

"Absolutely," David held up his good hand, and patted his head.

Max drew several manila folders from the portfolio and set them up by the laptop. "And, your uncle's hard stubborn head is the reason he thinks he can work while he's here."

"I just need you to check on a few closings," David said.

"You also need to rest. I told you I could handle those for you." I heard an edge in Max's voice, like a paper cut, small and quick, but undeniably there.

"Max has a real estate license too," David said, but he stared at the ceiling as he tried to shift his body ever so slightly. He winced and closed his eyes for a moment.

"Oh, so you're both in the real estate business," I said. That made sense; it was probably how they met.

"Technically, I'm not in the business anymore except for a few commercial properties or if a friend needs something." He pulled the card off the basket, read it, and then handed it to David. "I own a clothing store for men called Unique on Magazine Street. I opened it a few years ago. Three to be exact."

A men's clothing store. That explained Max's impeccable and classic look. But I wasn't sure they would have met that away. David's sense of style in clothing . . . He's not awful, just oblivious. But I'd heard of the store. I rifled through files in my brain, but came up empty.

"Whoa. Where did these come from?" Max pointed to the tray of mini pecan pies.

"From me and Mom. And I helped make them." Ben opened the mini-refrigerator. "And this, too. A chocolate cheesecake."

"That was a great idea. Thanks. Your uncle talks a lot about your mom's cooking, especially her desserts. I might have to break my 'no dessert before dinner' rule to taste them."

"Cool. Except . . ." Ben looked around the room, "we forgot forks and plates."

"I think I have a plan," Max said. "Ben, can you help by keeping your uncle company? Make sure he doesn't try to jump out the bed and run down the hall. Or eat all that cheesecake."

"Sure. I can do that," he grinned, and I detected a little swagger in his voice for being asked. David opened his eyes only long enough to smile at Max when he gave Ben his orders.

I couldn't figure out what role I played in this "plan" of Max's that I suspected wasn't as spontaneous as it sounded.

"While you're making sure your Uncle David doesn't cause any trouble, your mom and I are going to get coffee for our dessert party, and find plates and forks."

Ah, that was my cue; Max arranged for us to have alone time. Out of the range of David and Ben. This should be interesting. Awkward, but interesting.

Max and I were almost to the elevator when I heard Ben's, "Wait!" behind us.

Surely a catastrophe didn't happen in the last two minutes. But, then again, I knew lives could change in seconds,

We turned around and Ben trotted to where we stood. "Is something wrong?" I asked.

"I don't drink coffee. Can you get me a chocolate milk?"

# 28

When Max and I shared mind-numbing angst and uncertainty the day David was attacked, I suspended my hostilities in a self-declared truce. No one and nothing except David and his survival mattered. Senseless tragedy and violence almost always engender this response. For a few days or weeks or even months for others, depending on the enormity of the event, we saw others through the open eyes of our hearts. The country after 9/11, tsunamis, earthquakes, trapped miners—we wore adversity well.

Then the immediacy inevitably settled into complacency, and the eyes of our hearts eventually glazed over. Already my discomfort rode the elevator between Max and me.

In a week or so, David would be discharged from the demilitarized zone of the hospital and likely without a surrender or a peace treaty. Maybe Max hoped negotiations could start now.

"I'm guessing you didn't mean for us to head back upstairs, right?" I asked Max after we paid for our coffees.

"Right. Here's okay?" Max stopped by a table near a window that overlooked a small pond ringed with benches and copper planters stuffed with red and white poinsettias.

"Sure." If the conversation faltered, I had an outdoor view. Although, I had to admit, no place better than a hospital to have a private conversation. Between the constant paging, the clickety-click of carts, and patients and their families and friends were too focused on their own issues to care about anyone else's.

Max sipped his coffee, grimaced, and said, "It's not Starbucks, that's for sure," then proceeded to add five packets of sugar. He must have noticed me trying to look as if I wasn't counting every packet he opened. "I know. Sugar and caffeine are my last hold outs. I stopped smoking, stopped drinking except for a glass of wine sometimes, backed off the carbs . . ." He stirred, sipped, and shrugged. "That'll do. Anyway . . . I'll eventually wean myself off one or the other or both. Just not any time soon."

"David was always so much more disciplined about healthy eating and exercising." Neither one of which would protect him from AIDS, something I added to my list of "Things to Obsess Over When Your Sibling Comes Out."

"He still is." Max glanced out the window. He sighed, then looked at me. "I'm going to just cut to the chase here, okay? I should probably warn you I'm not always diplomatic. I don't mean to be hurtful or sound uncaring. David and I operate under 'full disclosure,' so I hope the two of us can as well."

I had a difficult time being honest with myself, and I've known me decades longer than I've known him. "I'm not sure where this conversation's headed. But I'll be honest about the fact that I'm not sure how honest I can be. At least for right now."

"Okay. I appreciate that. We just met. I probably know more about you because of David. But if this horrible thing hadn't happened, I have no idea when we would have met each other."

"Is this where you don't mean to sound hurtful part happens? This hasn't been easy for me . . ." I couldn't say Max was wrong, though, about when I would have been ready for the wall to come down or at least build a door to walk through. "I'm just finding out something about David that he's known about himself, apparently, for a long time."

"The thing is I know I'm not the sister-in-law you had in mind. I hope we spend time to get to know each other. Until then, we might have to push some stuff on the side. But the one thing we have in common for now is that we both care about and love David. Fact is, I need your help."

We both love David. I'm not sure I'm ready for this conversation. "What kind of help are you talking about?"

"I'm going to do whatever I can to help his clients. It's been tough for him to build his business with the economy the way it's been. He's worked hard, so I want to do whatever I can to make sure his business sustains it. The challenge is that I have a clothing store to manage. And, somehow, I need to be able to take care of David's business and my own, plus make sure he gets to physical therapy, to the doctor. I haven't even mentioned the basics, like eating, cleaning . . ."

The longer Max spoke, the more I heard desperation in his voice. I didn't know how he would be able to do everything he mentioned. None of that included taking care of David himself.

That's where I came in. He wanted me to help with David during the day when he couldn't be there. But how exactly? "So, what you're telling me is that you need someone to help with David. And you want that someone to be me."

"Yes, but I'm not the only one who wants that someone to be you. I told David we could hire someone whether the insurance company paid or not. I asked David how he'd feel about you helping us out. He'd love for you to do it, but he told me he didn't think you would. And he didn't want me to put you in the uncomfortable position of having to say 'no' or say 'yes' because you'd feel guilty not to."

"Why would he think I'd not want to help? My God, he's my brother . . . he could have been killed."

Max looked at me as if I'd announced I signed up to join the circus. "I'm going to ask this in the nicest way possible. You do know that you've avoided his phone calls, and the few times you have talked to him, the conversation clocked in at less than a minute?"

I squirmed, unsure what I had to say would make sense to Max. But he wanted to know. "I'll try to answer the same way, in the nicest way possible. My brother living is more important than his sexual orientation."

# 29

Ben and I got by that Christmas with more than a little help from our friends. Using my debit card, a reasonable limit, and Ben's list, Julie created magic for my son on Christmas morning. I perked up our puny tree with Saints and LSU ornaments; a purple, gold, and black surprise for Ben. He did, though, chide me for not including the Hornets basketball team or the Zephers baseball team. I promised to make amends before the next Christmas.

The best gift of all was delivering dinner and dessert to David, Max, and the nurses and staff on his floor. We fed their bodies, but their smiles fed our spirits.

Sidney Washington asked if we could meet at his office, which was actually a renovated home in a section of the city on its way to becoming commercial. I'd never met him in person, just seen him in television commercials and heard a few radio spots. He was a least half a foot under the six feet tall I expected him to be. Ah, the power of the media. The new Pygmalion. What the public wants, will get reshaped.

His handshake was too long, plus he was one of those two handed shakers. The kind who covers the whole handshake with the free hand, like it might be needed to prevent my hand from flopping out like a fish.

"So glad you could meet me today, Caryn," he said as he sat behind a desk that was more attractive than he was. But it looked suspicious, like a desk ready for or just coming off a photo shoot. Papers were too neatly disarranged or too tightly stacked to appear as if they'd been given real attention. On the right corner of the desk was a collection of framed photos, all family. Sidney and wife, Sidney and wife and collie, Sidney and wife and son, Sidney and wife and son in tropical places, snowy places, mountain range places, desert places. The desk screamed look at me enjoying my family and see how we travel around this great country of ours, and it's so obvious I love my wife because not only is she in all the pictures, she and I are notoriously scandal-free happy.

"And you, sir. I'm delighted to have been offered this opportunity." And now, time for token gratuitous family comment. "That's an attractive family. And it seems you travel often. How old is your son?"

"I'll bet Sid Junior is not much younger than you. He'll be twenty-one in a few weeks."

I tittered, and I don't do that often, but his remark clearly called for it. "Not much at all. I've been celebrating the anniversary of my 29th birthday for a few years now."

Each time he spoke to me his gaze dropped down from my eyes like an elevator, and it landed on floors as it went down the front of my body, floors where it had no business being. I recrossed my legs, thankful I'd worn a long peasant skirt that even hid my ankles.

I purposely glanced at my watch, which stopped working two years ago and I only wore it for its bracelet value. I wanted to redirect his attention to menus and to nudge the elevator into making its return trip to my face. "I'm sure you're a busy man, and I don't want to take too much—"

"That would be impossible. Someone as pretty as you are could never take too much of my time."

Which is exactly why every other week, a man in political office stood behind a podium and begged forgiveness for an indiscretion while a tight-lipped, vacant-eyed, lawyered-up spouse suffered what she'd make sure was his last indiscretion —at least on her watch. Even a wife with stage three cancer isn't reason for a man to keep his moral elevator from going straigh to the basement.

This is when I wished I could play the husband card. Where I'd smile saccharinely and ooze enough Southern charm to make a pitcher of sweet tea, and say, "That is so kind of you. That's exactly why my husband's glad he married me."

I choose to ignore the comment, because to dignify it in any way would suggest that it meant something to me. And it didn't. What it meant, though, was I needed to be careful to not do anything that would suggest impropriety, schedule meetings in public places, and only hope that he told his wife she was beautiful and could never take up too much of his time. And meant it.

After reviewing the catering options I presented, he promptly closed the folder, pushed it to the side and said, "I'll need some time to review these." He drummed his fingers on the desktop, then picked up his phone. "Lurlene, Ms. Becker and I need to meet with my wife sometime within the next few weeks. What do I have open?"

A bit presumptuous. Maybe he could have asked me what I had open. Proved he thought I needed his business more than he needed mine—which is true. But he just let me know, in that phone call, that his time was more important than mine.

I was tempted to say "no" to whatever date he picked just on general principles.

He uttered a series of "uh huhs" and then a "wait just a moment" before he turned to me. "Would the last Wednesday in January work for you?'

I opened my planner, and scanned the month, which actually was as empty as his moral code. But I pondered, made myself look perplexed, and then answered, "Yes, that will work. What time?"

"How about noon, we could meet somewhere for lunch?"

Just on my own, general principles, I said, "Is one o'clock too late for lunch? I have something that morning." I considered David "something," quite an important something. I left myself time to drop Ben off at school, go to David's, lunch, Ben and then, depending on Max's schedule, maybe David's again.

⌘

When Max called to tell me David was being discharged and he was bringing him home, I expected it would be Max's home as well. So, little wonder, they were both confused by my questions about wake up times and leave for work times.

I called David after I dropped Ben off at school to tell him I was on my way, and he said Max had wanted to talk to me, and would I mind waiting because he'd run home for a few minutes.

"What do you mean? Max went to his house? His house and your house aren't the same house?"

"No. Why would you think it was?" I'm almost certain I heard a grin in David's voice.

I assumed David and Max lived together. I don't know why, since David and Lori never did. They were in a relationship

211

where sex would be the natural consequence of them loving each other. But for David and Max, I assumed—because they were gay—their being together was about sex, not the relationship.

Wrong again.

My response surprised me, so I could only imagine David's face when he heard it, "Honestly, because you're gay."

"So being gay comes with property? If that were true, I'd be a retired and wealthy real estate agent." This time David did laugh. "Seriously, Caryn, Max and I have only known each other for a little over six months. I'm not saying we won't ever share a home. But not now."

Apparently, I had a great deal to learn about this new country I now resided in part time, with dual citizenship.

"I'll own that assumption. I should be at your house in fifteen minutes. Anything you need me to pick up on the way?"

"No, I'm good. Really. See you soon."

"Okay."

I was just about to click off when David said, "Caryn, thanks. I love you."

———— ⧜ ————

David lived in a shotgun house in the Fauborg-Marigny section of New Orleans. Max, as it turned out, lived five houses down from David's, and that's how they met. At a neighborhood Night Out Against Crime. Not very romantic, but maybe that didn't matter.

Max gave me a key to David's house and one to his. "Don't argue. Just take them. I feel more comfortable knowing if you needed something for David that was in my house, you could get it."

"Here's a list of phone numbers . . . my store, the neighbors between David and me, Dr. Armstrong, and this great Cuban restaurant around the corner. They deliver. You can program them in your . . ."

He glanced at my cell phone which must have seemed to him as prehistoric as the first Philco floor radio, and turned to David, "Have you seen what she's calling a cell phone?"

"Does it still have a cord and a rotary dial?" David asked and craned his neck from where he sat on the sofa to catch a glimpse of the artifact Max had scooped from me to show him.

"Your brother got the decorator gene and the technology gene. You, so far . . . got the chef gene."

"Are we keeping score?" I asked.

"Got the feisty gene, too. Okay. We can work with that," Max said as he returned my cell phone. "If I can wrangle a cell phone from the 21st century for you, will you accept it without trying to make it seem like you'll be in my debt forever? Because you won't be. You'll be in Sprint's debt forever. I'm just brokering the deal. "

"Just tell him 'yes' now; otherwise, he'll start calling you every hour. He's persistent that way," David advised.

Max looked at him. "All I wanted to do was get us tickets to a Saints game. If you'd have said yes the first time, the price wouldn't have had time to go up." He turned back to me, "So, what do you think?"

"I don't know. I mean I am due for a trade-in on this one, but the monthly plan will go up won't it?"

"Well, there you go. Proof positive you're related. Both of you have the thrifty gene."

Max explained there was a way for me to jump in on a family plan he and David shared, and that would reduce the cost of the monthly plan. And between a BlackBerry he no longer used or a special promotion he'd look into I'd be able to be the happy owner of a new cell phone. At least, new to me.

Max checked the time. "I need to run. Mayme, my store manager, planned to open for me this morning, but she needs to leave to take her mother to dye her hair. Again."

Awkward moment alert.

David and Lori would have said good-bye with a brief hug and a kiss. What was supposed to happen now? Should I disappear into the kitchen to give them some privacy? Did they not need privacy? I realized signs of physical affections between David and Max would be challenging. That's an area I didn't want to have to talk about yet, but I also didn't want to play the "let's pretend one or the other of us is invisible" game either.

Would they have expected Harrison and me to not show physical affection in their presence? And how would I have felt if they did ask that of us? Would I respect their wishes as I expected them to respect mine?

"Max, I almost forgot. Julie's picking Ben up from school this afternoon, so I can stay until 4:30. I'm sure you have more to do right now than you have time to do it. In fact, Julie said she'd handle after school rides for this whole week. You and David can let me know tomorrow what works best for you." I picked up the large Chico's bag I'd carried in with me. "Now, I'm headed to the kitchen to make coffee, put away dinners, and make a grocery list. Talk to you later, Max."

"I'll call around noon," Max said.

Finding the kitchen in a shotgun house was a no-brainer. Just keep walking straight through every room, and if you fall off the back steps, you went too far. As I left the room, I caught a glimpse of Max as he walked over to the sofa where David stretched out. Beyond that, I didn't know. I didn't want to know.

And that's all I knew.

# 30

I stacked the week's supply of meals I cooked in the freezer with the almost new carton of Blue Bell Caramel Turtle Cheesecake ice cream, assorted bags of vegetables, two containers of shrimp, and a box of double A batteries.

Even before I looked in it, I knew the refrigerator would be empty by the way the door quietly and quickly opened. Unlike my refrigerator where salad dressing bottles, jars of one thing or another, blocks of cheese, sticks of butter and margarine, eggs, ketchup, bottles of crab boil and pesto sauces all happily coexisted and weighed down the door. Another door slamming lesson Ben needed to learn. He'd taken out his leftover birthday cake, but the box required a two-hand hold, so he opted to close the door with his right foot. It wasn't until I came along and opened the refrigerator that I discovered one of the adjustable door bins had popped off its side hook, and set in motion an avalanche of bins that led to broken bottles, cracked eggs, and shredded patience.

David's refrigerator held water bottles, three take-out containers from P.F. Chang's, a gallon of soy milk, and Greek-style yogurts. Eliminated the need for a grocery list. "Restock" didn't require writing down. I emptied what I brought for lunch and dinner into the refrigerator, and checked the cabinets for boxes and cans, anything suggesting a food item, and what David had in the line of cutlery and cookware.

I was hunting for chopping boards when my cell phone rang. David's number flashed in the small window.

"Seriously? You're calling me from two rooms away?"

"I started to wonder if you'd just walked out the backdoor and kept on going. You are still in the kitchen and not walking down Constance Street, aren't you?"

"Just trying to get settled, figure out if I need to bring supplies from home. Speaking of, where's your cutting board?"

"Cabinet under the sink. Hey, would you mind making me a cup of coffee? Whatever flavor you pick is fine. And I drink it black with one of those yellow packets in the basket with the pods."

"Got it. Be there in a few minutes."

David's bright red coffee brewer was the only appliance on the limestone countertop. I picked through the collection of flavored coffee pods, found Hawaiian Hazelnut, and brewed two single cups to carry back to the living room.

I placed David's mug on the coffee table. He had his cell phone mashed to his ear; the conversation on his end consisted mostly of "Yes" and "Okay." He mouthed "client." I slipped my shoes off, sat in the armchair and propped my feet on the ottoman. The blue ticking fabric of the matching chair reminded me of the musty lumpy mattresses at my grandparents' home close to the lake. The times our parents actually went somewhere overnight, they'd drop David and me off at Mimi's and Papa's. One of their two acres was fringed with water too shallow and seaweed-slimy for swimming, but perfect for dropping a cane pole with a red and white striped bobber off the end of a pier.

After showers in water that smelled like rotten eggs, David and I would pull our mattresses out on the screened-in porch and cover them with scratchy white sheets. Some nights the four of us played "Go Fish" at the card table.

Mimi told us that stars were the bright faces of all the people in heaven that shined down to remind us of the light of God's love for us. So at night, lying on porch mattresses, David and I marveled at stars that throbbed in the dark body of the night.

Our grandparents died within a year of each other, one from cancer and the other of a broken heart. Mom sold the two acres. Too soon, unfortunately; five years later, the migration from the city started and it hasn't stopped since. Six houses, each valued well over a million dollars, now sit on that land. Everything once familiar to us there disappeared.

Except for the stars.

I looked at David's once purple and black bruises now faded to yellow and brown, and thought that my Mimi's story just didn't ring true any more. How could that light of God have shined on David's attackers? And, as if she heard me ask the question, Mimi's voice tiptoed into my consciousness: Light can also expose the truth.

---

"Do you need me to zap that for you?"

David had just taken his first sip of coffee, and he'd been on the phone so long, I figured it was on its way to iced coffee.

"No, this is fine. Plus I'm still a bit clumsy, so good probably it's not too hot. Saves me a trip to the burn unit."

"Did you want anything to eat?"

"No. Sitting on my butt doesn't require much energy. And I did eat breakfast this morning. Max brought over a bagel with

Nutella spread. Have you tasted that stuff? How did I get to be this old and not know about it?"

"Luck? Once you discover it, you're doomed. I could eat it right out of the jar using a spoon. Guess that's why we didn't know about it growing up. Mom might have considered it an addictive substance."

"Yes, she probably would."

A long space of silence. Except for what I suspect was foot tapping in heaven.

"We haven't really talked in months. Are we going to keep talking about food?" David wasn't confrontational; in fact, he sounded more like a parent coaxing a child into a pool. I guess that's where David wanted to lead me—out of the shallowness.

"No." I stared into my coffee mug, then looked at my brother. "That's kind of the problem. I wish we could go back to those days . . . when we had those kinds of conversations without thinking we used them to avoid talking about something else. When things were. . ."

"Normal? Was that the word?"

I sipped my coffee. I needed to think before I answered.

*You were on your way to being honest. Don't take a detour now.*

I know, Harrison. I know.

"I guess. I mean, if we were still talking about food or what-ever . . . you'd be at work right now. Not recovering from get-ting attacked."

David lowered his mug to the table and massaged the back of his neck as he looked at the ceiling. "You're right."

I'm surprised he agreed with me so easily, but I nodded as encouragement. Maybe this meant he was beginning to under-stand his own confusion.

"If I had just kept living the lie, the people who attacked me would have found someone else. And nothing would have

**219**

changed in your life. As long as I stayed dishonest, everyone else's world kept spinning. And all this," he waved his hand over his body, "is my fault. For not hiding the truth about myself."

Whoa. The train just stopped at the wrong station. "That's not how I meant it. I wasn't trying to blame you. I'm trying to be honest here. And the truth is, things were easier before you decided . . . announced, whichever, that you were gay."

"Are you being honest with me? Because I can't help but think that you're more concerned with how my being gay impacted your life than mine. As long as you saw the David you wanted to see, everything was fine." He flinched as he shifted on the sofa. "I get it. You want me to be gay on my own time."

"No. You don't get it. I didn't want you to be gay at all. I wanted you to get married, have kids, and grandkids, and just have a normal life."

"I can still have all those things. My being gay is my normal life. Do you . . . " He stopped, took a deep breath, "do you think I would choose to live a life that would cause someone to hate me enough to do this to me? The ironic thing is what they did to me because I was gay is what I did to myself inside, every day, for years, trying to live as though I were straight."

# 31

I could hardly bear to see the pain in my brother's face. And I felt responsible for it being there. Not because his being gay had anything to do with me. But because I struggled to understand him, and that he felt so alone and abandoned by me. Why couldn't I be the person who could easily accept this? I *wanted* to be that person.

I moved the ottoman near the sofa, and held David's hand. On one hand, I was grateful David had the courage to push open the door I spent months jamming with excuses and denials. On the other, I was afraid. We crossed into territory unfamiliar to me. And even if I tried to turn back, the shift had already happened. Once you know a thing, you can't *un*know it. And there was so much more ground to cover.

"David, I love you. I don't know how to make this work. I promise, I promise I won't shut you out again. That's all I can do  right now. But at least it's a start."

"Just tell me the truth. I know this is going to be a process. We're not going to figure it all out in one day. This is just as awkward for me as it is for you. If there's something you're uncomfortable with, I'll respect that."

"Well, there is one thing . . . and as much as I hate to bring this all back to where we started . . ."

He reached for the napkin by his mug, and wiped his face. "What? I don't think I have the energy or enough pain pills to do this again."

"It's not that complicated," I patted his shoulder. "I'm uncomfortable with the fact that there's no food in this house."

"It really is all about food for you, isn't it?" He laughed. "When I was in the hospital, Max cleaned out the refrigerator. Brought some things to his house. We eat out or order in, so not much cooking happens here."

"Well, that's about to change. I think you're due some medications, and then I'm going to start lunch."

"Good plan. I think I'll also pencil in a nap before and after lunch."

I brought David his pills and his bottle of water, and went to the kitchen to put together the chicken salad. Between chopping the shallots and the celery, I walked to the front room to check on him. I wasn't sure if he was asleep, but his eyes were closed. After the emotional toll of this morning's conversation, I could have stretched across the kitchen countertops to rest and been as comfy as David on the sofa.

I had just stirred the sour cream and mayonnaise for the dressing, when I saw someone walking through the side gate. All I could see was a well-built, nicely suited blond-haired man who appeared to be talking to his iPad.

I turned over a small frying pan and used it to check my makeup. Next thought: lipstick. And the thought that trampled all over the other two was a man that good-looking and that well-dressed didn't care if I wore lipstick. And if he was comfortable enough to knock on the backdoor of my brother's house, well, I didn't need a flashlight to find the clues.

The salad was ready, but I wasn't so sure I was. I didn't expect to start meeting David's friends so soon.

As soon as the door opened, he introduced himself. "Hello, I'm Gavin Singletary. I'm a friend of David and Max's. I apologize for not calling first, but I saw Max this morning, and he said you were here with David. So, you must be Caryn, right?"

A surprising number of words to compact into one breath, which unfortunately made him all the more adorable. Daniel Craig, James Bond, the early years, with smoother skin and bluer eyes that weren't shaded by a too-prominent forehead. "Right. Yes. I'm Caryn. Come in."

He propped his leather briefcase against the wall by the door. "Terrible habit of leaving this thing behind. Less likely to do that if I have to see it before I leave. His eyes scanned the kitchen, including the countertop where I'd set out glasses and plates.

"I'm fixing lunch. Chicken salad. I have enough if you'd like to stay."

"No, thank you." He continued to look around. "This is the first time I'm seeing the renovation. Nice job. Don't you think so?" He unknotted his tie, an understated gold and silver hound pattern, slipped it from around his neck and draped it over the handles of his briefcase.

"I didn't see it before, but, yes, it's a great kitchen," I said and ran my hand along the countertop, as if giving it attention made a difference. Guilt at having not been before flashed across my face, and I hoped Gavin missed it. But I doubted he did, especially when he responded with a nod and an "oh," that seemed to say, "Oh, that sister."

"David's on the sofa in the front. He was sleeping the last time I checked on him."

"Not anymore," David called out. "Glad you're here. Gavin."

"Okay, then." I shrugged. "Lunch is ready. Are you sure you don't want anything?"

"No, but I appreciate the offer." He pointed to the front. "So, I'll go see David . . ."

"Sure," I felt like Cinderella, but I wasn't even sure if it was pre- or post-ball.

David's and Gavin's voices were indistinct, but that might be a blessing since Gavin was probably asking why I'd never been to his house. But I suspected he knew. I bet most of David's and Max's friends knew. I was the sister who wanted David back in the closet.

After the pitas toasted, I arranged them around the plate next to the sliced avocados that circled the overloaded scoop of chicken salad. I found a cloth napkin, placed everything on a brass tray I found under the coffeemaker and carried David's lunch into the living room.

"I didn't think to ask if you liked anything I put in here. But just do what you always do. Pick it out or spit it out." I put the tray on the coffee table.

"Did you actually just say that in front of my friend?" David asked in feigned horror.

"Welcome to David's world," I told Gavin. David was not going to be able to maneuver lunch from a coffee table, especially one-armed for the present. "You wouldn't happen to have one of those lap trays?"

"No, add that to the list of things Max needs to pick up."

"Don't you have one you use for your laptop? I thought I'd seen you use it when we watched Saints games," said Gavin.

"Hey, great idea. Caryn, it's in my office, probably hiding under a stack of papers. They make good shelves too."

Gavin helped David sit with his back against the sofa and his leg cast on the ottoman. He set the brass tray on the lap table and looked at me sheepishly. "You know, I'm going to take you up on that offer. Or should I say offers?"

"Offers would be the right word. I'll be right back." I was flattered Gavin thought it looked good enough to eat. Maybe that would be some redemption. I headed back to the kitchen, but stopped when I heard Gavin call me.

"Caryn, you can hold the avocado on mine."

"Okay," I said.

I was on the prowl for another napkin when the voices in the front room escalated. And not in a "we just scored a touchdown" discussion. These voices were serious and intense. By the time I carried a plate for Gavin and for me into the room, I figured out Gavin was an attorney, and David wasn't enamored with whatever Gavin suggested.

Gavin sat on the ottoman. I handed him his lunch, and I sat cross-legged on the floor, my plate on the coffee table. Silence. "So, is this something I can help with or none of my business? I just don't want to overstep my boundaries."

"I want David to consider pressing charges," Gavin said. "Consider, David. Just consider."

"I don't think it's a good idea. Why would I subject myself to that kind of publicity?" David stabbed a grape and moved it to the side of his plate. "What do you think, Caryn?"

My gut already flashed a yellow warning light, which usually arrived in the form of knots boomeranging from one side to the other. Just a few hours before, I played the honesty card. Now it was time to ante up. Publicity. What kind of damage would that do to David's career? Max's store? My catering business when people make the logical connection? I didn't need to make that mess in front of a man who, an hour ago, was a stranger. "I agree with David. Why should he have to subject himself to that kind of emotional torture?"*Why should I have to risk financial torture?*

"Because it could make a difference, and not just for him. These are the kinds of criminal acts that don't get reported, and the scumbags who commit them know the odds are on their side because over three-fourths of these crimes never get reported."

"What if it makes a negative difference? Like what if David and Max find their businesses affected because of it?" I left my business out of the equation.

"See, Gavin. It's not just me disagreeing. I just don't want to rock the boat."

"David, I want you to really think about this. I told you I didn't need a decision today. Talk to Max about it." He spooned chicken salad onto a piece of pita. "And, of course, pray about it."

⸺✺⸺

Driving home, I realized I forgot to ask Max to pick up rice for the beans on his way from work.

At the light, I hit call and Max answered before the second ring. "Everything okay?"

Poor Max. He must have post-traumatic stress syndrome every time a cell phone rings or doesn't. "Yes, I'm fine. Nothing that a flying car couldn't cure. Louisiana must have the world's worst drivers . . . but that's not why I called."

"Good. Because if you were on a game show, I wouldn't know the answer if that had been the question. What's up?"

"I forgot to tell you on the way out that I forgot to bring rice for the beans tonight. I meant to ask you to pick some up on your way back to David's, but forgot that too. . . . But I thought you might have a neighbor you could borrow from."

"Perfect timing. David just asked about dinner. I'm wondering if we ought to think about a few low-cal meals. Not like the man's exercising."

David must have been nearby because the last two sentences were practically whispered.

"Put that on your list of things to talk to Dr. Armstrong about."

Earlier that afternoon, after Gavin left, I found a clipboard in David's office. I put it on the table near him and tied a pen to it. "I know it's primitive, but do you really want to open your laptop every time you remember what you want at the grocery or what you need to ask the doctor?"

"I can write notes on an app on my cell phone. That works just as well."

"Maybe for you. But I can't add to it or see your notes." I waved the clipboard in front of him. "This we can all see. See?"

Max laughed from the other end of the call. "On the clipboard? Sure, I'll ask David to do that. You know how he loves that oversized app you made him."

"I'll see you in the morning. Call me if you think of anything else you need me to do."

"I will. And Caryn . . . thanks for being here today. I can't tell you what it meant to me to walk out this morning and see you and David together. He missed you, and I don't know if he could make it through this without you."

"Thanks, Max. Have a good night. I hope you enjoy the dinner."

After spending the day with David, I knew I had to find someone or some place I could go with all this stuff I carried inside. I tried talking to Julie, and she meant well, but I couldn't make her understand the whole game changes when someone in your own family comes out. And, I didn't need God tugging on my ear to tell me I needed to get myself and my son to church.

Maybe I needed my own clipboard.

# 32

Mom!" Ben ran out Julie's front door and climbed in the car.

"How's Uncle David? When can I go with you? We're not doing anything tomorrow during school. I can miss one day. Please."

He sounded just like Gavin. So many sentences they were hooked like cars on a freight train.

Julie appeared a minute later, waved and made the thumb and little finger hand phone. "Call me tonight."

I leaned over and kissed Ben on his forehead. "Uncle David's getting better. His face isn't even black and blue anymore." He smelled like outside.

"It's not?" Ben pulled the visor down and peered in the mirror. Probably making sure I didn't leave a lipstick imprint.

"Nope. It's yellow and brown now."

"Mom, that's not very nice to make fun of Uncle David."

I pulled in the driveway, turned the car off, and leaned over to Ben. "I'm not at all making fun of your uncle. Sometimes, when sad things happen, it's good to find little things to be happy about. The yellow and brown mean that the bruises are going away. I'm sorry. I forgot you didn't know that." I kissed him on his forehead. "Understand?"

"Yes, now I do." He opened the car door, "I did my homework already. Can I watch television for a little while?"

"Sure," I said. "In fact, after your bath, why don't you come to my office? You can watch your shows while I get some work done."

The day's mail sat on top of a UPS package left at the front door. I recognized the box. I didn't have to open it to know it was the new books I'd ordered.

With an "I'll see you in your office," Ben went to his room. I heard the water running within a minute. I didn't even want to guess where he'd already tossed his shoes and clothes.

I walked past the telephone and ignored the flashing red light on the answering machine. In my bedroom, I exchanged my flats for my slippers, and traded my jeans and blouse for a T-shirt and sweats. I tore the packing tape off the box and took out the four new paperbacks. One of the books I flipped through seemed to be a bit more explicit than the ones I'd ordered before. I put that one first on the stack in case I decided to return it.

A detour to wash my face and brush my teeth and I was on my way to my office to see what adventures in catering waited for me.

With school back in session after the holidays, my email inbox started filling up again. Orders increased at every school, and some asked if two days a week would be possible. I did the math and if I kept all the once weeklies and conservatively added half of those if I offered another day, plus the side jobs that sprouted off of those, and the Washington political event,

I could cover the mortgage payments. The Junior League gig pushed me through the holidays, and the election celebration would be the padding for those first and second months when the note ballooned.

How much easier my life could have been if Harrison and I had drawn up our wills after Ben was born. Legal entanglements drained so much of Harrison's insurance money that, after putting aside what I thought would help Ben in college, the bank account needed an infusion. And I was the donor.

When I started my business, I envisioned myself as the go-to woman for the food snobs, who created hot and cold canapés with exotic and epicurean ingredients that were as pleasurable to pronounce as to consume—pecorino, porcini, quince jam, basil aioli. But women who worked all day didn't want foods with mysterious and unpronounceable names. They wanted recognizable, comfort food. Meals that didn't require more maintenance than they did. The last few times I delivered my school meals, I imagined each one as a family with a woman who just added another hour to her evening. Maybe what started for me as a murmur, God intended to be my calling. But, more important, He might want me out of my kitchen long enough to get into His church.

---

Ben, his pillow and his blanket arrived to overtake the sofa. His face and neck glistened because, as usual, the towel didn't make it that far up his body. I wouldn't have been surprised if he had puddles of water in his ears.

"Not too long, buddy. School tomorrow." I gave him the remote. He handed it back. "No television tonight?"

Maybe he wanted to talk about everything being in an upheaval. We hadn't spent much time together.

"Wrong remote, Mom. That's the one for the DVR, I need the other one." He opened my desk drawer, close enough for me to steal an orangey whiff of his shampoo, but not a minty scent of toothpaste.

I plopped my hand on the top of his head. "Don't move. Am I going to smell clean teeth or cruddy ones?"

"Cruddy. But I'll brush them right before bed. Promise." He mashed and bashed his pillow into shape, covered himself with the blanket, and was channel surfing within thirty seconds.

All those genetic predisposition studies I'd been reading since finding out David was gay—why was it no one studied men and their remote controls? Ben knew how to use the remote control before he wore training pants. I'd watch movies where the fate of the world hung on the press of a button—by a man who probably held a remote before he learned how to use a fork. And I'd thought, we're doomed.

I clicked through to a few of my favorite recipe sites, *Southern Living* being one of my top three, and browsed their slow cooker recipes. Max and David were about to be the proud owners of a Crock Pot, which meant I could start meals in the morning that David wouldn't have to bother with when I left, and would be ready when Max arrived home. I printed one for turkey chili and another for peppered beef soup served in toasted bread bowls. Even as I searched the recipes, uninvited images of Max and David in domestic bliss, appeared in my mind's eye, like those annoying pop-ups on Internet sites. But I didn't have a filter I could activate to block them. Would there ever be a time when I'd think of my brother with this man and not experience a ripple of uneasiness? Was I even supposed to? I shook my head as if I had an Etch-a-Sketch brain that wiped the slate clean.

I browsed a few more sites, even considered Googling both Max and Gavin, when I heard soft murmurs instead of snippy retorts. Ben had been watching *Smallville*, the show about the pre-tights and cape Clark Kent, but all the characters must have been struck mute because the dialogue that had been my background noise, ended. I glanced at the television and saw a shot of candles surrounding a bed, and I didn't need to see more to figure out Lois and Clark weren't about to roasting marshmallows.

"Eye muffs, Ben, and change the station!"

"How am I supposed to cover my eyes and change the channel at the same time?" He turned the television off, then flashed his scowl. "They were just kissing. I've seen people kiss before."

"Candles in a bedroom" and "just kissing" never belonged together in a conversation with my son. I'd read enough romance novels lately to predict the sequence of events. But I didn't want to explain that to Ben. One day. Not today. I went for the easy question. "Really? And who have you seen kiss like that?"

"Trey and Julie," he said, to the tune of "so there."

"Ben, there's a difference between two people kissing like Nick's parents and kissing like Lois and Clark on the show."

"Not really," he said, flopped over on his side and looked at me. "One time me and Nick tried to find popcorn in the pantry. We heard his mom and dad, so we kinda hid there because they told us to play outside for awhile. When it got quiet, we thought they left. But when we peeked, they were kissing all weird and stuff. And then Miss Julie said something about getting lucky. We ran out after they left."

Television. Julie and Trey. Those were Ben's points of reference for physical affection between couples. Not the Treadways, a few houses over, who walked every afternoon, holding hands. Well into their 70s, Dootsie joked she and Billy

**233**

held hands to keep each other from falling. I doubt they were even on Ben's radar. He had no memory, of course, of his father and me. I barely had a memory of us. How was I going to teach my son about intimacy and affection when I couldn't figure it out myself? And would I soon need to add Max and David to that list?

⌘

Just as I thought it was time to shut down for the night and roll myself and an already sleeping Ben into bed, I spied an email from Pastor Vince and one from Mr. Washington, both sent that morning. It was evident, once again, that not having a Smart phone made me a not smart businesswoman. While I was at David's, I could have been taking care of this, and at a time when I'd be more awake and more coherent. Tomorrow, Max would be given a mission to sniff out a cell phone deal. He seemed the bloodhound type.

Both men wanted to meet next week. Vince to discuss wedding catering and Washington, actually sent by Lurlene his assistant, that he changed the venue to River Oaks, a new banquet hall, and he wanted to meet me there. The thought of another appointment with the ogler made a root canal seem appealing. I'd seen his wife on television commercials and, unless he used a stand-in, the woman bore an uncanny resemblance to Jackie O. And considering he looked like Richard Nixon, she definitely won the attractiveness card in that relationship, which made his creepiness all the more confounding. Maybe I could convince Julie to join me. Washington might be less inclined to take inventory with his eyes in front of someone else. Or he'd think he'd won the jackpot. But I didn't want to commit to any appointments without checking with David and Max. I emailed them both that I'd check my schedule and get back to them.

The next morning, I woke up in one of those bolt upright panics. My heart galloped in my chest as I fumbled to find my cell phone. The novel I'd been reading—heavier on the intimacy, lighter on the affection—flew to the empty side of the bed when I pulled up the sheets. My hands followed a muffled beep coming from the headboard until they wrapped around the phone. The battery was almost dead, but I had beaten the alarm by two minutes.

I closed my eyes, breathed deeply, and imagined myself sinking chin deep into a warm bath. When was the last time I actually relaxed, in a bathtub or otherwise? When I opened my eyes, the cover of the book I lost myself in last night looked tawdry spotlighted in the soft morning light.

*It's not as if you're hurting anyone.*

Exactly.

But when I'd heard Ben calling me, I shoved the book in my nightstand before he reached my room.

# 33

Ben dashed into my bedroom and waved a folded sheet of red construction paper in front of me.

"Look what I'm making," he said as he climbed on the bed.

Bordered on what I hoped were footballs, the words "Get Well Real Real Soon" hobbled on the front flap. Inside he had written, "Dear Uncle Da."

"Can I finish this so you can give it to Uncle David today? I'll be fast." He tugged the card from my hand, slid to the floor, and waited.

"How about finishing it tonight when you have more time? I'll be here tomorrow too." I pushed my feet into slippers and patted him on the back, mostly to get him moving forward.

Ben didn't budge. "Pa-leeze?"

How could a barely awake mother resist her doe-eyed son wearing his LSU pajamas who begged to finish a card for his uncle?

"Okay, okay." I yawned, and he was already on his way when I said, "Don't mess around. You need to be ready when Julie gets here."

"And so do you," I said to my matted-hair reflection as I passed the wall mirror on the way to the kitchen.

I scrambled an egg, wrapped it in a warm wheat tortilla, and left the plate on the island. "Ben," I called out in the direction of his bedroom, "I'm going to get dressed. Come eat your breakfast."

Of course he didn't make it to the kitchen to eat breakfast, and of course he still wore his pajamas when Julie arrived, and of course I drove him to school. Late.

Max must have been on lookout duty. He opened the latticed French door before I even walked up the whitewashed concrete steps of David's house.

"Sorry. Ran a little late this morning," I said and handed him the Crock Pot.

"Ran into traffic?" Max asked over his shoulder as I followed him in.

"No, a persistent little boy," I said. "Uh, where's David?"

"Slept late," Max said as he walked into the front room. He held a plate out. "Scone? I made orange cranberry and a lemon curd dip."

He cooked too? I must have looked as surprised as I felt because Max handed me a napkin and said, "Not a cook, but I can bake. A little." He set the plate on the table. "Generally, not a talent I broadcast. Makes me seem even more of a stereotype. You know, gay man who bakes."

I nodded and chewed.

"I'll check on David," he said.

---

"If anyone calls about stopping by, would you mind telling them to wait a few days? He already looks tired."

"Max, I'm not invisible. I can decide if it's a good time or not," said David, who sounded very much like Ben when he pouted.

237

"Just looking out for you. Don't let those pain meds delude you into thinking you're invincible," Max said as he moved toward the door.

"Well, obviously I'm not. All I have to do is look at myself to know that."

I stood between the two of them and felt like a line judge at a tennis match as they volleyed back and forth. I needed to stop them before I had to call an out of bounds. "Max is right. You do look tired." I held up my hand when I saw his mouth forming an answer. "Stop. But if it makes you happy, I'll check with you before I tell anyone not to come over."

Max glanced at his watch, "We'll have to wake up sooner if this is going to be our morning routine." He smiled.

David and I both laughed. "You win. And sorry for—"

"Apology accepted. I'm supposed to meet that couple with four kids, Cindy and Tommy Burkhalter. The ones who want a big house with a small note. I have backup at the store. Going to be a long day in the suburbs."

David rubbed the bridge of his nose. "All these medicines, and I still remember the pain of that family. Nice, but clueless. I tried to explain the Katrina-effect on property values. Their home's worth more, but so are all of the ones they're trying to buy . . . Oh, and be careful . . . the little one isn't fully toilet trained."

"Maybe I'll skip the store. Come straight here . . ."

He was still shaking his head when he closed the door.

⌘

"This is the reason we were late this morning," I said and handed him Ben's card.

238

"My nephew, the budding Hallmark man," he smiled as he read the outside. It was the inside of the card that caused David's damp eyes. "Did you read what he wrote?'

"No. We were running behind schedule, so I just slipped it in the bag I toted over. What did he say?"

David cleared his throat. "Dear Uncle David," he read, "I pray for you every day. When you're better, we can play football. I love you and Jesus loves you too. Your nephew, Ben."

---

I chopped and measured for the turkey chili while David ate breakfast and channel-surfed. Every few minutes, dialogue streams would chop off mid-syllable, and start again seconds later. Maybe he couldn't take his Adderol with all his other medications because his attention was definitely at a deficit.

"Caryn, can you come here?"

David sounded more annoyed than injured, which saved me from running on the polished hardwood floors where even walking fast could lead to a head injury.

"Have you ever tried to read a newspaper when you have just one arm?" Open newspaper sections covered the sofa, the floor, and his lap. Some of the pages were crumpled, others folded. Black newspaper print smudged the underside of the arm he waved as if he needed to point out the problem. Even his hand looked as if he'd been doing charcoal finger painting. "And the ones I drop, I can't even reach to pick them up." He grabbed the pages on his lap and threw them to the side. He laid his head against the sofa. "I don't know how I'm going to make it through this," he whispered.

"Why aren't you using your Kindle?"

"Because Max left the paper here," he said pointing to the coffee table. "My Kindle's in there." He jerked his thumb toward his bedroom.

I picked up newspapers, folded them, stacked them. "Plates. You need plates."

"What?"

"After Harrison died, I stayed numb for weeks. Then, like it came out of hibernation, this rage grew inside. Here." I put the paper down that I'd been holding and put my hand on my stomach. "It filled up every space it could find in my body. Some days I even tasted it, like curdled milk." I picked up more pages to fold. Stared into the past. "I had to get rid of it before it hijacked my body. Somebody, I don't even remember who it was, told me to go to Goodwill and buy a stack of cheap plates. Fling them on the ground one at a time, the whole stack. Whatever. Something about hearing the hard noise as they hit the concrete and smashed into pieces that made me see my anger was those plates. And the breaking and the noise . . . that's what it was doing to me. Once I figured that out, it didn't see the inside of me. And it stopped controlling me."

"I'm not sure Goodwill has enough plates for me." He clicked off the television just as *The Price Is Right* music started. "It's difficult to ask for help when you're used to taking care of yourself."

"Of course not. That's what family and friends do for—"

"I didn't mean family and friends. And, yes, you are support. But I meant God. He isn't going to abandon me. In some way I don't even understand yet, God's strength will help. My bones may be broken, but my spirit doesn't have to be."

How was it possible my gay brother had more of a relationship with God than I? Not that I didn't plan to work on the church thing and God. But I thought being gay meant an automatic expulsion from God's kingdom. How could David love a

God who didn't just put him in the back of the bus, He kicked him out entirely? One of us was confused, and I didn't want to be the one to tell David the God he worshiped when he was a straight man was probably not going to punch his ticket into heaven now that he was gay.

I didn't know what to say, so I just nodded and changed the subject. "Do you want me to get a damp towel so you can wipe that print off?"

"No. I'm going to crutch my way to the bathroom, and I'll wash it off then. This might take a while, so no need to check on me. Unless you hear a loud crash."

I convinced him that it would be faster if I wheeled him to the door of the bathroom. Faster for him, easier for me to not have to watch him struggle to take every step there.

"You could grab my Kindle for me. It's on the table next to my bed."

I hesitated, maybe because I wouldn't send anyone into my bedroom without a warning. Even though I passed David's bedroom every trip to and from the kitchen—one of the downfalls of a shot gun house where the only really private room is the bathroom—I didn't linger.

Now that I could walk in without feeling as if I trespassed, I saw not just a sparse, uncluttered, and tranquil space. I saw my life and David's juxtaposed in that one place in a house that was our most intimate—our bedrooms.

When I left this morning, my bed was unmade, as it was most mornings regardless of being late or early. I used the comforter as a blanket because I couldn't justify the hundreds of dollars I'd spend for one I deemed more sophisticated. The bright yellow and cornflower blue plaid looked more suited to a teenage girl's room, so I wasn't too motivated to find it covering my bed. On one side of the room, cookbooks and clothes battled for floor space. The drapes I intended to hang years ago were on a shelf in my closet, still wrapped in the Pottery Barn bag. Sometimes the dresser held two or three coffee cups, leftover from the night before or mornings as I dressed for the day.

While my room made me eager to leave it, David's was an invitation. Earth tone shades and textures expanded the room. Under the rustic pine sleigh bed and dresser, a sisal rug edged in chocolate brown covered almost the entire wood floors. The stripes in the silk duvet reminded me of shades of coffee, from espresso to café au lait. The wheat colored silk drapes only looked as if they had been carelessly tossed over the bronze curtain rod.

I found the Kindle on the antiqued black desk table that covered the wall between the bed and the floor to ceiling window. Under it was a paperback New Testament that billed itself as a "fresh translation" and on the cover, the water that splashed resembled a crown. David was still in the bathroom. I set the Kindle down, and picked up the paperback with its thumb worn edges. I flipped through pages with sections underlined or maybe a line or phrase highlighted. A few pages were tabbed with sticky notes. One marked James 4:12, which read, "There is only one lawgiver and judge, and he is able to save and destroy. But you who judge your neighbor, who are you?" Another, Philippians 4:5: "Let your gentleness show in the treatment of all people." On page 264, the subheading "Grace now Rules" had been circled, and on the next page in Romans 5, the text read: ". . . grace will rule through God's righteousness . . ."

I returned the book to the table with one question ramming into my brain: can someone be gay *and* a Christian? I know David told me he and Max attended church. Did they attend as an openly gay couple? When David came out, I assumed the announcement meant he sacrificed heaven. Never mind I wasn't much more than a holiday Christian; it would always be a viable option for me because I was straight. I could choose to go. Or not. But even if David chose heaven, there was no gate through which gay men could enter. At least that's what I thought to be true. It didn't matter that David lived a life of kindness and compassion.

Julie and I used to joke that whatever happened in our marriages, it always came down to one thing for our husbands . . . sex. So that's what heaven came down to for God? I gave Him credit for being a bigger man than that.

Maybe I needed this confusion to push me into making that appointment with Vince. Catering his daughter's wedding would be a sandbox compared to this. I picked up the Kindle and turned to leave when a thought exploded into my consciousness. My gay brother kept a New Testament near his bed. His straight sister kept sensual romance novels by hers.

# 34

I checked in with Julie. The boys needed poster paper for a social studies project, so she asked if I could stop at Walgreen's. "When I picked up the boys this afternoon, one of the teachers said she didn't get an email from you with the monthly meal options. I told her I'd find out."

If I hadn't been driving, I would have slapped myself in the head. How could that have totally fallen out of my brain?

"Since you're mute, I'm guessing you didn't send the email." Her microwave beeped. "Wait a minute, Caryn. Getting the popcorn out for the boys. Wash your hands first. Get a bowl. Yes, you can take it outside."

"I'm mortified. I can't believe that email didn't go out." I merged onto I-10; cars moved slower and slower, until all I saw ahead of me were brake lights and a long night. "Great. The interstate is officially a parking lot, and I see the flashing lights of a fire truck coming up the service road. This is not good."

"No, it's not. But be grateful it's not you stopping traffic. Look, don't worry about the project stuff. I can pick that up tomorrow since they're not doing anything until the weekend. You need to get that email out."

"Well, I can't do it from here. Not with my phone." I shifted to park and put the phone on speaker. I raked my fingers through my hair and rubbed my scalp. A massage. That's what I needed to rid my body of toxins. But would there be anything left of me after that? "And what am I going to write? 'Dear Teachers: I'm an idiot. Even though I've been cooking for you for months now, I forgot to send out a January menu.'"

"How did you know? Sure, that's exactly what I thought too. Why don't you just tell them the truth minus the details? Your brother was hurt, you're helping—"

"No. Absolutely not. I don't want to spread my personal life all over the school system or answer questions or figure out how not to answer them." I opened the windows, then turned off the car after I realized even the 18-wheelers were shutting down. On my left, two teenaged girls had pushed themselves through the moon roof of the Acura they were in. At first they relayed whatever they saw from that vantage point to the other occupants of the car. I was just about to ask them myself, when the music cranked up and a song I didn't understand and probably wouldn't have wanted to, transformed them from road scouts to "I was glad they weren't my daughters, and my son wasn't in the car with me" girls. At least their hip gyrations were confined to the car's interior. I hoped the other two bodies were females.

"Are you afraid people will find out David's gay or that you'll lose orders because you have a gay brother?"

They both sounded ridiculous, but they didn't feel ridiculous when they gnawed like mice on the fringes of my doubt. "I don't think I'll lose customers because of David, except for the ones who might think I'm using my profits to support him or something. The fact that he was engaged and people expected a wedding makes it all a mess. I feel like I'm playing twenty questions. 'When's the wedding? There is no wedding. They

**245**

broke it off? Yes. Lori or David? Both. Is it just postponed? No.' Do you hear the problem?"

"I hear you convincing yourself there's a problem."

"I could send an email that said my gay brother was attacked by homophobes, I'm taking care of him because his partner needed help, that's why the menu was late, and don't ask me any questions."

"Now I'm relieved you don't have the cell phone to send it. You have the ride home to decide. Just send something. I think most of these people care more about their own stomachs than the drama in your life. Or mine. Or almost anyone not them."

"Guess I never thought about it that way."

"I need to pay the pizza guy. He's walking up to the door now. Don't worry about Ben. If you're not back by the time it's official lights out, Ben can just sleep here. Why don't you just stop here anyway? I'm sure you'll be hungry, and since Trey ordered three different kinds of pizza, I'm sure we'll have leftovers."

"I'll call when I'm closer. We might actually be moving." I hung up, and when I saw the lights of the 18-wheelers, I felt encouraged. Those truckers knew what was going on and, if they didn't they could find out. They social networked on their CB radios long before the internet.

Even five miles an hour was progress after thirty minutes of no movement, but still slow enough for me to return Zoe's call. She wanted to know if Ben and I would be interested in coming back to the center with desserts, and maybe staying for a while to play games or just chat with some of the residents. "My brothers think Ben is a cool kid, so they plan to be there whatever weekend works in your schedule."

"Thanks for the invitation. I'm in my car, so can I check my catering schedule and let you tomorrow? Would you want to ask your residents if there are any certain desserts or cookies they want?"

"Sure, and I'll explain you're not making everything they request," she said with amusement. "I appreciate your getting back in touch with me so quickly."

"You've been on my list of people to call, but for a reason entirely unrelated to my catering business." I waited a moment to continue for the howling of the ambulance to fade as it passed on the other side of the interstate, "And I realize we don't know each other well, so please understand I won't be offended if you say 'no.'"

"Okay." A matter-of-fact okay, not a hesitant, questioning one.

"A few months ago, my brother told me he was gay. I haven't handled it well. I don't have anyone to talk to, except for my friend, Julie. And even though I love Julie, and she's been a tremendous support person, I don't think she fully understands how challenging this is for me because her brother's not the one who came out . . ."

"Like yours and mine, right? I'll be happy to talk to you, especially if it means helping you not make the mistakes I made when my brother came out."

Closer to the accident, the police funneled three lanes into one. Less than a mile later, the traffic slowed again. But this time, it was because the wreckage captured attention. One car crumpled like a sheet of paper, another seemingly cracked in half by the light pole it hit head-on. I tried to look without gawking.

"Caryn? Hello? Are you there?"

"Yes. I'm sorry. I've been stuck in traffic forever, and just drove past the accident."

"That's always a heart-wrenching time, isn't it? It reminds me how temporary we all are."

I thought about Harrison, about almost losing David. "You're right, which makes me want to work out this relationship with my brother even more."

"Let me see, I could meet you sometime Saturday or . . . I'm scheduled to work Sunday . . . we could meet around one o' clock. You can bring Ben. He can help the boys at the Bingo game while we talk. Oh, and don't worry about bringing anything then. We can set up desserts for another day. How does that sound?"

"Perfect. That way I won't have to leave Ben." I turned into the Walgreen's parking lot. A few minutes picking up poster board wouldn't make that much difference considering how late I already was.

"Unless one of us has a change of plans, I'll see you Sunday afternoon."

"Thanks. See you then."

I checked my face in the rearview mirror, dug through my purse for lip gloss, pulled out a pen instead, and gave up. A trip into a drugstore shouldn't require that much attention. I tossed my keys in my purse and headed in, hoping everyone I knew was somewhere else.

Two poster boards, a jar of unsalted peanuts for David, who wanted more one-handed snacks, and a 2-for-1 on my favorite Maybelline mascara later, I called Julie. She informed me Nick and Ben had just gone to sleep, and asked if I wanted him to spend the night or go home with me. "We walked over to your place earlier and picked up clothes for school tomorrow, so he can just leave with us in the morning if that works for you."

"Maybe I need to give him my picture to put in his binder so he'll remember what I look like."

"I'll look for one. In the meantime, what kind of pizza do you want? Pepperoni and sausage, ham and pineapple, or veggie?"

"Veggie. And what—wait, that's a call coming in—let me make sure it's not David or Max."

"You'll be here in five minutes. Talk to you then."

The incoming call was the number I didn't recognize. I let it go to voice mail.

# 35

I can't believe I just ate three pieces of pizza." I handed my plate to Julie.

"That's because you didn't. You ate one piece and the tops of two," Julie said as she loaded it in the dishwasher. "I can't believe you talked me into brewing a pot of coffee this late. Who eats pizza and drinks coffee?" She said the word "coffee" as if it was synonymous with "sludge."

"You're drinking a Diet Coke."

"Still only half the caffeine. Already had this discussion with my mother last week." She pushed the dishwasher door.

"Are you spending the night here, too?"

The thought of not having to put shoes back on my happy toe-wiggling feet almost tempted me. But I wanted to be able to relax at the computer wearing my pjs and not worry if the pizza gave me gas. Even after only two days, I realized that alone time wasn't entirely awful after being around people constantly. "Tempting as the slumber party sounds, I need to download some information for Vince. He called today, and I need to set up an appointment with him." And probably for more than just information about catering choices, but feeding my soul hadn't been in my top ten list of urgent things to do. Maybe I wasn't hungry enough yet.

"Trey's going to slumber, but the 'party' is questionable. Probably a good thing for both of us he's at the gym tonight. All I wanted him to do today was pick up a gift card from Talbot's for his mother's birthday. His mother. He forgot. We're supposed to meet them on the other side of the universe tomorrow night for dinner. He claims he'll remember tomorrow. When he taps my shoulder tonight after we're in bed, I might try that 'I'll remember tomorrow line'."

"If that was supposed to be a sell job for staying, you're fired. Sounds like I'm the one who needs to host the slumber party." If Julie continued with her reward and punishment game with sex as the prize, would Trey ever have an incentive for doing the right thing all the time? Was there a prize for that?

I topped off my coffee and noticed a page torn from a Williams-Sonoma catalog hanging from a magnet on the refrigerator. The baked ziti recipe called for fresh eggplant and Kalamata olives.

Recipe. The email Julie reminded me about earlier. I already missed one week of orders. Now, I risked another week. Dependability mattered as much as the menu.

"I have to get home."

Julie stopped wiping the countertop and looked at me. "You're as white as my sheets used to be."

I poured my coffee in the sink, meant to set the cup on the counter, but missed. When it hit the floor, the handle broke off in one direction, the cup in puzzle-sized fragments in the other. "Can it get any worse?" I bent to pick up pieces, but they might as well have been underwater for the tears that blocked my vision.

Julie bent next to me and tugged me to standing. "Hey, it's not a big deal. The mug came with a flower arrangement Trey sent me last year. I've already forgotten what it was he forgot to do that made him send it."

She walked me to the sofa and handed me a box of tissues she'd picked up along the way. "You're scaring me. What just happened?"

I blew my nose. The cup must not have been as empty as I thought. Coffee spatters the size of raindrops were splayed on the front of my khaki pants. "I'm an idiot." I pounded my forehead with my fist as if to prove it. "That email you reminded me about? It just hit me that my customers haven't heard from me in weeks, and everything I've worked so hard to build, and what if they won't order because they don't think I'm dependable, or what if they don't want to recommend me . . ." I ran out of breath, but not words. They pushed against my brain like impatient prisoners. "And when they do start ordering again, how am I going to manage? Some of them already want two meals a week, and I can't figure out how to do one a week, and help David at the same time, and between cooking and David, Ben hardly sees me, and—"

"Let's stop there for now. And stop wringing your hands like they're wet towels. You're about to lose a layer of skin." Breaking one of her own rules, Julie sat on her coffee table across from me. "You're exhausted. You're not eating well. Probably not sleeping well."

The front door opened, and Trey's "Just me, ladies" voice echoed from the foyer. "Guess how many . . ." he walked in, spotted us, and mumbled ". . . miles I ran?" Every part of him leaked sweat. Even his clothes. He wore the smell of outside, grass and dirt, and night. "Everything okay?" Man-talk for "Do I have permission to leave because I'm out of my element here."

I nodded.

"We're good. We're good," Julie said.

Trey probably translated that as, "permission to escape granted" because he turned to head down the hall.

"There is one thing you could help with." Julie patted my hands and spoke toward me, but Trey knew the directive was meant for him because he stopped before she finished the sentence.

"What's that?"

Julie told him a cup fell in the kitchen and asked if he would clean it up, "especially those tiny slivers that go everywhere," and if he could mop it "just a bit to make sure the sticky is gone" and ended it all with, "if you wouldn't mind."

"Not at all," he answered and looked like he meant it.

Julie watched her husband as he walked toward the kitchen. I watched them both, and I wanted another life. No, not another one. I still wanted my family and friends. A "light" life. That's what I wanted. Like light margarine, light pudding, light ice cream, light cream cheese. I wanted a life with all the heavy taken out.

I jammed the used tissues in my pants pocket. "I have to go," I told Julie. Every stress in my life pressed down on me, like someone revving an engine. All that noise and energy, but I stayed in the same place, and the rut became deeper and wider. I didn't even care about the email right now. I wanted my life from underneath everyone else's foot.

"You don't have to go home to send an email. You can do that here. I'll even write it. All you need to do is send a menu out. You don't have to say anything else, at least not tonight. We can come up with a plan tomorrow after you leave David's. Most of your customers won't even read it for a day or two. Not everyone checks email as compulsively as you." She handed me a wad of fresh tissue. "Deal?"

The racing in my stomach slowed a bit. Tomorrow. We could fix it tomorrow. I trusted Julie with Ben, surely I could trust her on this.

"Deal."

⎯⎯⎯⎯⎯ ⦷ ⎯⎯⎯⎯⎯

Before I left, I tiptoed into Nick's room to kiss Ben good-night. He was on his stomach, his arms stretched over his head, and right leg bent at the knee. He looked like an h in his purple and gold pajamas against the white sheets. I kissed him on his forehead and whispered, "I love you," and closed the door behind me.

Julie sat on the sofa, folding towels while she watched the news.

"Would you like some help?" It sounded more like a token offer than I meant it to. But then if I hadn't meant it that way, I would have just sat on the sofa next to her and started folding without asking.

She looked at the basket at her feet. "Not many more. But thanks for offering. Besides," she picked up a stack of folded kitchen towels, "you need to get some sleep."

I drove home, walked straight to my bedroom, showered, and without even bothering to blow dry my hair, went straight to bed. I had a new voicemail, but it wasn't from Vince. The one person I probably should have called first, I didn't call at all. It was the second phone call from the strange number. Maybe someone calling about catering. I pressed play.

"Hi, Caryn. This is Gavin. I called earlier, but just now figured you didn't recognize the number. I told David I wanted to talk to you about catering menus. Which I partly do, but I'll

254

explain later. I have a deposition in Houston, so I'll call when I'm back in the office. Have a good evening."

David thought Gavin wanted to talk to me about catering. And he does. Partly. If all gay men were this confusing, I was going to need a beginner's class.

# 36

David and I made a pact to limit deep moral and philosophical discussions to every other day. Fortunately for him, that was before my meltdown at Julie's last night.

At the moment, our most harrowing conversation required deciding dry cleaners versus washing. Over half of what I thought should go into the wash stack, David vetoed.

"Now I understand how you get by with that grown-up Fisher-Price washer and dryer stacked on each other," I said as I jammed button-downs, polos, jeans, khakis, and assorted pants into a canvas duffle bag. "Next month your dry cleaning bill should be light. I doubt you'll have to send one-legged sweats and jeans."

"I have an appointment with Dr. Armstrong next week. Not quite sure what's going to happen with the knee. But I'll get my arm back. By the way," he added sheepishly, "I'm supposed to be doing these. Max reminded me yesterday."

I looked at the handout. Three of the seven exercises he couldn't do yet because they required lying flat on the floor. Between the two of us, we might be able to get there, but he'd have to stay there until Max came home. "This paper said these should start after surgery. Are you telling me you haven't done any of these?"

"No. I've been doing them. So much going on yesterday, I really did forget."

⧓

By the time Max arrived home, David had finished two of the three daily range of motion exercises, the turkey chili had been divided into containers and frozen, and David asked the four people who wanted to visit if they could come another day.

Max landed in the chair as if a giant hand had pushed him in it.

"Do you want something to drink before I leave? I made a pitcher of sweet tea and one of unsweet," I shoved my feet into my sandals before I tripped on them on the way to the kitchen.

He locked his fingers, put his hands behind his head, and closed and opened his eyes in one long blink. "You know you're in the South when you get two options for tea."

"Where are you from then?"

"Originally, here. Lived in Texas, California, New York for a long while, then moved back." He closed his eyes again for a few seconds, and when he opened them looked as if he hadn't quite made it back from wherever he'd gone. "Sometimes the smallest of things make the biggest difference." Max took a deep breath. "Yes. I'd love a glass of sweet tea," he said and sat straight in the chair, slapped his hands lightly on the armrests, and leaned forward to talk to David. "So . . . let me tell you about these nutcase clients of yours . . ."

I poured the tea and added a sprig of mint from stems I cut that grew out of the neighbor's yard and into David's. Hearing the laughter between him and my brother, I considered that I didn't know much about him. But, I hadn't asked. I still felt uncomfortable when they were together, so I was glad Max had somewhere to go everyday. It wasn't that I didn't like him. I did. But I knew when I shut the door behind me, they'd be Max and David, the couple in love. And I didn't know what to do with that.

⸎

As I backed out the driveway, I glimpsed Max.

"Caryn! Caryn, don't leave yet." he trotted down the steps. "Glad your window was open and you heard me."

He crossed his arms on the window opening so we were face-to-face. "David and I talked about the schedule for this week. If you can make it work, being here everyday would help tremendously. We don't want to interfere with your time with Ben, so I'll do my best to get back by late afternoon."

"I'll ask Julie if she can still help out. Ben's already trying to work me over to get him out of school a day so he can come with me. As long as I'm home in time for supper with Ben, it should be good." I'd not been this close to Max's face or had reason to, and I saw the faintest hint of a scar right above his left brow.

"We appreciate everything you're doing. Plus I know you're still not sure about . . . things . . . but you show up anyway."

I wondered if David had the same insight about my being there as Max and just didn't say anything. In one way, it was a relief to know Max sensed my discomfort. I didn't want my standoffishness to be interpreted by David or Max or their friends, like Gavin, as my being the Ice Princess.

He patted the roof of the car. "You be careful going home. And tell Ben that was a great card he made for his uncle."

"Thanks, Max. I'll see you tomorrow."

The entire time I spent with my brother. I didn't allow myself to think about last night's email fiasco. But the angst hovered in the car waiting for me. I hoped Julie worked out a plan because I had nothing.

## 37

Remember last night when we talked about a plan for your email, and options for what you could say?" All Julie needed to match her tone was a whiteboard and a marker, and we'd be both transported to middle school.

I looked at her as I dumped on the floor the pile of clothes I'd gathered in Ben's room and my bedroom. "You mean, my option as in telling everyone my gay brother was attacked or as in owning my stupidity?" She trailed behind me to the laundry room where I threw a load of towels in the washing machine and tossed Ben's uniforms in the dryer.

"Can you work with me here?" She tightened her ponytail. "I'm going somewhere with this. Really. I am."

"Follow me into the kitchen first." The papers in Ben's homework folder were scattered all over the table. His math assignment for tomorrow involved solving word problems. We were about to tackle: "There are 10 spoons and 9 forks in the silverware drawer. How many pieces of silverware are there in all?" when Nick called to ask Ben if he wanted to go to Dairy Queen. A no-brainer. Unlike the math question Ben would have probably had to answer with, "I don't see my silverware drawer because we always eat at the Pierce's house."

Julie grabbed a Diet Coke out of the refrigerator. "Last night I had to walk you off the ledge, and tonight trying to save your business isn't important? Or am I the only one who remembers that?"

I stacked my son's papers near his backpack. Ran my fingers over his name, his letters like awkward stick figures bumping into one another. "I remember. After spending all day at David's, then finally being able to have a little time with Ben, I guess I'm just not ready . . . I don't know, to have to think that hard? I pulled a tub of cookie dough out of the freezer. Once it defrosted, I could bake a few dozen to bring to Zoe. "I do remember I didn't want my personal life all over the school system."

"Right. And the reason you didn't write the email was you didn't know what to say."

"Julie, let's sit down and you can get to the point. It's late. You're stressing my stress."

"One more thing." She opened a bag of Doritos she found on the island and slid into the chair. "You know that scripture passage from Isaiah, the one about 'a child shall lead them'?"

I looked at her. "Seriously?"

"Guess you don't. He talks about wild and domestic animals being able to live side by side—like a wolf and a lamb, and a leopard and a young goat—how Jesus makes that all possible." Julie paused to finish her chip. "And Isaiah says that little child will lead them. You know how children possess a wisdom and clarity about life that adults don't."

Her hands were as animated as her face, which made listening to her entertaining, but didn't provide me any more information than I had before. She leaned forward. "Ben was that little child. Everything you worried about. Not sending the emails, what to say in the emails. Ben made a way."

I felt the egg salad I had for dinner take flight in my stomach. "Ben knows David is gay? How would he know that? How would he even know what that meant?"

"I'm so glad you're my best friend, and I love you, otherwise, I'd be ready to smack you about now." She paused. "Is everything in your universe going to revolve around David's choice of a partner? Is that it? Is that all David is? If you can't see past that, I'm afraid Ben might not either." She stared over my head for a moment, then looked at me, "And that would make me sad. And I apologize if I didn't handle this right."

"I still don't have the slightest idea what you've been trying to tell me." I stood and tugged my polo shirt down from where it bunched up around my waist. "Can you just say exactly what Ben did? Maybe after I've slept, all this will make more sense to me. " Before I sat again, I grabbed paper towels and handed them to Julie.

She closed the chip bag, wiped her hands, and took a deep breath. "Ben was upset at school, so his teacher talked to him privately. He told her his uncle had been in a terrible accident and you were taking care of him until he could get better. I think he might have said something about David's face being purple. Ben told them how tired you were, so he's doing his homework before you get home, and he's sad that he doesn't know how to help you. So, using your emails to them, Ben's teacher sent emails to your school customers. They wrote that you'd been helping your brother who was seriously injured. They weren't sure when you'd start delivering again, but asked everyone to give you time to sort things out. They've received so many emails they're having to organize all the people who want to help."

She pulled a lumpy brown envelope out of her purse and handed it to me.

"What's this?" Someone had written "To Mrs. Becker and Ben" on the outside.

"Joanie in the front office gave it to me today. I haven't opened it, but she said it's filled with gift cards to restaurants, pizza places, and a few grocery stores. They're from Ben's school and from teachers at some of the others. She said they're expecting more, and some teachers wanted to cook, so they're in the process of coordinating that."

"I'm . . . I . . . I'm overwhelmed. And I'm so sorry. So sorry." I wiped my eyes with the hem of my shirt. "And they're doing all this and they don't even know my brother."

"No, not all of them. But Ben's class does." Julie reached in her purse again. "Remember, David brought them the cupcakes when you forgot." She handed me a framed picture of David and Ben, surrounded by all the kids in the class, each one holding a cupcake."

If shame could bury us, I'd be in the earth's core.

---

"Max, did I give you the grocery list the other day?" I'd stirred the contents of my purse at least five times and still couldn't find it.

He stopped midway in helping David into the front room. "Yes. Yes, you did."

"Why don't you give it back to me, and I'll go to the store. I didn't realize how busy you'd be, and I think David would welcome a chance to have an hour during the day all to himself."

"Is he tired of you already?"

"I'm tired of me already. David's going to go stir crazy. Eventually, somebody needs to figure out how to get him out of the house."

David plopped on the sofa. "The two of you are talking about me like I'm invisible again. I'll be sure and let both of you know what I need and when." He flipped open his Kindle. "Now that I've learned to read a newspaper without it ending up on the floor, maybe I could learn how to make my own breakfast?"

"Are you talking to me, Oscar the Grouch? Why are you such a grump this morning? And I thought Max already fixed you breakfast. He usually does." I looked around. "Where did he go?"

"To the bathroom?" David shrugged. "Sorry. I didn't sleep well last night. My arm hurt. Probably too many of those range of motion tortures. I'm also trying to stretch out the pain meds. How am I going to know the pain's going away if I'm on medicine that masks it?'

"Why don't you stretch out the medicine time during the day when you have more distractions? Then, if you need them at night, you won't feel guilty." I tucked the linen drapes over the front windows behind the tieback. "Look, it's sun. I could get some sand, we could pretend to be on the beach. You could even get a tan if I pulled the chair six inches to the left."

David looked up from the Kindle, shaded his eyes with his hand and squinted. "You know, you can be funny at times. Is it something on loan or are you trying to develop it?" He shot a grin my way. "I like it." He peered out the front door. "What is he doing?"

I joined him in spying on Max, attempting to balance what appeared to be a pastry box, two gift wrapped boxes, his brief-case, and a coffee cup from Starbucks.

"Maybe one of us ought to help him," David laughed.

"Guess that would be me," I said and met him at the bottom of the steps. "You did all this in the time you were gone?"

"Glad I could provide entertainment for the two of you." Max handed me the Starbucks cup. "That's for you. Low fat vanilla latte, no foam, Right?"

"How did you know that?"

"It's on your Facebook page . . . under Favorites."

"You read that? I didn't think anybody ever read those." The awe factor just increased.

"Then why did you write it if you didn't think people were going to read it?" He handed me a set of car keys. "My car is parked across the street. The white BMW. Could you set your cup down, and get the two coffees I couldn't juggle to further amuse you and your brother?"

A few minutes later, the three of us sipped Starbucks coffee and devoured chocolate croissants from the French bakery around the corner. The gifts made themselves at home on the coffee table. "What's the special occasion?" I asked.

David shrugged his shoulders. "It's Wednesday?"

"That's it exactly!" Max handed one wrapped box to me and the other to David. "Happy Wednesday to both of you." He slid his iPhone out of his suit pocket. "Be prepared for pictures!"

David, with a little help from Max, opened his box to a find an iPad in a black leather case monogrammed with his initials. Max hugged him in one of those back-slapping man hugs. I didn't flinch like I thought I would, especially when I realized I'd seen more physical contact between football players on national television.

Max gave me a new iPhone with the promise that he and David could teach me everything I needed to know. "We'll have cell phone school starting with setting it up, which David will conduct as soon as I leave. And pay attention because there might be a test," he said, sounding like one of Ben's teachers.

"I wanted you to help me buy a new phone. I didn't expect you to buy one for me." I appreciated Max's generosity, but I wondered about it as well. He either had an endless stream of cash or endless number of credit cards.

"If you expected it, then it wouldn't be a gift. The surprise is the fun part. Right?"

"Right. Absolutely," I agreed. But my cynical self, the one who looked a lot like Betty White, yammered, *"He could be trying to buy you. Win you over by spending money. Hope you'll accept him because he's just so gosh darned nice. Pretty soon he'll be buying presents for Ben too."*

"Wait," Max said. "You don't like it, do you? I should have asked first. Did I overstep any boundaries here? If I did, I apologize. It hasn't been activated, so it can be exchanged. What do you think, David?"

"Hmmm. Not sure." David hooked the iPad to his laptop.

"Odds are he didn't hear the question," I said to Max. "And, no. It's not that I don't like the phone. I do. Very much. But it's a generous gift, and I just—"

Max's face dropped a bucket of worry. "If it's the money you're concerned about, please don't be. I'm not about to lose all my worldly possessions nor have I mortgaged them. Does that help?"

"It does," I said. I opened the box to check out my new phone. It wasn't even on yet, and I already felt intimidated.

Max gave me the grocery list and said David would help me tour the App Store. "Make sure and download the app that takes pictures of your notes and stores them. And there's a bar scanner too. You can scan items to check prices or, if you just used your last bottle of Tabasco Sauce, you just scan its bar code and—voila—on your list it goes."

If there was a lifetime quota on using the words "wow" or "cool," I came close to reaching it. When Max mentioned cell phone school earlier, I thought he meant it as a joke. Not anymore. I might even need summer school.

Less than ten minutes after Max left for work, he called David, who handed me his phone. "Here, Max wants to tell you something."

"Hey, Caryn. I didn't call your number because I thought you might be trying to set up your new phone. I wanted to tell you I had a present for Ben and totally overlooked it when I was getting things out of my car. Please remind me this afternoon, so I can give it to him."

---

By the time Gavin called later that day, I had learned how to answer the phone without hanging up on the caller.

"What kind of event did you want to talk about having catered?" Something profitable and large, I hoped.

"Oh," he cleared his throat. "I do want to discuss your catering, and I apologize in advance for not telling David the whole story of why I wanted to talk to you. Your brother values your opinion, and I wanted to have some time to explain why I think it's so important for him to file charges against whoever it is who beat him up."

I wandered out the front door and sat on the steps so I could talk without David overhearing. I doubt, though, he paid any attention to what I did because that would have meant punching his ticket out of iPad universe. "David and I already agreed that taking legal action would be overwhelming. I don't think he wants to go through that. And I don't know if there's anything you could tell me that would make a difference."

"I appreciate your honesty, and I promise not to pressure you or David. I thought it might help for us to talk. And, it's a lunch you won't have to cook."

We planned to meet Monday at Mona Lisa's, an Italian restaurant on Royal Street. I immediately started building a wall of excuses as to why I wouldn't support Gavin's desire to take legal action. I owed it to my brother to make sure Gavin's intentions weren't to further his own career by exploiting David. Protecting David from the public meant protecting my name and my catering business too. But Gavin didn't need to know that.

<hr />

"How does it feel to wake up in your own house?" I sat on the edge of Ben's bed after I'd spent a few minutes gently tugging his ear to wake him up.

He opened one eye and peered at me suspiciously before rolling over on his back. "You pulled my ear."

"Yep. I sure did." I pushed his hair off his forehead. "If you want, I can bang pots at the door instead."

"You're weird, Mom." He yawned and rubbed his eyes. "Are you staying home today?"

It might have been a question, but it sounded more like skepticism. Sadly, it didn't surprise me. I didn't blame him for being doubtful. "Actually, no."

"Figured," he sat up and shoved the sheets off his legs.

"Whoa, buddy." I put my hands on his shoulders. "Guess that didn't come out the way I planned. You're not staying home, either. You have a birthday party to go to today."

"Oh, yeah, I forgot. Justin's party at Putt-Putt," he said, his voice flat with disappointment.

"But, before you do that," I paused, "the two of us are using one of the gift cards from your school and going to The Broken Egg for breakfast."

He looked at the ceiling, then back at me. "For real?"

"For really real." I hugged him, grateful he couldn't see the tears in my eyes. I wanted to share his excitement, but his genuine surprise only reminded me of how little of myself I shared with him.

❧

"Are you sure that's breakfast and not dessert?" I asked Ben after the waitress served his Belgian waffle covered with Bananas Foster sauce, whipped crème, pecans, and sliced bananas.

He tasted a spoonful of the topping and, with chef-like seriousness, declared, "Both."

"Yours," he said and pointed at my plate of Eggs Sardou, an English muffin topped with sautéed spinach, artichokes, two poached eggs, and a dollop of Hollandaise and Florentine sauces, "is breakfast, for sure."

"Do you want a taste? You might change your mind."

He wrinkled his nose. "Uh, no. Those eggs look like space ships."

"You know, that sounds like something your dad would have said. He wasn't so crazy about eggs either," I said, leaving out the part where Harrison explained his aversion by detailing the process of a hen laying an egg.

Spending time with Ben that morning, I realized I missed just hanging out with him. Hearing his school stories, laughing with him, and seeing him delight in being important. I resolved that I wasn't going to lose Ben. I didn't want to lose one more man in my life.

❧

After Julie and I dropped Nick and Ben off at Putt-Putt for a classmate's birthday party, we started our mission: finding black boots for Julie.

"I hate when clichés come to life right in front of me," I whined as I followed Julie around ShoeTu Deux.

"What about these?" She held up a black leather mid-calf boot with a leopard cuff. "Hmmm. I'm thinking 'no.' Unless you're embracing your funkiness."

She returned the boot to its match displayed on the center table and patted it. "Good-bye my walk-on-the-wild-side alter ego," she said. "Now what cliché are you talking about?"

"The one about the good ones are either gay or married. The good news of having a gay brother is you don't have to feel awkward with his friends because they're not looking at you as relationship material. The bad news is that you wish some of them would."

"Are we talking about this Gavin guy?" She reached for a black patent platform with a gold heel.

"Yes, and back away from that shoe," I said. "Look, I found these." I held a black suede boot with smocking at the ankle and waved it like a matador waving his red cape in front of a bull.

Julie showed it to the sales clerk who wore a "Sales Specialist" button and platform sandals with enough straps to entertain Houdini for hours. "Size seven?"

We sat on a bench between the boots and pumps and waited. Julie for boots, and me to figure out, after years of telling friends the only dates I wanted were the kind used in fruitcakes, why I'm interested in a man disinterested in women.

"You sure you're not making him gay by association? Are you assuming your brother doesn't have straight friends?"

Miss Gladiator sandals returned with three sizes for Julie to try. "I'll get these ready for you." She opened the first box, pulling out cardboard and paper.

Julie turned to me. "Well?"

"Yes. No. It's stupid, really. I've met the man once and talked to him on the phone once. What am I? Fifteen?" I spied a red satin stiletto shoe with an ankle bow. I wandered over to the display to check the price. It cost more than my mixer, but less than the ravioli maker I wanted. I set it back on the table. "Maybe that 'all gay men are fine dressers' perception's a stereotype. I just don't know any straight men who are that impeccably dressed and well-groomed."

"Metrosexuals," blurted Gladiator sandals.

"What?" The question popped out of both of us at the same time.

"I'm sorry to butt in like that. Sometimes it's hard to pretend you're not hearing a conversation." She busied herself opening another box of boots.

"Metrosexuals? Sounds like *Sex and the City*. And we're talking straight men? Maybe I need to start paying more attention to the Urban Dictionary," Julie said.

"You haven't heard of this either?" I asked Julie.

Julie smirked. "Sure. The subject comes up all the time in carpool line. And you've seen Trey's clothes . . . when he's home, he's frumped out."

"So, explain this term to me," I asked Michelle, our sales person.

She held out the next pair of boots for Julie to try. "Metrosexuals are men who spend time and money on their clothes. Get their hair styled, not cut. My boyfriend gets manicures with me, and he doesn't even care some of his friends think he's crazy. It sort of bothered me at first. But in a weird way, it's like Paul's pretty confident in himself as a man to not be embarrassed or ashamed that he cares about how he looks. He's a fine-looking guy, and if using moisturizer on his face helps him stay that way, what's wrong with that?"

Yes, and who knew I'd get a gender education class at the shoe boutique?

# 38

After a volley of phone calls, Lurlene, Washington's assistant, and I finally made voice contact. I caused most of the confusion because I hadn't yet adjusted to the keypad sensitivity of my new cell phone. Invariably, I'd call people I never meant to call, a problem Facebook compounded because I didn't know when my phone synced to it, I'd end up with a list of numbers for friends of friends of friends. Some of the people I needed to talk to, I disconnected in my eagerness to answer quickly when I tapped the phone too many times. David continued to reassure me I'd make it over the learning curve.

Washington insisted I needed to visit the venue before I met with him and his wife a few weeks later. Since I passed the place daily on the way home, I arranged an appointment the next day. I left David's house early, asked Julie if she'd hold on to Ben another hour, and drove up to find him waiting at a wrought iron arch flanked by tall gas light poles.

I didn't see Lurlene. She was probably already inside sniffing for bombs or WiFi.

"So glad you could meet me today, Caryn." He shook my hand, but his eyes soaked in the rest of me. Which, because I knew I'd be meeting Mr. Make My Skin Crawl, I packaged in khaki pants and a long-sleeved black tee. About as appealing to the eye as cardboard to the mouth.

"Lurlene told me it was important," I flashed my all-purpose, one size fits all smile. "Is she inside? She mentioned she might be here." I wanted to meet the woman who tolerated The Ogler.

He glanced at his watch, "She's probably boarding her plane about now. Gave her a week off to spend time with her momma in Dallas."

See, Caryn, there is clean water underneath that oil slick. "That's kind of you, Mr. Washington. I'm sure she appreciated that," I said as he extended his hand toward the courtyard and motioned for me to, of course, walk ahead of him.

The building design was reminiscent of wrought iron balconied homes in the Vieux Carre. A wall built of old St. Joe bricks surrounded the courtyard entrance. The courtyard, a long rectangle, had a fountain in the middle, a few benches along the interior, and a garden on each end. Impressive and already a notch above the other places available.

Washington rang the doorbell to the left of the leaded glass doors.

"She better appreciate it. I told her she needed to take time off now because once the campaign started rolling, no more trips unless it's to the bathroom. I've already informed Big Lurlene if she wants to see her daughter, she can fly here."

Guess there's more oil on that slick than I thought. "Well, so Lurlene is named after mother."

He shook his head. "She sure is. I asked my sister why she passed on that name to her own daughter when she hated it growing up herself. She said it would make her strong like it did her. Me? I think it's keeping her single. Know what I mean?" He winked.

I knew exactly what he meant, and I'm certain so did his niece. Maybe she tolerated him for the same reasons I did. Future payoff.

"Lovely, isn't it?" The man who must have opened the doors, but who became invisible in the drama, waved us in. "Welcome to Fontainebleau."

Both doors opened, creating the exact effect intended—a gasp of surprise at the gleaming oak of the wide grand staircase that started with curved wood railings, then a landing, then split in each direction and rejoined on a balcony with iron railings cast with fleur-de-lis designs. The marble floor looked like a frozen lake of melted caramels swirled in white chocolate.

"Thanks, Tommy, for meeting us today." Washington patted him on the shoulder.

"Happy to help you, Mr. Washington," Tommy said, who appeared about the same age as David minus the broken nose and yellowy complexion. He wore a V-neck sweater the color of plums over a steel gray round necked T-shirt, faded black jeans and loafers. While I measured him with my new metrosexual yardstick, he and Washington exchanged "how's the family" pleasantries.

Washington's hand on my back interrupted my assessment.

"Caryn, this is Tommy Arceneaux, owner of The Fontainebleau. Tommy, meet Caryn, the little lady I told you about."

I swallowed my irritation at his introduction, looked Tommy in the eye, and hoped my firm handshake conveyed the rest.

As Tommy toured us through the facility, the story of the two men meeting as members of the same Mardi Gras parade organization unfolded.

"Last year was Tommy's first year riding. Had to teach the new dog old tricks." Washington slapped him on the back.

Tommy flinched as if a stranger just bumped into him. "My man, here, is throwing out those long pearly white beads to just anybody in the crowd." He shook his head, a lot like Julie did when she saw me using a hand-held can opener. "So, I showed him how it's done. Picked out one of those girls riding their boyfriend's shoulders. Pointed at her, held out the beads, then made my move." Washington pretended to hold up the hem of his shirt and pull it almost over his face. "When I do that, they know what to show me. I see a pair, they get a pair." He laughed.

Tommy smiled weakly as he ushered us into his office. He arranged two chairs in front of his desk, and then sat down after Washington and I did.

"Yep," said the would-be representative of the people. "I told Tommy that's the beauty of those masks. You get to play, and don't have to pay. My son's going to be riding this year. He can't wait to see all the sights."

What kept me bolted to the chair was the thought of how profitable this contract would be. And the vision of wrapping a pair of those beads around Washington's neck. Unless I misread the distance in Tommy's demeanor, we hitched ourselves to the same coattails.

———— ✺ ————

I called Julie and told her I was on my way home, but I felt like I needed a shower to rid myself of the slime.

"The politician was politically incorrect again? Delicious irony in that."

"I'm avoiding all food references. I already feel sick."

"It's interesting how God connected our moral sensibilities to our stomachs . . . Tell you what, go home, and call me when you get there. You probably do need a shower. I'll walk Ben home. I could use a change of scenery."

I didn't argue.

An hour later, a freshly showered version of myself thanked Julie for delivering Ben. I told her I'd call later with the details.

I ate turkey chili while Ben reviewed his school day for me. The highlights were the A on his spelling test, the B on his state capital test, and the chicken strips for lunch.

"Am I ever going to see Uncle David again?" He broke his chocolate chip cookie in half and dipped one end into his milk.

I handed him a napkin to wipe the trickle of white making its way to his chin. "Of course. I'm working on that, I promise."

"Can we go this weekend?" This dunk wasn't so successful. Half the piece fell back into the glass. "Guess it stayed in there too long." He ate what was left, held up his glass and peered into it. "I can still drink this, huh?"

"Sure, but this weekend we already have plans." I explained Saturday had to be my cooking day, but he could be my assistant if he wanted to. After his pouty shrug, I told him about my conversation with Zoe. When I mentioned the boys wanted to hang out with him, he grinned broadly.

"They remembered me? That's cool." He drank his milk, but he needed a spoon to finish the soupy mix at the bottom of the glass.

"One more surprise." I handed him the bag hanging on the laundry room door. "This is from Mr. Max. Uncle David's friend who you met in the hospital." Calling Max David's "friend" would have to do for now. I rationalized calling Max and David friends wasn't misleading. They were friends, first.

"Did he get me a phone too?" He sounded doubtful, but hopeful.

"No. But I still don't think you'll be disappointed."

He reached in the bag. "Look! It's a Spiderman game for my Wii! Wow. Can I call him and thank him?"

"Why don't you write him a note? I know he would really appreciate that because it's easier to keep than a phone call."

I thought a "but" was about to slip out of his open mouth, Instead, he paused, scratched his head, and said, "I'll do that. Can I play first?"

Usually I insisted the thank-you came before permission to play. This time, I went for the road more travelled. "Sure, as long as I have it for tomorrow."

"Thanks, Mom." Ben kissed me on the cheek and off he went.

I cleared the table and carried everything to the sink. I turned on the faucet, waited for the water to almost burn my fingers. Haven't talked to you in a while, Harrison. *But then I see you everyday in the face of our son. And now I have to figure out how I'm going to tell him about his Uncle David.* I wanted to drag my pillow in the closet and sleep on the floor just so I didn't feel so lost in the space that constantly surrounds me.

# 39

I forgot how much I loved this place," I told Gavin as I looked around at the various portraits of Mona Lisa covering the walls of the restaurant named after her. Tucked away on the quiet side of Royal Street, Mona Lisa's unapologetic funky, dim lighting no matter what time of day, and generous portions of hearty Italian meals contributed to its popularity.

"When was the last time you were here?" Gavin lowered his menu long enough to make eye contact.

"Six years ago? Maybe longer. A couple of months after Harrison died, three of my friends thought a girls' night out would be entertaining. We're all fancied up walking down Bourbon Street and so totally out of our element. Every barely dressed and over-served young person who passed us—some didn't even pass us, they were just passed out—one or more of us would say, 'If that was my son or daughter . . .' like we were authorities on the subject of teens gone bad. All of us had kids under the age of five. What did we know? We were looking for a place to eat, and I had been here a few times with David, so we landed here."

I quickly ducked behind my own menu when I felt puddles forming in my eyes and that same irrational sadness I experienced like when I was pregnant. Mourning over Ross and Rachel's breakup on *Friends* or crying when I couldn't find the dryer sheets. Instead of being a funny, fond memory, it became pathetic and sad because it reminded me of how long it had been since I found myself in the company of adults —Cyndi Lauper's right—sometimes girls just want to have fun.

The waiter came, and I composed myself long enough to order the spinach lasagna. Gavin ordered the Mardi Gras linguine with shrimp and sausage. As he took our menus, the waiter said, "Thanks, Gavin, have it out for you soon."

"You must eat here on a regular basis," I said.

"Once, maybe twice a week. Usually for lunch when I meet clients."

Awkward. Under other circumstances when I met people I'd ask if they were married or had children. No way was I going to bake that political potato. I didn't know how he knew David and Max, so I started there.

"I met Max after a friend told me about his clothing shop. A few weeks later, I saw Max at church, and he introduced me to David. We see each other at Bible study and a group of us hang out at Ray and Linda's during football season. They had a boy two days before the Super Bowl. Poor baby didn't get any sleep that day."

"Harrison and David used to tell me Ben's schedule should rotate around LSU and Saints games. I won't tell you what I told them because I said it, I'm sure, after one of those nights when Ben woke up every two hours."

Gavin's cell phone vibrated on the table. He checked the number. "A call I can make later."

I assumed Ray and Linda were straight, but maybe not. Beyond that, the church thing confused me.

"You'll probably laugh, but I didn't know gay Christians were possible. I didn't know Jews for Jesus were either."

He raised his eyebrows and the hint of a smile appeared.

"Maybe not laugh. But you grinned. But, seriously, I went online and found out there are over 350 links for gay Christian websites. That shocked me."

"Careful, hot plate." The waiter set the two plates in front of us and asked if we needed anything else.

"No. We're good. Thanks, Drew."

I stabbed my lasagna with my fork a few times when I saw Gavin bow his head for a minute before he started twirling his pasta. *Well, there you go, Caryn. That's one small thing you could have been teaching your son.*

While the lasagna cooled, I started n my salad.

"Since you go to church, I guess you think of yourself as a gay Christian, right?"

Gavin starting choking. Or coughing. I wasn't sure which. He held his napkin to his mouth until the hacking subsided, then drank some water.

"You okay? Something go down the wrong way?" I looked around for Drew just in case Gavin had another spasm, but I didn't see him.

"No. Everything's okay. Your question surprised me. But the answer is 'no'."

"You're not a gay Christian? I guess I shouldn't have assumed—"

He laughed and shook his head. "No. You shouldn't have assumed. But what you assumed was that I was gay. I'm a Christian, but I'm not gay."

I'd never blanch vegetables again without thinking of myself in that moment. I felt like I'd just been scalded in boiling water.

"I feel like an idiot." I buried my face in my hands. I looked up when I heard Gavin laugh.

"If you could see your face . . . too bad I couldn't have captured that for Max and David," he said.

"Well, ditto, for you. I thought you were having a heart attack or I'd have to do a Heimlich maneuver, which by the way and for future reference, I'm not expert in, so the outcome might have been iffy."

"Caryn, I understand why you might have connected the dots and ended up in Oz. That's why I represent hate crime victims. We judge people by externals, make assumptions about them. For some people, it ends tragically."

"I'm embarrassed to admit that until those six young men all committed suicide in the same month after being bullied because they were gay, crimes against gays weren't on my radar. But now it's David, and that changes everything."

"I know, and that's why I think you can be the person to help David see how important this is . . . not just to him, but to others who are victimized. Probably 75 percent of all hate crimes go unreported, and men are the targets more than women. I've heard some people say the percentage of crimes against people because of sexual orientation is miniscule compared to the national averages of people murdered." He tapped his spoon on the table, and looked off for a minute. "What are they saying? Those lives don't matter? Too few people were murdered for us to pay attention to them, their families . . . ?"

"David can be stubborn, but do you think he's trying to protect me or me and Ben by not coming out about this? Or is he protecting Max and himself?"

"Not Max. He doesn't need protection. He's about as out as out can be. Every organization he's active in is to support the gay community or to build a bridge to the straight community. As for David, telling you the truth was as difficult for him as admitting it to his fiancée. Maybe more. Now that he's done that, and you're reaching out to him, I don't think he cares who else knows."

"So, that leaves me and Ben. Well, my father, but I know he wouldn't want David to not right a wrong because of him. And, I wouldn't either, really. But I'd be lying if I told you I don't worry about Ben getting teased at school. Or people not hiring me because they'd be one degree of separation from being in contact with a gay person. I've already heard someone in my book club say she won't let her children anywhere near her uncle because 'he's gay and might have AIDS'."

"Then I guess that's what it comes down to. Supporting David means you might have to 'come out' too. I wouldn't be pushing so hard if I felt David didn't have a chance to win. He can identify the attackers, at least one or two of them, since they met at the door at some point."

I ate a bite of lasagna without bothering to compare it to my own. Not having to buy it, cook it, or clean after it could make the ordinary taste great. And this was miles past ordinary. What Gavin talked about would require miles past ordinary for me too. I didn't know if I was ready for the trip.

"Caryn, I didn't expect you to decide this today. Pray about it . . . wait, what did I say? You had half an eye roll going on there."

"Pray about it? That doesn't seem to work well for me. College, my husband, now this. But the really funny part is, David is the one who kept telling me to not give up on God. That God hadn't given up on me. He invited me to his church or at least the one he and Lori used to attend. I even went a few times."

"I missed the funny part," Gavin said, buttered a heel of French bread.

"The gay man God condemns leads the straight person into church? I can even see God's sense of humor in that one."

"Not all churches and not all Christians think God condemns gay people. You already know that if you've spent any time on the Gay Christian Network. I may be overstepping a boundary here, but I don't think David would want you to use his being gay as a reason to stay away. It hasn't kept him out of church." He relocated a shrimp to the other side of his plate and then looked up again. "I apologize if I sounded critical, especially after you opened up to share what you did. Here's another funny part. I wonder if we well-meaning Christians sometimes keep out of church the very people we want to see in there." He shrugged. "I just want to do the right thing for David. For me, that means I pray. For you, however you think through these kinds of decisions, I just want you to be sure."

An odd thought formed in the back of my brain: this store is open for browsing. It's so wrong to think this when you're engaged in this serious discussion about your brother. For just a moment, I realized I didn't have to look at this intense and attractive man with my nose pressed against the glass like I did when I gazed at diamonds in Tiffany's. He was available, and I was okay with shopping.

---

As soon as I walked in the backdoor, I started my rant. "David Collins, get your nose out of that iPad. I don't even have to see through these walls to know you're on it. I have a little matter to discuss with you. And if you weren't already in a big mess of broken, I'd be tempted to take it outside." I stopped as soon as I saw David. He was reading the newspaper. "What are you doing?"

"Olympic arm-wrestling. What do you think?"

He answered without moving the paper.

I stepped over and whopped the middle of the newspaper down until I saw his face. He stayed serious for about 2.3 seconds, then laughed almost convulsively. "I'm sorry. I'm sorry. It's just too perfect."

"You already know?" I sat on the other side of the sofa.

"Gavin called as soon as you left Mona Lisa's. He thinks maybe he ought to buy fewer clothes at Max's." He stopped to wipe his eyes from his laughter hangover. "Now he's wondering how many of his clients might think the same thing." He leaned over and pushed my shoulder. "Come on. It is funny. I don't remember the last time I hurt from laughing so much."

"So happy to entertain you." I tried to sound angry, but hearing David I couldn't help but laugh myself. "But David, honestly, why didn't you tell me?"

"Because it never occurred to me you'd think every man who walked in my house must be gay too. Why would you think that?"

"I've only been here when Gavin was here. And he seemed to fit the profile . . ."

"Oh, so you're gender profiling now? Not all gay men dress nicely, they don't all decorate, they don't all like Cher or Streisand or Lady Gaga. . . . Well, maybe almost all. I'll have to think about that one. They're not all Adam Lambert, and they don't wear boas . . . unless there's a costume party somewhere."

"Maybe I need to be enrolled in Introduction to Gay 101 along with cell phone school."

"If you ask, I'll give you a crash course because you, my dear," he patted my hand, "have terrible gaydar."

He didn't ask too many questions about anything we talked about outside of my grand discovery of Gavin's straightness. I know I needed to bring up the subject of filing charges, but today I felt like David and I had a breakthrough. We talked about being gay and laughed. Together.

———— ∞ ————

After my lunch with Gavin, I drove home without the usual noise of talk radio and thought about prayer and how important it seemed to him in making the right decision. The right decision for David.

If I could talk to Harrison in my head, then it wasn't so impossible for me to believe that I could have these same conversations with God. After all, they hung out in the same place, so it wasn't even a different area code.

My prayer experience was Santa God prayers. "Here's my list God, arranged in order of preference. I'll be waiting." And that was exactly what happened. I waited for the answers on my list. If God chose to answer with His list, then I still considered my prayer unanswered.

This idea of praying for someone else? Radical. I didn't know what might be on someone else's list. I didn't know what was best for that person. I know for certain that I wouldn't want anyone going to Santa God pretending to know what would be on my list. God already had His own list. Which meant if He had a list for someone else, then He had one for me too.

In wanting the decision to be right for David, God was teaching me about myself too.

# 40

Ben, it's time for us to leave to go to the Goldstein Center."
I stood at the door of Ben's room trying not to think of the dangers that lurked in the carpets I hadn't vacuumed in months. Or what treasures were shoved under my son's bed. Earlier, Ben and Nick had invited Sean over and the three were playing Madden football. I gave a cursory glance at the new friend. All I knew about him was that his family moved from here from Chicago a few weeks ago. They bought the Billings' old house a few doors down, and he was in Ben's class. He seemed a bit rough around the edges, like nine on his way to juvi . . . something about his slouch and no eye contact.

Obviously, since Nick and Sean kept playing Madden football, they didn't get the message our leaving meant they needed to leave too. "Okay, guys, thanks for coming over, but we have somewhere to go," I said.

Ben held up the Spiderman Wii game from Max. "Can I bring this?"

"Of course," I said and walked away. Two steps later heard, "Dude, you have Spiderman? That's so gay." It might have been the first time I knew what it meant to "turn on a dime." I stepped into the room and asked, "Who said that?" I already knew Sean did, but that was part of the test.

"Me," Sean said without hesitation. "That Wii game's gay."

"You've never been to our house before, but just so you'll know, we don't say that here. We don't use the word 'gay' like that."

He looked at Ben and Nick and then back at me. "Like what?"

"To mean 'stupid.' Because when you use it that way, it means 'stupid.' I don't think you would want me to say, 'Oh, that game's so like a boy who just moved here from Chicago.'"

"Whatever," he said. "I'm leaving now. See ya." Before the boys could answer, he walked out the door.

After we dropped Nick off on our way to Zoe's, Ben said, "Mom, when did we have a rule about using the word 'gay' like that?"

"Right after I heard Sean say it."

---

We walked through the front doors of the Goldstein center, and the young man sitting at the desk said he'd page Zoe.

"You're the lady who brought those desserts over at Thanksgiving. We were hoping you would come back for Christmas. Or Hanukkah." He grinned as he picked up the phone and said Zoe's name.

"I planned to, but we had an emergency in the family."

"My uncle got in a bad accident. So, my mom's been taking care of him. And he has a friend named Max, and he's helping too. He bought me this game." Ben handed it to him. "My name's Ben."

He looked at the game, then handed it. "Hi, Ben. My name is Dennis. Very nice gift from your uncle's friend. I think everybody needs friends like Spiderman. Don't you?"

"My friend said the game was gay. But my mom told him we can't use that word in our house."

Dennis leaned on the counter with his arms crossed in front of him, and when he looked at me, I thought his eyebrows crossed too. "Really? And why is that?"

"Cuz it means stupid."

Oops. Something got lost in translation. "Ben, I didn't mean the word 'gay' was stupid. I meant Sean shouldn't use the word to mean that something's stupid."

"I'm confused. Then what should it mean?"

Dennis cleared his throat. "Oh, look, Mom, here comes the cavalry."

Sam and Eli walked up, and one of them said, "Ready to ditch your mom and have some fun?"

"Sure!" Ben said, then turned to me. "Sorry, Mom."

I squeezed his shoulder. "Hey, don't be. I'm ditching you, too. See?" I pointed to Zoe who'd just arrived.

He grinned. "Funny."

"See you later, Ben's mom," said the other, and they left.

"Well, that didn't work out like I planned," I said to Dennis, and wished I had an app that made me invisible.

"So I heard." He pushed his bangs off his forehead. "I know you didn't ask me, but maybe you should define the word for him before someone else does."

---

We sat outside in one of the garden areas where brick walls on three sides and fountains made it peaceful and private.

"It's too bad you have to be old or ill to live here. I felt like twenty pounds of stress fell off my shoulders just walking through here." I kicked off my shoes and leaned back on the lounger.

"You know, we used to try to figure that out, then it occurred to me Ethan had the same effect on people. He was peaceful, and gentle, and yet even those qualities wrapped themselves around a quiet strength. Ethan's spirit lives on through this place. I'm grateful God has blessed us with that, and I don't try to question it anymore." She reached out to pat my hand. "So, tell me about your brother."

I told her everything from when David first called me until now, and how I struggled still trying to adjust to this new David and my confusion with church and how to tell Ben. "I don't know how to be the sister of a gay brother. When I'm with Max and David, I'm fine until I remember that they're not just two guys hanging out. They're partners. And then I start thinking about what that means, you know, in practical terms."

"I do know. I told Ethan once I didn't like thinking of my brother in bed with another man." She laughed. "He looked at me and said, 'Good, don't. Why would you want to think about that? I don't think about you and your husband in bed.'"

"True." I sat with the sense of that for a moment. Across from me, water cascaded from a trio of antique earthen pitchers. If only I could spill out myself as easily. I watched the water falling and said, "But then I also know the reason I can be comfortable around Max and David is that they aren't physically affectionate in front of me. Harrison and I didn't think anything of holding hands or putting our arms around one another or kissing each other hello. I don't know if I can handle that, and I don't know if I have the right to ask them not to show any affection for each other when I'm there."

"Just be honest. Tell David that. I learned with Ethan we could agree to disagree and still love each other. But, on the other side of that, I came to recognize that I wouldn't always feel comfortable. You learn to live with your *un*comfortableness. Besides, the number of straight people who make me uneasy far outweighs the gay ones."

I thought about Washington's "ick" factor and my level of discomfort with him, which I tolerated because I could benefit financially. "Yes, I get that too."

Zoe wandered over to adjust a cluster of irises whose blooms had tipped into a nearby fountain and looked like they were lapping the water.

"And you need to be honest with Ben. I don't think he needs anatomy and psychology courses. Ed and I don't have children, at least not yet, so it's not like I'm an authority. But I'd start by explaining to my own child how some people are born with brown eyes, some with green, and some people with blue eyes." She paused and let the water cascade over her hand. "Even in the same family, different children can have different eye colors. You don't choose eye color. It just is. And blue-eyed people fall in love with brown-eyed ones. Sometimes two green-eyed people fall in love. So sometimes a girl and a boy love each other, sometimes a girl and a girl love each other, and sometimes a boy and a boy love each other."

Though I knew her analogy would be easy to understand, I didn't know how easy it would be for me to be the one to explain. "I think Ben's more resilient than I am. More than I give him credit for." I watched a sparrow hop around the fountain, peck at the water and then fly off. "I give him lots of practice."

Drying her hand on her linen slacks, Zoe sat back, hugged her knees to her chest. "I didn't want my friends to know my brother was gay. In some weird way, I thought it defined who

I was too. Then, when I told them, I was suddenly supposed to be some authority on Gay Nation. Should gays get married? Should they have children? Be open in the military? At first, I tried to be the expert witness, and go in armed with statistics and research. Finally, when I heard about Matthew Shepard and read about other hate crimes, I realized I didn't have to be an authority on anything except loving my brother."

"I'm embarrassed to admit that I don't know much about Shepard or any other hate crimes."

Zoe stretched out, and said, "Come with me."

We walked to her office where she opened a file her laptop She stood near me as I read about Matthew. A 21-year-old University of Wyoming student, he had been pistol whipped, tortured, had fractures at the back and side of his head, severe brain damage, lacerations on his head, face, and neck, and tied to a fencepost, and found eighteen hours later. An African-American man, James Byrd, was tied to the back of a truck, dragged and decapitated. Another man was beaten with nail-studded two by fours and kicked with steel-toed boots until he died. Another beaten, stabbed twenty times, and his throat slit.

"I can't read anymore." I shut the laptop and wished I could shut out the images reeling through my brain. I couldn't stop thinking about my brother. The anger, disgust, and sadness roiled inside me, left me speechless.

Zoe pulled a chair near mine. "I know. I know," she murmured. What I felt in my soul I saw reflected in her eyes.

"It took eleven years after those two men murdered Matthew for the Hate Crimes Prevention Act to be signed into law. What happened to David is unconscionable, but it could have been so much worse. I hope the people who did this to him can be brought to justice. Unfortunately, the crime that killed Ethan wasn't so much hate as it was rejection, intolerance."

"What do you mean?" How could she say dying of AIDS was related to rejection?

"When he first told my parents, my father said he just hadn't slept with the right woman. He told me and I just couldn't understand how this muscular, attractive, intelligent man could be gay. A few weekends later, Ethan and a group of his friends, none of whom knew he was gay, went on a drinking binge in the quarter. He told us later that he spent a considerable sum of money sleeping with women. One of them was HIV positive. How's that for irony? My gay brother died from AIDS because he slept with a woman."

# 41

I need you to listen to me with your heart and your head and not talk until I'm finished."

"You *were* serious about this being a serious discussion," David said, a hint of humor in his voice.

I opened my mouth and almost dispensed a typical sisterly response, but I managed to contain my sarcasm behind a firewall in my brain. That I didn't respond with the expected comeback would speak volumes about my intention here. And I could see the acknowledgment of that in David's eyes.

"I know how much you love your nephew. Fiercely. No one, with the exception of his father, cherishes him the way you do. In fact, you've been like a father to him. When you first came out and I ignored your calls, Ben suffered. He missed you, and no matter what I did, I couldn't make his sadness disappear. And I want you to know that I was wrong. That even if I couldn't find a way to reach out to you, I should not have stopped Ben."

David held up his hand. "Stop. Did something happen to Ben?"

"And if something did . . . like being bullied at school . . . what would you do?"

He shifted on the sofa. "I hope this is a hypothetical, Caryn, because if you're trying to soften the blow of someone being cruel to Ben, then don't. Tell me exactly what happened because you know I will do everything in my power to protect him. And if kids at school are being mean, someone needs to stand up for him. No kid deserves to be bullied."

"I could count on you to defend him, right?"

I saw the tightness in my brother's face, the way he clenched his teeth and how his chin jutted forward, and I knew he would be angry. In fact, I counted on it. "Are you really asking me this stupid question? I don't understand why you'd even need me to answer it."

I took a deep breath. "I know you're mad, confused, maybe even ready to go wreak havoc on whoever was responsible for causing someone you love to endure that kind of pain. Nothing's happened to Ben, but this happened to you . . ."

He held up his hand. "Stop. You manipulated me by pretending someone hurt Ben to make a point?"

"I . . . I didn't see it as manipulating you."

He glared at me.

"Okay, maybe I did. I wanted you to see that your being attacked is the adult version. And that anger you felt is what those of us who love you feel as well. If you would do anything to protect your nephew and to make sure whoever caused him hurt would have to take responsibility for that, then you understand why people you love would do the same for you."

"Are you talking about pressing charges? Is that what all this is about?" He threw his hands up in the air. "I can't believe you're sitting here with your self-righteous indignation after agreeing with me that I shouldn't."

"You're absolutely right. And I'd be mad at me too. Actually I am angry at me. I wasn't totally honest with you about my reasons for not wanting you to pursue criminal charges. But then, I'm suspecting you weren't either."

His eyes narrowed. "What does that mean?"

"I think you wanted to protect us—me, Max, Ben, Dad—because you knew you couldn't do it without fallout. And maybe, a little bit afraid because of the 'what if' monster. What if we do all this and the thugs walk away? What if we do all this, and I'm afraid to relive this experience? How can I be sure, if they don't walk away, that there won't be retribution somewhere down the line?"

"And what weren't you honest about?"

This was a moment of truth for me, but one I'd rather not have to look David in the eyes to say. But I couldn't expect courage from him and be a coward myself. "If you press charges, then you're out. To everyone. My friends. Ben's friends. Dad's friends. And I've worked so hard to build my business. I wasn't sure how much I could risk. And, I'm still not sure. But you don't deserve the indignity and pain you suffered for no other reason than because you're gay. If someone from one political party physically attacked another simply on the basis of how that person voted, the public would be outraged."

I sat next to him on the sofa and held his hands. "I love you. Ben loves you. And the two of us want you around for a very long time. You should be able to live your life without fear of losing it just because you aren't hiding who you are. Your courage could save someone else's brother or sister or son or daughter. I want you to think about it. Talk to Max. Pray. I'm not *behind* you on this one, David. I'm right beside you."

---

Once David decided to pursue charges, I knew I couldn't postpone my talk with Ben. If he was going to hear about his uncle and Max, he was going to hear about it from me first.

We were on our way home from shopping for new pants for Ben. He grew out of the ones he started school with before the year ended. I said what I hoped was a prayer and decided to open the discussion about David.

"Ben, remember the day Sean came over and said your Spiderman game was gay?"

He looked up from his Game Boy. "And you said gay doesn't mean stupid?"

"Right, that day. Do you know what gay means?" I glanced at him to gauge his reaction. None. He hadn't lifted his head from his game. "Ben, did you hear me?"

"Yes, I heard you. I'm not sure what gay means. I just hear kids at school say it sometimes. All I know is what it doesn't mean."

I avoided the interstate thinking traffic lights and stop signs would extend the time we spent in the car. I learned a long time ago cars could be great places to have a serious discussion, provided it's not one that angers the driver.

Waiting for the signal light to turn green, I drummed my fingers on the steering wheel and wondered how to transition from gay doesn't mean stupid to your Uncle David is gay.

"One time I heard you call Uncle David gay," Ben said and kept pushing game buttons.

The horn blaring from the car behind me reminded me to pay attention to the traffic light, which had obviously turned green. I was about to turn green with it. "You did? When did you hear that, Ben?"

He shrugged. "I dunno. A long time ago. I just figured you meant he was doing something dumb."

"Oh. So, why didn't you say something after Sean came over. When you knew it didn't mean that?"

"Guess I just forgot. Why?"

"I want to explain to you what gay means, and I need you to stop playing and listen. With both ears."

"Okay. Is it going to take long because I have to go to the bathroom?"

I found a McDonald's, pointed the bathroom out to Ben, and ordered two chocolate shakes. With whipped cream. We sat at a table, and I related Zoe's story about people with different color eyes and how sometimes boys and girls love each other or girls and girls or boys and boys.

He didn't say anything when I finished talking. He sucked up the last smidgen of his shake, looked out the window, then back at me. "So, Uncle David and Max love each other."

"Yes."

"Like you and Dad loved each other."

"Yes."

He looked outside again before he turned back and asked, "Are they going to have kids?"

Now it was my turn to stare out the window for a bit. "You know, I don't know. They would have to adopt one, but I don't know if they will."

"Okay. Are we going home now?"

I sipped what was left of my shake. "We can. So, you understand?" I must have forgotten something. This did not unfold as I expected.

"Yeeesss."

My kid was patronizing me.

"Uncle David and Max love each other. And I love Uncle David and Max. I got it. That was simple, Mom."

I laughed. "You're right. It was simple." So simple. What was that Julie said about a child leading?

Could that be what God was up to?

# 42

"Fasten your seatbelts," Gavin told us.

The day David called Gavin to tell him he was ready to go forward with the lawsuit, Gavin called me, David and Max and set up a meeting at his office.

"As soon as the suit's filed, there's going to be publicity, especially in an election year. Under no circumstances should you talk to anyone in the media. Refer everyone to me. Don't say anything to anyone outside of this room that you wouldn't want on the evening news or the front page of the paper. Nothing on Facebook, Twitter, blogs, or any social networks on the Internet."

He gave us a rundown of what we could expect, then told us not to hesitate to call him with questions or concerns. "We all know the potential this has for some politicians to make names for themselves, so don't get sucked in to their rhetoric. This is also going to be pulpit material in many churches— some supporting David, some not."

We didn't have to wait long. Sidney Washington's response to David's lawsuit almost preempted the article in the newspaper. Of course, being a political candidate he parlayed it into an opportunity for coverage, press releases, and any other attention he could lasso with his rope of influence.

When interviewed about the lawsuit, Washington said the percentage of hate crimes has been over exaggerated, and the resources required to pursue these cases would be better spent on crimes that affect a majority of the population. "Gays and the like," he said, "are rips in the fabric of society. And they need to be repaired. Meaning that if gay people choose that lifestyle, then they're capable of not choosing it."

He said the gay agenda would take over and destroy America and that it started in the schools with things like anti-bullying campaigns. "All that's just a cover, a gateway to sneak homo-sexual promotion in the schools. Do we really need hate crime laws? Isn't a crime a crime? Why do these people think they need special protection?"

Alongside Washington's rant was a brief interview with Pastor Vince who said the Hate Crimes Protection Act was a response not simply to violence, but to the brutality and often torture of men and women simply on the basis of gender or race or religion.

Vince shared that *Love Is an Orientation* by Andrew Marin helped him understand the need for the church to elevate the conversation beyond the orientation of gender to the greater orientation of love. "Marin said, and I quote, 'Love is not just a word. It's a measureable expression of one's unconditional behaviors toward another.' I know not all pastors will agree with me. But I think if young men and women are reaching out and wanting to learn about Jesus, who am I to say no? Look who Jesus hung out with. And he never made repentance a pre-condition to love."

Julie came over the day the news about the lawsuit appeared in the paper. "I wanted to tell you how proud I am of you. I know there's so much you're still struggling with, but if it helps, I see you living out what Jesus told us to do. He said we should love one another. Period. Love one another followed by a period. Not a comma, not a semicolon, not a question mark. If I do that, just love His people, I can let Him take care of the rest."

# 43

My routine expanded to include driving David to physical therapy and appointments with Gavin. I looked forward to going with him to Gavin's office and, unless I misread straight men too, he seemed happy to see me. David even noticed and hidden somewhere in his, "I like the way you're paying more attention to yourself," comment was a compliment waiting to happen.

The ever-honest Max on my last arrival to pick up David, scanned me and asked, "When did you start substitute teaching?"

"What? I didn't."

"Well, then stop dressing like you did. Next thing you know, you're going to show up here wearing a jumper with dancing pencils."

"A denim skirt and a cardigan. Is that bad?" I adjusted my skirt, made sure the zipper hadn't spun around to the front.

David laughed. "Lighten up on her Max. She's never seen your shop. Or maybe you could just take her shopping."

"It's not enough that I'm enrolled in cell phone school and Introduction to Gay 101, now I have to have a wardrobe consultant?"

"Possibly. But we'll wait until brother David over there can walk faster because we might have to do something about that hair while we're at it."

I recognized that crazed look. I'd seen it on hairdressers when you sit in the chair and say, "I'm tired of making decisions. Just do something."

"David, let's go before I'm undergoing liposuction and permanent eyeliner." Neither one of which I would've minded.

———⊶⊷———

I'd started delivering meals again, but told everyone I'd have to stay at one a week for the next few months. Since I had no idea who had contributed to the "brown envelope" of gift cards, I had sent an email blast to everyone on the list thanking them for their generosity. Having them gave Ben and me time together going out to eat and meant fewer trips to David's to deliver meals, though we often ended up there on weekends so he could visit his uncle.

I planned to spend a marathon cooking day on Saturday morning, but Ben begged to spend time with David and Max. I let Ben pick out a dessert, but I explained that since I planned to cook, we couldn't stay long.

I noticed a few more cars than usual, but they could have been there for the neighbors. I really hadn't met too many of David's friends, and I wasn't sure I was ready to. But, I couldn't back out now.

We weren't even up the steps when I heard yells and whoops that could only mean one thing: football. Max, David, Gavin, and an assortment of people were watching an afternoon game. They introduced me to the neighbors from across the street, Phil and Ariel, and another couple, Mitchell and Paul. Ben announced that he brought carrot cake, passed it off to me, then wedged himself on the sofa between Max and David. "What's the score?" he asked, and plunged his hand into a bowl of popcorn Max held without taking his eyes off the television.

Getting Ben to leave was like asking me to leave a live cooking demonstration by John Besh or Paul Prudhomme. After a few attempts, interspersed with Ben begging to stay, Gavin offered to bring him home.

David and Max looked at each other and nodded, and I could have punched them both. "Caryn, let him stay here. He hasn't had a chance to hang out with the guys," David said.

"Really, he'll be fine. I don't mind taking him home," Gavin said.

I shouldn't have been that excited to leave my son, but I knew it was knowing that I'd spend time with Gavin that made me sing along with the radio on the way home.

———— ⚬⟩⟨⚬ ————

When Gavin called that he and Ben were on their way, I had already polished furniture, vacuumed, cleaned the bathroom, spritzed the den with something that said Spring Rain but smelled more like Forest After a Thunderstorm, taken a shower and picked out something I hoped didn't give Gavin images of chalkboards and erasers. After Max's observation of my clothing status, I dropped in at Ann Taylor's and treated myself to a dusty teal silk crossover blouse that accented my waist. I wore it with a pair of black jeans that I found in the back of my closet.

Ben was surprisingly cooperative after he arrived. He went to take his shower without being asked twice.

I was alone with a man in my den. I couldn't remember the last time that had happened when it didn't involve a hospital bed. We sat on the same worn sofa where, all those months ago, I poured out my David story to Julie. And now, because of David, I shared the sofa with Gavin.

He explained Ben had a fast-food stop on the way, so I brewed a pot of coffee and offered Gavin his choice of brownies or cookies. He wanted two of each.

On my way to refill our coffee, Ben reappeared to announce he was going to bed.

"Are you feeling okay?" I placed my hand on his forehead. Voluntary bedtime was not standard operating procedure.

He looked up at me. "I'm fine. Just tired." When I bent closer to kiss him good-night, he whispered, "You don't have to tuck me in tonight, okay?"

On the way to his room, he stopped to thank Gavin. "I had a good time today, Mr. Gavin."

"I did too. We'll have to watch more football games together. I didn't know you knew so much about penalties," he shook Ben's hand. "Good night, Ben."

Ben smiled and walked to his room. I thought I saw him give Gavin a thumbs up, and I wondered if they had planned this performance.

Gavin surveyed the room. "This is a comfortable space." He looked at me. "But then you're easy to be with."

"So, I'm comfortable and easy? Is that how you flatter all your women?"

"Absolutely," he said. "Is it working?"

"Almost. But, we spend too much time talking about my family. I don't know that much about you," I said, and imagined, just for a moment, how soft his lips would feel on mine. What his arms would feel like wrapped around me.

I recovered in enough time to hear him tell me that he was the oldest of three, two boys and a girl, and that he was divorced, no children.

"Most people assume I left my wife. Interesting, the judgments that follow that. Guess that's another one of those skewed perceptions. But she left me. As in emptied the closets, the house, and most of the checking account. She didn't tell me where she went. Then one day the papers came, and that was it. She didn't want to talk, to compromise, to mediate. Nothing. Just wanted out. That was five years ago. She's living in Florida, so we don't even have to face the possibility of bumping into each other."

"You didn't suspect anything? One day you're happy, the next day she's gone?" Gavin didn't strike me as the kind of man who lived in an alternate reality. Even talking about it now, he looked sad.

"I asked myself that question often after she left. What did I miss? I was in law school, and then studying for my bar. I'm sure I was clueless about a lot of things. But then, if someone's unhappy, they shouldn't pretend. Maybe I should have asked more questions. I don't blame her entirely. I wonder, sometimes, if we would have had a chance."

My stomach tightened. "So, are you saying you think you still love her?"

He looked surprised by the question. "Oh, no. That's not what I meant. Whatever I did to fail her in the marriage, I wish I would've known. I want to make sure that history doesn't repeat itself, you know?

"Yes. I do," I answered. "Yes, I do."

# 44

Max called Monday morning and asked if I had time to deliver a package for him.

Strange request, but by this time, I knew Max well enough to know that ordinary wasn't in his vocabulary. "I have a few deliveries lined up for this week; in fact, making a chocolate mousse cake as we speak. Just tell me what and when and where."

"It's David. I need you to deliver David to his therapy appointment on Friday. We're doing inventory at the store, half of my employees are out with some grunge in their systems, and I need to be there. If you could take him that would really help. And the appointment is at nine."

"Sure. I can drop Ben off, unload these desserts, and still deliver the package on time."

I called Gavin to ask if I could stop by his office while David had his physical therapy appointment so he could review my catering contract with Washington.

"That would be fine. It'll be nice to see you."

I loved hearing those words.

———— ⊷⊷⊷ ————

Gavin's office was one of several in a renovated house not far from David's. Most of the people worked solo, so they shared a receptionist. Trudy knew my family by now. "Go on back. He knows you're here already."

I walked in and almost walked into him. Not that I minded; he had to put his hands on my shoulders to steady me. I would've been willing to practice that one again.

"Here, have a seat." He picked up a stack of papers on a chair by his desk. "I want to make sure I don't run you over."

"That wouldn't be so bad. I know a great lawyer who could take my case." I smiled and wished we'd moved pass this awkward stage of not yet ready to kiss when we meet, but beyond the friendly peck on the cheek. I sat and handed him my contract. "How's the case going?"

"Progress. We may have found a witness, but we have to interview her just to be sure. We have composite sketches of the two guys David remembers. We're moving forward, so that's a good thing." He leaned forward on his desk. "Tell me what's going on with Washington."

"I know he's going to connect the dots eventually, if he hasn't already, and figure out David is my brother. I'm thinking he might fire me because of it, but he'd have a contract issue, right?"

Gavin read the contract, his eyes darting back and forth over first one page and then another. He folded the pages and handed them back to me. "Right. You have terms for cancellation. But I think the bigger question is why you're still going to do this job for him when he can't make his feelings about gays any clearer."

"I'm doing this job because the money from this contract is important. I'm a single mother, remember? Not only that.

It's the contacts I can get from this job. He knows people who know people. Where else could I get these referrals? I don't have to like him to take his money." I shoved the contract in my purse.

"No, you don't. But at some point, you need to decide what or who you're willing to stand up for. For some of us, there's a defining point in our lives. A place we draw a line, step over it, and decide we're never going back over it again."

I wasn't expecting a lecture from Gavin. "Are you suggesting I don't care about David?"

"It's not my place to pass judgment on that. Maybe if I tell you why I represent hate crime victims, it'll make more sense."

Gavin told me he was in high school when his older sister Amanda came home from college during spring break and told their parents she was gay. "They offered to buy her a washer and dryer," he said and shook his head. "My parents thought if she had her own, she wouldn't need to move in with the woman she told them she loved. One of those things that, if it wasn't your own family, it would be funny."

I nodded. That I understood.

He eased back in his chair and tapped a pen on the palm of his hand. "Here I was, like most high school kids, totally ego-centric, always worried about my reputation. While my sister told my parents, what I know now is something that required incredible courage, I listened from the kitchen. My first thought was would I make it through football tryouts if the guys on the team know my sister's gay or if they think I'm gay."

"Gay by association? I'm familiar with that one . . . unfortunately." I smiled remembering our lunch. He didn't.

Gavin placed the pen in the pewter holder, leaned forward, forearms on his desk and clasped his hands. He looked at me and continued.

**309**

"My father shouted, my sister shouted back, and my mother refereed. He told my sister she was a disappointment. She could only come home if she stopped sinning, admitted she was wrong. I don't know what she said. I just remember her feet pounding the stairs so fast they sounded like heartbeats. I waked in, tried to talk to my parents, but they refused to discuss it with me. I don't even think she knew I was home."

He stopped, but he looked past me, as if he waited for the pieces of the memory to fall into place. I reached into my purse and silenced my cell phone. A tidal wave of voices in the hall waned as the conversation moved into the office next to his.

Gavin sat back, pressed his fingertips of each hand together, and said, "I walked right past Amanda's closed door to get to my own room. I didn't know what to say. Not so long later, I heard her door open and she trotted down the stairs as fast as she'd gone up them. More shouting and then the backdoor slammed. She was leaving, and I had no idea where she was going. I bolted out of the house to catch her. I wanted her to know I loved her even if I didn't understand. Her Camry was already down the driveway and about to turn onto the highway. I ran down the block and watched as she turned into the wrong lane. She died without hearing that I loved her."

My fingers throbbed from twisting my purse strap as he spoke. I didn't know if I should speak and crack the stillness or let the room swell with it. I shifted in my chair, and when he didn't continue, I said, "Gavin, I'm so sorry." I reached across the desk and let my hand rest on his. "Your parents—"

"My parents never recovered. The tried to keep Vicky, the woman Amanda told them about, away from the funeral. That's when I told them the last memory my sister had of them was their faces as they shouted at her. The least they could do was allow her a peaceful funeral."

He slipped his hand from underneath my own, reached over a stack of files, and handed me a silver picture frame. I didn't need him to tell me that I was looking at Amanda. The same square chin and blonde hair. Taken the day of her graduation, the picture showed a generous smile, but it also captured an unmistakable wistfulness in her eyes.

"My parents died a few years ago, within a year of each other. Truth is, they died inside the same day Amanda did. Her death divided our family. Blame and guilt were all we could share."

# 45

I left Gavin's office, the story of his sister like a fresh throbbing burn on my hand. The more I thought about it, the more it hurt. The pain in Gavin's face when he said, "I watched my sister die because of intolerance. At that moment I decided I wouldn't let that happen again, to anyone," was as difficult to witness as his words were to hear.

I knew my decision to still cater for Washington disappointed him. Maybe surprised him, too. I tried to explain what the job meant for me and for Ben. I could have time to spend with my son because I wouldn't be so frantic about money. I couldn't make him understand Washington was the means to the goal. It was one job. But it could lead to so much more.

He didn't even walk me out like he usually did when David and I were there. I stood up to leave, and he told me he wished me luck and hoped everything turned out the way I expected.

I didn't allow myself to cry until I reached the car, but even then, I held back because I didn't want to have to explain to David why my eyes were puffy and ringed with black.

Days later, Washington stepped up his verbal attacks as the suit gained more publicity and there was speculation that at least two of the attackers could be identified. He suggested David lied about his money and watch being not stolen so he could use the Hate Crime Protection Act for publicity. After Washington's last press conference, I thought I'd have to tie Max in a chair to prevent another crime from occurring. The newspaper reported Washington said, "How do we know that he didn't lure those young men there intending to do *them* harm? Perhaps they were only defending themselves."

Max actually laughed when he heard that. "What an idiot. As if David could, what, immobilize four men at once?"

Every time I heard Washington speak, or I read something in the papers, I tried to pretend the David he was talking about wasn't my brother. I stopped listening to talk radio in the car. Gavin's calls, though infrequent, usually started with some reference to David before we lapsed into casual conversation. But he stopped calling. It's not like we had a relationship, I told myself. If he couldn't understand what I had to do to support my son, then maybe he wasn't someone I should be interested in anyway. Then, I'd think he probably said to himself if I was the kind of woman who could sell out her brother, why should he want to spend time with me.

David called to tell me he'd heard from Lori. She had been following the story in the newspaper, and she wanted him to know we were all in her prayers. "She asked me to tell you she's impressed that you came out, too."

When I didn't respond, David said, "You know she meant that as a compliment."

"I know. I'm glad she got in touch with you. That was probably a difficult call for her to make."

"I agree, and I told her that I admired her for making the effort. I wouldn't have thought less of her if she hadn't called. But the fact that she did said a lot about her character."

"Are you trying to tell me something, David?" I said as I pushed aside containers in the refrigerator looking for a brownie or leftover piece of anything.

"I'm hanging up now. I can't talk to you when you're in one of those moods," he told me. "Call me when you're human again."

———— ⊗⊗⊗ ————

When Julie asked me if I was still going to cater for "the creature," I told her if David asked me not to, I wouldn't. "If it's okay with David, then why is everyone upset with me?"

"What makes you think this is acceptable to David? Because he hasn't said anything? Maybe I know your brother better than you do."

I mentioned it to God, but He wasn't sending much information in my direction.

A few days later, Lurlene contacted me to set up the lunch date with Washington and his wife. I called David to tell him we were meeting to finalize plans for the reception. "But David, if you don't want me to do this, I'll back out."

"Caryn, I'm not going to be your conscience. You have to do what you think is best for you and Ben. I love you no matter what you decide."

Some people complain their families constantly tell them what to do. Me? I'm cursed with a family that expects me to make my own decisions and stand by them.

———— ⊗⊗⊗ ————

I was in my office collecting dinner orders when I heard the front door open and close.

"I'm in the back, Ben. Come tell me about your day."

He didn't dash down the hall with his usual bam-bam-bam of shoes thudding on the carpet. It sounded as if he walked in slow motion and dragged his backpack behind him.

When I saw him in the doorway, I almost bruised myself knocking against the desk and chair to get to him.

"You look terrible. Do you feel sick?" I felt his cheeks. No fever. "Come sit down. Tell me what happened."

He scratched the crease on his pants as he talked. "Mom, remember Uncle David brought my class cupcakes?"

I nodded. "Sure. Everyone loved them."

"Yeah, they did. Except a few kids saw Uncle David's picture in the paper and asked me if he was gay."

Something sour exploded in my stomach. "And what did you say?"

"I told them what you told me about people having different color eyes and all. Then Mario and Tyler asked if I was going to grow up gay, too."

I rubbed his back. "I'm sorry they said that. That was mean."

"Well, I don't want you to be mad at me because of what I said."

"I don't think I'll be mad unless you used words you shouldn't be using."

"No. I told them that if I was gay then I'd want to be like my Uncle David because he's nice and funny and strong. He got beat up bad and he had to go through a lot of surgeries and stuff. And I think he is brave for wanting to make sure the people who hurt him never hurt anyone else."

⬤⬤⬤

I purposely arrived at Tony Angelo's a few minutes late so the Washingtons would already be seated. And they'd have to wait. And maybe wonder.

The hostess led me to their table. Even in the middle of the week, the restaurant vibrated with conversation and clattering dishes.

Sidney stood up when I reached them. He introduced me to his wife, who looked more like Jackie O. in person than she did in the photos.

"So nice to finally meet you, Caryn," her handshake was feeble and tentative. "We worried something might have happened to you," she said. "Weren't we, Sidney?"

He patted her hand. "I wasn't so much worried about Caryn. I'm sure that little girl can take care of herself."

More than you realize, Sidney.

"Here you go, Caryn. Why don't you have a seat right here across from my pretty wife, and we'll order before we start hammering out the details." Washington pulled out the chair next to him, the one facing his wife. "How's that sound ladies?"

I didn't move except to set my briefcase on the table. "No, thank you. I can't stay long, but I do have something to give you."

He and his wife looked at each other, then back at me. Washington moved the glass in front of him in small circles; the ice clinked like pennies in a bowl. He watched it for a moment and a lazy smile slithered across his face. "So," he set his glass firmly on the table, "you have something to give us?"

The insolence he generated fueled my determination. "David Collins is my brother. Of course, you probably knew that already. Your asking me to cater your election night party meant a great deal to me . . . in money and referrals. And, I'm ashamed to admit I tried to ignore all those pathetic, terrible things you said about my brother because I needed the money."

I reached in my briefcase and pulled out the envelope I'd prepared.

"But, my son recently taught me an important lesson . . . and he's not yet nine." I turned my attention to his wife. Mother to mother. "Ben taught me that you stand up for who and what you believe in. That you stand up even if it means losing your friends. Or, in my case, even if it means losing money." I handed him the envelope. "Because, Mr. Washington, my son taught me that once you sell yourself out, you can never buy yourself back."

He tossed the envelope on the table.

"The contract is in there. Torn. I know it's only a symbolic gesture. But that's enough for me."

"And you think you're going to get away with this?"

"I just did."

On my way out, I heard Washington talking loudly about contracts working both ways and lawsuits.

I didn't care. God already sent my answer. Through Ben.

<hr>

I drove straight to David's house. I wanted to apologize and to tell him, in person, that I walked away from Washington's job.

Max opened the door even before I knocked, and he didn't seem shocked to see me. He looked like he just tossed back about ten cups of espresso.

"You heard? Come in. Come in."

David sat on the sofa looking about five cups less tanked than Max. He was so fixated on whatever he was watching on the television that he barely glanced at me. But the intensity between David and Max seemed to charge the room with energy, as if they'd both been plugged in to a generator.

"Did I hear what?"

Max closed the door behind me. "One of the attackers has been identified as Sidney Washington Jr."

# 46

I had just left the Washingtons less than an hour ago, and the media already swarmed over the story that the son of the candidate for Congressman had been named as one of the young men responsible for the crime against David.

David stared at the picture of Sid Jr. on the television. "I almost feel sorry for the kid. Look who his role model has been."

I recognized the photograph as one I'd seen on Washington's desk. The one taken on their family vacation in the Bahamas. I was about to mention that when Max said, "If you didn't stop by because you heard this latest development, is everything okay? Not that you need a reason to be here, of course. When I saw you drive up, I thought maybe you'd talked to Gavin or—"

"No, I haven't talked to Gavin lately," I said and tried to sound less concerned than I felt about not hearing from him. "I wanted to talk to you both, but this news about Washington's son . . . I'm stunned. Did he turn himself in? What happened?"

Max looked at David. "I know you're worn out telling this story, do you want me to explain?"

"Sure, go ahead." David picked up the remote and turned off the television. "I don't need to watch that. I lived it," he said quietly.

"A week or so ago, David identified one of his attackers. He knew he'd seen him before that day, but couldn't make the connection as to where. I shouldn't call him a kid. I think Tim is almost 23. Anyway, David and Gavin were going through a list of agents, and that's when David remembered that he was the son of a real estate agent David had worked with," Max explained.

"That's disturbing," I said. "This kid's mother knew you?"

"Wait," David interjected before Max could answer. "I've worked with his mother Nancy for over a year. She's devastated. I don't want you to think he acted out of some homophobic influence from her."

"So, how did he know you're gay? I don't get it. Why did he target you?"

"Actually," Max said, "I'm the one Nancy knew first because we'd worked together on a few local committees for revitalizing neighborhoods. And she knew that David and I had started seeing each other."

I looked at David, then Max. "Forgive me for how this is going to sound, but why David, why not you?"

Max shook his head gently, "I forgive you, and I wish it had been me instead." He looked over at David, and there was no mistaking the depth of that truth.

"Honestly," David continued, "I was an easier target. Pretend to be clients, ask to see a house. No one else is there. The house is empty." He rubbed his hand over the bandaging covering his elbow. "It makes sense. Sick. But logical."

"So, to connect the dots . . . this kid and some of his friends, one of whom was Sidney, took up gay bashing as a mission. Mostly a drunken mission," Max said. "They just hated gays, they said. Hated hearing about gay rights. Hated hearing about Gay Pride marches . . . They didn't seem to need too much beyond that."

———— ✺ ————

"I did come here to talk to you both, but if you wouldn't mind, Max, I'd like to talk to David alone for a while."

"Of course not. I have to make a run to the cleaners and make sure the plants at my house aren't on life support. Call me when you're finished," Max said, and on his way out, passed David sitting on the sofa, and patted him on the shoulder. "Let me know if you need me to pick anything up while I'm out."

"Thanks. We'll see you soon."

I moved the chair so I could sit facing David. "First, please forgive me for being so concerned about money that I put it before my relationship with you. You know I'm not exactly a regular passenger on the God train, so this trusting business is new to me. And despite what you and Julie and even Vince would say about faith, it's difficult to have it when so much else in my life hadn't gone the way I planned. But, the reason I drove here today was to tell you that I canceled my contract with Sidney Washington."

David's expression softened. "Really? The Washingtons have had one heck of a day . . ."

I nodded. "Yes, they have."

"I know you felt trapped, that you were trying to do what you thought was best for you and Ben. It didn't mean I liked it or that it didn't hurt," David shared.

"Well, for a long time, I was angry because you'd kept who you were a secret for so long. I mean, I thought we were close. So to be told that you hid from me who you really are, I felt like you'd deceived me. It made me wonder if maybe we weren't as close as I thought we were."

"I'm not proud of that. I should have told you sooner. I should have told myself sooner. Eventually, I was so tired of hating myself, that I needed to just tell you the truth when I did because I might have talked myself back into the lie."

"I understand. Because here's the thing: you weren't the only person keeping a secret."

At that moment I wanted to suck those words in like my vacuum swallowed all those tiny bugs. But the disbelief that shadowed my brother's face flipped the switch.

"I realize now I measured you against a code I wasn't willing to use against myself. When you first told me, I was more worried about being the sister of a gay brother than your being gay. I didn't know what people would think of me. I didn't want people to know because I thought it might affect my business. And, I just didn't know if I could accept this man in your life or even be with you, him, your friends without feeling weird."

If his face was a map, I would be lost. I couldn't read his expression, and he wouldn't steer for me. Time to move forward with the truth. "I didn't tell you that Harrison and I started having sex long before we were married. I'm bashing unwed moms and stocking early pregnancy tests because we had so many close calls. Or that after he died, I hid books in my bedroom so I could read about the romance and sex I wasn't having. . . . And God is teaching me, maybe in very small steps, that He is the final judge, not me. And that my job, for as long as I am here, is to reach out and love. There's still so much I'm struggling with, but I wouldn't want to risk losing you or your never hearing me say I love you."

When Max returned, I told him and David the story of how Ben taught me what it means to stand up for those you love. I detailed the Washington meeting at the restaurant and my decision to walk away from the job.

"So, the two of you may be stuck with Ben and me for a while if the catering jobs start dwindling."

"Maybe not," said Max. "While you and David were talking, I made a few phone calls. I think I found a way for you to replace the money you would have earned with Washington."

"You're running for office?" That would be an interesting campaign.

He looked at David, shook his head, and said to me, "No. That would be a disaster second only to Katrina. This is much better."

"Good, because anything is going to beat nothing," I said.

"I've been told I can offer you a contract to cater a fundraiser for Project Lazarus. I don't know if you're familiar with it, but it's the oldest and largest agency in the New Orleans area providing housing and assisted living to people with AIDS. It's yours if you want it."

"Want it? *Want it?* I can't believe they want me. Thank you. Thank you." I threw my arms around Max and squeezed.

"You're welcome. Promise me though you won't get freaked out knowing you're going to be in a mishmash of gay and straight people."

"I promise to be on my best behavior," I said, then turned around and hugged my brother.

———— ∞ ————

The final shock of the Sidney Washington Jr. story came when Mrs. Washington asked to meet with David and Gavin.

She told them Sid was physically at the location of the attack, but she knew he didn't actually have a part in beating David.

David said Mrs. Washington's answer when Gavin asked why they should believe Sid wasn't one of the guys who actually took part in the pummeling astounded them.

"Because," Mrs. Washington had said, "my son is gay, too."

Apparently and understandably, Sid Jr. didn't want his friends to know. "So, that's why he didn't back out. We tried to not tell his father. But now, if we admit Sid Jr. is gay, perhaps some charges against him would be reduced."

David said that if they don't tell the truth about their son, then they're selling him out for his father's career. But if they do, then Washington loses everything he'd worked for.

It was a conflict of emotions I knew all too well.

---

Every catering job I'd had helped prepare me for the weeks leading to the Project Lazarus gala. The planning seemed all the more special because of the important role Lazarus House played in the New Orleans community for over twenty years.

As driven as I was to make sure the catering was as spectacular as the event, my brother and Max were even more determined to make sure I wasn't the frump of the evening.

After countless shopping trips, I fell in love with a frothy dress with an ankle-length blushing pink tulle skirt and champagne-shaded silk halter top. Even Ben would become a prince that night and wear his first tuxedo.

Julie, Trey, and Nick would be sharing a table with my dad and stepmother, who managed to "squeeze us in" between vacations.

I hadn't heard much from Gavin. David said he was busy with the lawsuit and other projects. I promised myself that, after the gala, I would call him. I owed him that. He not only challenged me to confront what I most feared, he reminded me—just by our spending time together—that relationships require more than steamy love scenes to endure. The kind of romance in the books I'd been holding on to seemed empty and pointless. So much so that I packed all the books in a box and carried them to the street curb so the waste maintenance company would take them where they belonged.

That night, my Cinderella transformation left me barely recognizable, even to myself. I tottered into the den, still wobbling on my spikey heels, until my sharply dressed son reached out to steady me. "Mom, you look like cotton candy."

I held my son's face in my hands. "And, you, mister, are one sharp-looking guy. If you don't have a date, I'm yours."

I looked around the room. My brother, finally free of casts and braces and crutches, and Max, both tuxedoed, standing together. "Would you look at us?" I reached out to David and Max. "Who would have thought? What a difference a year makes."

David leaned over, kissed me on my cheek, and whispered in my ear. "What a difference God makes."

"Time to go. You can't be late for your first gala." Max reached for the door, wearing a grin the size of the Gulf of Mexico.

David held my elbow and steered me to the door. "Don't worry, Princess, we made certain you'd have everyone you needed to make tonight wonderful."

"Everyone? I think you meant everything, right?"

"No," said Max as he opened the door. "He meant everyone."

I managed to glide toward the open door in time to see a handsomely dressed Gavin standing halfway between the front porch steps and the door. He held one exquisite red rose.

"Gavin . . ."

He grinned at me and asked, "Are you ready?"

"Well, Sis?" David asked behind me.

I peered over my shoulder at him and Max, smiled and nodded, then turned to Gavin.

"I'm ready," I said. I stepped out the door and into Gavin's arms.

# Discussion Questions

1. How would you have responded to David's phone call that Saturday morning? Or have you been Caryn, having someone you love confirm that he or she is gay?

2. If you were Julie, what would you have told Caryn? What did you think about their conversation?

3. Did this novel challenge any of your assumptions? If so or not, explain.

4. David's fiancé, Lauren, seems to adjust to his announcement better than Caryn. Why?

5. How does Caryn's faith increase in the novel? Or does it?

6. Did the story being told from Caryn's point of view help or hinder it as it unfolded? How might it have been a different story in third person?

7. At the basic level, beyond the issue of a person being gay or straight, what do you think this novel is about?

8. Caryn fills the voids in her emotional and physical lives after Harrison's death with highly charged romance novels. Is this "emotional pornography" an issue in the lives of married women as well?

9. When it comes to sexuality, how do we pick and choose the things we condone?

10. What other instances are there in the novel of "broken sexuality"?

11. Did you, like Caryn, assume Gavin was gay? What does this reflect about Caryn, about us?

12. Max and David consider themselves Christians. Do you see being gay and Christian as mutually exclusive?

13. How is the title significant to the events in the novel?

14. Why would this novel be considered "not-your-usual Christian fiction"?

# RESOURCES

**Project Lazarus** (www.projectlazarus.net) was founded out of compassion and service to all people. Project Lazarus provides services to people with AIDS who can no longer live independently or whose family can no longer take care of them.

**The Trevor Project** (www.thetrevorproject.org) is determined to end suicide among LGBTQ youth by providing life-saving and life-affirming resources including our nation-wide, 24/7 crisis intervention lifeline, digital community and advocacy/educational programs that create a safe, supportive and positive environment for everyone.

**The Marin Foundation** (www.themarinfoundation.org) works to build bridges between the LGBT community and the Church through scientific research, biblical and social education, and diverse community gatherings. Andrew Marin's book is *Love Is an Orientation: Elevating the Conversation with the Gay Community.*

**The Gay Christian Network** (www.gaychristian.net) is a nonprofit ministry serving Christians who happen to be lesbian, gay, bisexual, or transgender, and those who care about them.

***When Christians Get It Wrong*** Adam Hamilton tackles the issues—homosexuality, politics, faith and science, other religions, and suffering—that keep young adults away from church and demonstrates what Christianity is supposed to look like.

**The Matthew Shepard Foundation** (www.matthew shepard.org) tries to raise awareness and promote human dignity for everyone by engaging schools, corporations, and individuals in dialogues. These dialogues take many forms; some are presentations, some are interactive seminars, and some are web-based. Ultimately, they try to cross boundaries between straight and gay in order to bring people together.

A portion of the royalties from this novel will be donated to
The Trevor Project and Lazarus House

Want to learn more about author
Christa Allan and check out other great
fiction from Abingdon Press?

Sign up for our fiction newsletter at
www.AbingdonPress.com/fiction
to read interviews with your favorite authors, find tips
for starting a reading group, and stay posted on what
new titles are on the horizon. It's a place to connect
with other fiction readers or post a
comment about this book.

Be sure to visit Christa online!

*www.christaallan.com*

*Twitter: @ChristaAllan*

# What they're saying about...

### Gone to Green, by Judy Christie

"...Refreshingly realistic religious fiction, this novel is unafraid to address the injustices of sexism, racism, and corruption as well as the spiritual devastation that often accompanies the loss of loved ones. Yet these darker narrative tones beautifully highlight the novel's message of friendship, community, and God's reassuring and transformative love." —*Publishers Weekly* **starred review**

### The Call of Zulina, by Kay Marshall Strom

"This compelling drama will challenge readers to remember slavery's brutal history, and its heroic characters will inspire them. Highly recommended." —*Library Journal* **starred review**

### Surrender the Wind, by Rita Gerlach

"I am purely a romance reader, and yet you hooked me in with a war scene, of all things! I would have never believed it. You set the mood beautifully and have a clean, strong, lyrical way with words. You have done your research well enough to transport me back to the war-torn period of colonial times." —Julie Lessman, author of *The Daughters of Boston* series

### One Imperfect Christmas, by Myra Johnson

"Debut novelist Myra Johnson ushers us into the Christmas season with a fresh and exciting story that will give you a chuckle and a special warmth." —DiAnn Mills, author of *Awaken My Heart* and *Breach of Trust*

### The Prayers of Agnes Sparrow, by Joyce Magnin

"Beware of *The Prayers of Agnes Sparrow*. Just when you have become fully enchanted by its marvelous quirky zaniness, you will suddenly be taken to your knees by its poignant truth-telling about what it means to be divinely human. I'm convinced that 'on our knees' is exactly where Joyce Magnin planned for us to land all along." —Nancy Rue, co-author of *Healing Waters* (*Sullivan Crisp* Series) 2009 Novel of the Year

### The Fence My Father Built, by Linda S. Clare

"...Linda Clare reminds us with her writing that is wise, funny, and heartbreaking, that what matters most in life are the people we love and the One who gave them to us."—Gina Ochsner, Dark Horse Literary, winner of the Oregon Book Award and the Flannery O'Connor Award for Short Fiction

### eye of the god, by Ariel Allison

"Filled with action on three continents, *eye of the god* is a riveting fast-paced thriller, but it is Abby—who, in spite of another letdown by a man, remains filled with hope—who makes Ariel Allison's tale a super read."—Harriet Klausner

www.AbingdonPress.com/fiction

# Discover Fiction from Abingdon Press

## BOOKLIST 2010

Top 10 Inspirational Fiction award

## ROMANTIC TIMES 2010

Reviewers Choice Awards
Book of the Year nominee

## BLACK CHRISTIAN BOOK LIST

#1 for two consecutive months,
2010 Black Christian Book
national bestseller list;
ACFW Book of the Month, Nov/Dec 2010

## CAROL AWARDS 2010

(ACFW) Contemporary
Fiction nominee

## INSPY AWARD NOMINEES

Suspense     General Fiction     Contemporary Fiction

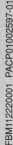

FBM11222001 PACP01002597-01

**Abingdon Press** fiction
a novel approach to faith
AbingdonPress.com | 800.251.3320